KEYNAN MASTERS

AND THE REMIXED MONSTER

ALSO BY DaVAUN SANDERS

Keynan Masters and the Peerless Magic Crew

KEYNAN MASTERS
AND THE REMIXED MONSTER

DAVAUN SANDERS

HARPER

An Imprint of HarperCollinsPublishers

For Azure & Dakari

CHAPTER ONE

THE ONLY PERSON IN THE WORLD

Can I confide? Made a small mistake for my fall break, tried to show my parents something new for old times' sake. I'd love to show you what I did there, but kinda busy hyperventilating. Freaking out. Losing my . . . you get the idea. Remember what I said last time? About your eyes lying to you? I didn't know how right I was about that part.

So let's run it back.

Magic is a thing, and turns out, I'm good at using it. Like, really good. Saved my school, the Peerless Academy, by trapping a cantankerous talking gecko and light-spewing bird—Slickback and Disco—before they ruined the school. True, I kinda helped create them, and I let them get loose. Minor details! Then there's Ratchet, the scary crystalline leopard thing. We're pretty sure Amari's guess is spot on—Ratchet is an ancient sorcerer twisted into a horrible monster by corrupt magic. A Glory.

My rhymes stopped them all.

The most important part? There is no way I could have seen any of that through without help from my friends. There's Leah, my bestie from our *Build-A-Scholar* days, dancer supreme, the one and only Starbreaker. Amari, artist extraordinaire and resident ponderer of all things. And even Dez, our tried and true beatboxer and reformed destroyer of snacks.

I doubted we were going to save the day when Ratchet broke into Peerless, but Dez showed me that late really is better than never. I'm good on my own, but together? We're amazing. A bona fide magic crew. The Peerless Magic Crew.

Problem is, my folks and friends back home are clueless about magic. I wasn't supposed to show anyone on Bizzy Block, not even my mama and baba, but I got greedy. I couldn't wait. I made a beautiful little glowing orb. The tiniest sneak peek at what my rhymes can do wouldn't hurt anything—right?

Wrong. My bedroom? Flaked apart like someone somersaulted through a pile of old leaves. Turns out, it's not real. It's made of magic. My one little rhyme showed me the truth.

I'm Peerless, fearless, with important things to do.
Gotta show my parents not to fear this when I know it's right and true—
and real—like the laws of physics, like light and air.
Reveal the realness of this magic if I'm really being fair!

That's not even the worst part.

My parents? Also. Not. Real.

My baba's brown hands, strong enough to crack walnuts, are unraveling like sparks above a bonfire. So are my mama's. They're huddled together, trying to stop the glittering crumble, squeezing each other. All because of my one rhyme. *Reveal the realness of this magic.*

How was I supposed to know that meant my parents, too? Their eyes are fixed on me, terrified and confused. How can I fix this? *How?* My heart is crashing against my ribs. Breathing hurts. I feel like if I say the wrong thing, the wrong rhyme, I'll start unraveling, too.

I try to remind myself. *My name is Keynan Masters, and*

I'm made of strong stuff.

My parents have been telling me that for as long as I can remember, and somehow the words still pull me together. I drag myself to my feet. My magic isn't finished snacking on my room, and I watch as my wall and bedroom window shiver and collapse into the tiny glimmering sphere, disappearing completely. The books on my nightstand tumble to what's left of the floor. Strange, spongelike material replaces the wood. There's no mistaking it. This is the same smudged rainbow ground as the radiant waste. That broken land full of corrupt magic and impossible creatures is camped out beneath my bedroom floor. I barely see it because my mind won't stop wheeling back to the most important thing.

They aren't real. My parents *aren't real.*

Tears blur my eyes as I run for the street. "Help!" Bizzy Block, our cul-de-sac full of old cozy houses, overflowing gardens, and easygoing neighbors, might as well be on another planet. An unbothered planet, while my entire world is falling apart inside. "Someone! I need help!"

A few houses over, Old Zeph trundles down from his porch, hitching up his faded overalls as he huffs over in concern. "Keynan, what's all the fuss?"

"I . . . I messed up!" For a split second, the sky's blue fades like a shade swept over the sun. Sickly yellow material puffs up from the cracks in the asphalt. My heart won't stop pounding—there's corrupt magic everywhere! The radiant waste is bleeding into Bizzy Block. "My parents are in trouble!"

"Okay now, okay!" Old Zeph grumbles, but he peers back at our house worriedly. "Now what's happened that's got you interrupting my nap?"

I just point—there's no explaining this. He rubs his chin but won't even touch our fence's gate. "Why . . . what happened to the wall, boy? And that strange light . . . like nothing I ain't ever seen . . ." His face contorts, like he's swallowing down something fearful and foul, squeezing it into different words. "A . . . fire? Why you just standing there? Grab the hose! I'll get Yua!"

He hobbles back toward his house, and I stare after him in disbelief. Fire? There's no smoke, no orange-and-red flames licking our home. Why fire? But my mama had said the exact same thing when my magic first sank its teeth into the wall.

Zeph lets out a yell, tumbling down to the sidewalk. Orange squash rise around him, bouncing off the fence and each other. Writhing green vines encircle one of his legs, hissing like cranky cats. I knew I hated squash for a good reason! He kicks himself out of the tangle, losing a flip-flop.

"Gotta get help," I mumble. I could rhyme at it, but what if I make things worse? A sideways rhyme might churn up some tickle leaf or a three-headed caterpillar. "Yua!"

Yua's head pops out of the shop tent in the middle of the cul-de-sac. "What in the—?" She peels off her shop goggles and stares in disbelief. "Buster!"

Her puppy bursts out of the tent. Buster dives head-first into Old Zeph's garden, growling and tearing up the squash. Eating it, too! Yua races up. We help Zeph to his feet. "Rodents in the garden," Yua says with a scowl, swiping her dark bangs out of her eyes.

"What *rodents*?" I gawk at her as Buster gnaws through a hissing vine.

"Never mind that," Zeph says. "The house—Heck's house. There's a fire smoldering!"

Yua stiffens and immediately strides for our house. Papa Chandler joins her, bustling over from across the street with his apron on and a towel over one shoulder. I trail behind them—so glad Yua's here and taking charge. Our house is . . . quivering, like it's afraid of what's inside it. Yua stops.

"Is that an . . ." Papa Chandler licks his lips. "Earth-quake?"

"Bizzy Block doesn't get earthquakes," Yua replies

absently. Light flashes through the windows. My magic is still inside. Still eating our house. "Unless storms are shaking the ground now." Both grown-ups peer suspiciously at the sky.

They can't be serious—an earthquake would have us *all* shaking, not just one house. "That's not it," I say breathlessly. "You need to know about—"

"Zeph said it's a fire." Yua's scowl deepens, like she's upset with herself for not solving the puzzle. "Can't smell anything burning, though. Weird fire."

"Better get the hose anyway," Papa Chandler says worriedly.

I stare at them both. Why don't they see it? Unless . . . no. My mind skitters from the obvious answer. *No, no, no.* I lick my lips. "Yua . . . if it's a fire . . . where's the smoke?"

Yua's jaw works. Papa Chandler purses his lips, peering at the house. They can't see what's obvious because they've been *made* not to see it.

For them, anything out of the ordinary is a storm. They believe Buster's chasing rodents instead of whatever busted magic did to Old Zeph's squash. And not one person has uttered a peep about the puffy orange growth in the street's cracked asphalt!

My neighbors are made of magic, too.

Buster romps over to us, tongue lolling. An awful gurgle vibrates through his black-and-rust-colored fur. He whines, and Papa Chandler leans over to scratch his ears. "What's got into him?" asks Old Zeph. "Bubble guts?"

The squash, that's what! Buster's markings glow faintly orange. Vines wriggle out of his ears. They encircle his neck like a leash.

I want to shake them all. "Busted magic got into him!" I exclaim.

Buster growls, sneezing and drooling everywhere. Wherever the puppy's slobber flies, baby orange gourds start growing on the concrete!

"There's no such thing as magic, Keynan." Yua laughs anxiously. Buster nearly bowls Papa Chandler over, zipping around us. "He's just got the zoomies."

No point arguing with them. "Whatever—just distract him, I've got an idea!"

Buster stops and stares straight at me, like he knows I'm about to rhyme. He's not puppy-sized anymore. More vines encircle his chest and front paws. A low growl rumbles from his throat—way louder than it should be. Any hope of rhyming flies out of my head. My tongue might as well be sandpaper.

Yua seizes his vine collar. "Bad dog!"

Papa Chandler grabs it, too. "Strong little fella. Maybe you should get moving, Keynan." Buster wrenches away, but Yua seizes him again, yelping as a vine snares her wrist.

"But the house—"

Buster breaks loose again. Pretty soon he'll be more shrub than dog. He rounds on my neighbors, and they take off shouting. "We'll draw him off," Yua shouts. "Zeph, Keynan—run!"

Run . . . sure. Where? Old Zeph's garden is quivering again. More vines, thick as my wrist, snake through the fence, straight for us. A strange new glow radiates from behind my house now—in the garden. What now?

I tug on Zeph's arm, but he shakes his head. "Go on now, Keynan. Just need to rest myself a minute." I gasp—a squash vine has wriggled around his ankle! Zeph firmly pushes me back. "You made yourself a mess. Best find a way to clean it up. Go on now!"

I flee across the street. Where am I supposed to go? I can't bear to return home and see my parents—my fake parents—like that. I just can't. Corrupt magic is everywhere. Our new squash puppy is chasing my fake neighbors around the basketball court. Everywhere on Bizzy Block, radiant waste is pouring through the seams.

Only one place might be safe. Where I can breathe and

make all of this *make sense*. Where me and my friends found out magic is a thing to begin with.

The Peerless Academy. But how to get back?

My tablet—the navigation? On the nightstand in my room. No way am I going back inside. I'm so scared I can't think. I've rhymed my way out of a garbage fire before. I gotta dig deep. Strong stuff ain't feeling so strong right now. What would the bravest person I know say?

"I've got this."

Definitely not as convincing as Leah, but it's a start. Now let's get these rhymes where they need to be!

I need a way up out of here, that much is clear
so let's ride, uh—need to find a place to hide
without changing up what I need inside,
rearranging my Break, ummm . . .

The air crackles, tugging at the shop tent's canvas. Yes! Not perfect, but still got it! Pinkish-blue light flashes timidly in an almost-circle. A gust of wind nips at my shirt. Wait.

This isn't the Break I meant to make—a nice safe portal back to Peerless. The blue shimmer brightens, contorting

10

itself into an angular silhouette, almost as wide as the street. No! Way too big for a Break!

One last brilliant flash leaves spots on my vision. I blink them away to reveal . . . a shuttle.

The Peerless shuttle. I circle around it, stunned. My rhymes did this? "I mean . . . it's better than a bike!" Small problem, though. I don't know how to drive! What am I supposed to—

The side door accordions open. A mystified Jocelyn peeks out. She's traded out her afro puffs for long box braids streaked with blue. "Keynan Masters! What on earth have you done?"

A howl sounds out behind us. Buster. Jocelyn's eyes nearly fall out of her head. *"What kind of dog is*—never mind! In! Get! In!"

Jocelyn peels off the second I figure out my seat's buckle. I sink back into my seat as the shuttle hums forward. "Look out!" Jocelyn shrieks.

Buster's chunky head is right outside my window. Close enough for slobber bombs! And he's huge. He lopes alongside us easily, jaws widening, vines wiggling at us from his throat.

The puppy abruptly stops. He lets out an exasperated bark and turns back for Bizzy Block.

I flop in my seat, breathing hard. The wipers are on; coruscating colors shine through all of the windows as if we're sloshing around inside an aquarium made of stained glass. Jocelyn peeks up at her rearview mirror. "We're good, kid. But boy, do you have some explaining to do."

"What had happened was—"

"Oh, I didn't mean for me! Save it, mister. This is way above my pay grade."

Great. Headmaster Kinder's gonna be overjoyed for my return. This is gonna be even worse than the first time I popped up unexpectedly at Peerless. I had finally made it onto her Favoritest Student List, too!

For an instant, the quiet, abandoned streets I remember from my very first bike ride to Peerless stretch like bubble gum pulled too far. I shiver, fearing the worst. If busted magic is lurking in Bizzy Block, who knows how much of it has crept into the abandoned neighborhood along the route to Peerless? Between one breath and the next, the covered bridge is suddenly in front of us—the place where I first tried magic on my own and fixed a light bulb. I still remember the rhyme.

Sometimes we need light to shine,
without it we can't see.

Today I'm here to get what's mine,
so I need this light to be.

Short, sweet, and effective. Those were the days.

We trundle over the creaky wood and curve up the drive to Peerless. The sight of the massive building helps me breathe easier—the granite columns guarding the main entry, the high walls of solid brick. Peerless feels solid in a way I didn't know I needed until now.

"Here I was minding my business . . ." Jocelyn coasts to a stop and lets out a sigh. "Okay, spill it!"

I hesitate, remembering Professor Touré's warning. *There's so much corrupt magic in the world now, most people think it's supposed to be there. Or they lie to themselves to hide what their own eyes are telling them.*

"Professor Touré can explain it better," I manage. "Is she here?"

"Of course she's not—no one is! It's break! Not that I get to rest. Someone's got to tell her . . . what happened." Her face scrunches up as she fiddles with her tablet. She's got the same bewildered expression that Yua and Old Zeph had when magic crashed into their world. If she starts talking about a fire, I'm going to cry real tears.

"Can I just stay in my room?" I ask, trying to keep my voice from cracking. "I've got nowhere else to go."

"The headmaster's not gonna like this," she finally mutters. "Timing is all off. Can't take you back, though. Not without the world's biggest doggy biscuit."

"You saw . . . all of it?" I bite my lip. "My neighbors weren't able to . . . to . . ."

"The big old monster dog with the necklace made of vines? How could I miss it?"

I can't help but hug her in relief. At least Jocelyn sees the magic for what it is. She sighs, but squeezes me back. "You'll be aight, baby. We'll be okay. Headmaster Kinder will know what to do."

"Yeah, she'll fix it," I agree, but my heart isn't in it. I'm just glad she recognizes the same realness I did. That means she's not made of magic, too. Right?

"Why do messes follow you around? Is there some record for biggest bother of a student you trying to break? Hold on. I know this lady isn't ignoring my messages . . ." Jocelyn taps at her tablet, shaking her head. "There. Door's open. Keep to the dorm while I figure this out. And *try* to stay out of trouble? Please?"

"Promise."

She stomps back up the shuttle's stairs. "Good. Or next time I see you coming, I'm going to turn around and go the other way!"

The door closes and Jocelyn peels off, back down the

drive and over the covered bridge. I take a deep breath and push open one of the huge double doors into the Peerless Academy. It opens soundlessly—I guess Touré found time to fix it after Slickback made a snack of one of the hinges. That all feels like a lifetime ago. Jocelyn is right. I've started a whole new mess.

My footsteps ring out on the cool slate floor as I make my way down the main entry hall, familiar columns on either side. The overhead chandeliers offer no light, but blue sky is visible through the windows. The spotless white walls and gleaming wood floors are reassuring and awful at the same time—it's safe, but I'm completely alone. I can't stop thinking about my parents and my neighbors. My home. Bizzy Block is all a lie—an illusion created by magic. Why? Why would anyone do this?

Every breath I take echoes in my ears as I climb the stairs to the first-year dormitory. The silence is scarier than just an empty school. I feel like I'm the only person left in the whole world.

CHAPTER TWO

NOT MY FRIENDS

The dorm room I share looks exactly as I left it. Uniforms hung up in the closet, red and green shirts. My bed is nice and neat, while Ian's is a rumpled mess, like he just rolled out of it. We were pretty tight when I first got to Peerless, but something changed before fall break. He's gotta be real—his snoring sure felt real. But what about everything else? The rest of my friends? We've gone to class together, eaten meals together. I miss them all so much, and I hope they're doing better than me.

A glint pulls my eyes to my desk—Yolanda's golden heart-shaped necklace. Leah dropped it on accident, and I meant to give it back to her after fall break. Now I don't know if I'll ever see her again.

I can't just hide under my bed until Headmaster Kinder

shows up. *If* she shows up. The headmaster has a habit of disappearing for long stretches of time. Jocelyn will track her down, though. I push away the small voice screaming in the back of my brain—insisting something happened to Kinder, too. What if her neighborhood is a bubble just like Bizzy Block? Would we even be able to find it? Get her out? We've argued over whether Glories are still around, those ancient sorcerers turned inside out by busted magic during the Wars of Illusion. I think this answers the question. Who else would mess with us like this?

I shake my head, irritated with myself. I'm letting my imagination run away with me. Kinder's fine—she's the most amazing sorcerer we know!

So first things first . . . my stomach is growling so loud, I'm almost ready to snack on some magic-seasoned squash. I make my way to the courtyard, ignoring the echoes and too-quiet study nooks. The space is just as beautiful and peaceful as ever, meandering paths through garden flowers, veggie patches, and fruit vines.

I plop on my favorite stone bench, nestled at the base of our massive oak tree. It's tall and regal and timeless—and our go-to place for purging corrupt magic. The courtyard makes me feel safe, and the tree most of all. Not just because trees absorb any magic from the waste that's trying to latch on to us. Some of my best memories were born here. Six long claw gouges in the bark are the only sign of Ratchet's attack on Peerless. A reminder that our crew can do anything together. All we need is our art and each other.

A trickle of corrupt magic floats from my fingertips, like a puff of turquoise pollen caught fire, and disappears into the oak tree's bark. I stare at my hand, astonished. Where did that come from? After everything that just happened on Bizzy Block, it does make sense. A knot in my chest loosens, too. If magic is coming out of me, that means I'm real, doesn't it? Of course it does—the other option is too scary to even consider.

There's so much corrupt magic in the world now, most people think it's supposed to be there, Professor Touré's warning comes to me again. *Or they lie to themselves to hide what their own eyes are telling them.*

My gaze wanders through the courtyard. Our berries are either picked or too green. Soup must be around to collect them and tend the gardens. Or maybe Touré. I'd be overjoyed for either of them to pop out of a hallway, even if they treated the rest of break like one long detention. Why didn't I ask Jocelyn for a new tablet? I could have at least checked in with my friends in our favorite game, Mirror Maze Castle. Make sure they're all right.

A sound from deeper in the courtyard pulls me to my feet.

I creep cautiously along a path behind the tulip beds. There it is again. A sniffle. A hammock sways back and forth between two of the smaller trees. "Hello?" I call cautiously.

The snuffling abruptly stops. Leah Jamison's face peeks over the hammock's edge. Her eyes are as big and brown as I remember, but rimmed red from crying. A ponytail holds back her gold-tipped locs, and she's wearing an old pink T-shirt and jeans.

If she's not real—if she doesn't call me *brick brain* right this second—I'm running back to my room and pushing my bed against the door! But if she is real . . . she's probably thinking the same thing about me. We're both waiting. Everything I'm afraid of is reflected in her face. Someone has to go first.

"Why is my name Keymaster?" I blurt out.

Her eyebrow arches. "If we're going to do this, at least make it challenging. Most embarrassing thing that ever happened to you?"

"My own magic creatures tried to eat the school, obviously."

She snorts. "Something only I would know. At your . . . home."

I scour my memories for stories we'd told each other back in virtual classes. "I tried to make dinner for the last night of Kwanzaa. Not even Buster would eat it. I shared the recipe with you in *Build-A-Scholar*." She nods doubtfully, and I fire back. "Best day in Mirror Maze Castle?"

"The time I tricked the gargoyle to lock itself in the dungeon. We would've cleared the level if you hadn't kept checking the other dungeon cells!"

"How was I supposed to know some of the prisoners were snitches?" So this slander is the real deal—and she's not done, which is even more confirmation she's authentic Leah.

"Favorite rhyme?" she demands.

"Psshh! They're all my babies, how could you even ask me to pick just one?" Leah's mouth twists . . . is she *laughing*? The nerve! "Okay then . . . if you are really Starbreaker—happy dance break!"

Leah jerks like I flicked her ear. "Are you serious? Keynan . . . the magic . . ."

I swallow. Duh. Who knows how a spontaneous dance could mess with Peerless? But we've got to trust each other on stuff like this, even if it's a little dangerous. "Them's the rules." She nods, and hops into the most miserable two-step I've ever seen, which is saying something because I nearly trip when my toe catches on a cracked paver.

The lights flicker. We peer around anxiously for any signs of busted magic bleeding into the school. This was worth the risk, though. Leah Jamison is my BFF, my homie, my ace beaucoup—we were Keymaster and Starbreaker together back in virtual school, way before Peerless. Everything feels a little less horrible now. "Did . . . everything fall apart for you, too?"

Leah springs forward for probably the best hug in the history of hugs. We're both shaking. "I was so *scared*," she whispers. "If you were fake, too . . ."

"What happened?"

"I was dancing and . . . you know, playing around. I just wanted my parents to be proud of everything I've learned, and know I'm just as good as—" She cuts off, but I know she means her older sister. Leah competes with Yolanda in everything, although she would never admit it. "Anyway, they started flaking apart like grated cheese!"

"Same—when I did my rhymes! It was awful. I can't stop seeing it."

"I just ran, Keynan. I'm not even sure how I got here. My feet . . . just ate the ground up and—*bam*. Peerless.

I came in through the teachers' lounge, the broken wall still isn't fixed." She frowns. "How did *you* get here?"

I run back how my rhyme conjured up Jocelyn, and that help is on the way. "That's one good thing, at least," Leah breathes.

"Except that Kinder isn't here." How much time has passed since Jocelyn left me on the steps? Kinder would show up the second she knew we were here. She'd probably skip the shuttle ride and open up a Break! Unless . . . Jocelyn ran into trouble and never gave her the heads-up, or—

"Don't worry, Keynan. She'll come. What do we do until then?"

Now how is she asking me what I was about to ask her? No way I'm deciding things for us, not after this. Professor Touré and Headmaster Kinder—shoot, even Professor Mendoza—all warned me that I didn't know a thing or two about a little bit when it comes to magic. Over and over. I'd proved them right in the worst way. "I wish everyone else was here."

"Do you really, though?" Leah asks softly. "Keynan . . . what if they're not real? What if it's just me and you and Yo?"

"No way. We couldn't have saved Peerless without the headmaster and Professor Touré. And Professor

22

Mendoza . . ." My throat gets tight. She's gotta be real, after everything we've been through. She's not just a professor—she's kinda my friend. What if something happened to them over fall break, too? "Did, umm . . . did your sister come home for break?"

"Well . . . no," Leah admits. "But we grew up together! She couldn't be . . . she's not . . ."

"No way," I agree hastily. "We found the video from her tablet—where she's arguing with Kinder and Touré about telling us that magic is real." Yolanda might be the meanest third-year in Peerless, but that's still better than fake.

Leah nods, a little relieved. But now I can't stop worrying about everyone else. Me and Amari made magic together—and not just Slickback and Disco. Dez crushed my snacks and ruined my notebook of poems, but he turned out okay in the end. Better than okay—he stepped in when our crew needed help the most against Ratchet. Ian was the first one who tried to warn me about magic. Warning me about . . . himself? Makes no sense.

They're all just as real as me and Leah and Jocelyn. But . . . I would have said the same thing about my parents, a day ago. Not to mention Old Zeph or Yua. Even Buster! How do I know for sure?

"I can't stand this," Leah mutters. "I don't trust my own eyes anymore."

"Me neither." I hate this, doubting myself, not trusting the memories I have of people who I care about. What's even real, and how do I decide? "I don't know if—" I stop, craning to listen. A distant clatter pings through the courtyard, like metal on metal. "Did you hear that? Sounded like pots and pans."

"But the kitchen's half a building away!"

"Yeah . . . something's off." Which probably means busted magic is involved. Our one little happy dance didn't let it sneak into Peerless. Did it?

"We better check it out." Leah bites her lip. "Have some rhymes ready."

We follow more loud clattering, like the echoes don't know they are supposed to fade away. They lead to the dining hall, weirdly empty with all the tables pushed back, jumbled up beside Soup's wall of fresh herbs. Cans of all kinds of food are stacked randomly on the tables. "Soup?" I call hopefully. "You, uh, cooking?"

Amari emerges from the kitchen with a dozen more cans, pouched into his tank top. He freezes and drops them. Echoes jounce off the walls as cans roll around his feet.

"Amari!" Leah exclaims.

Dried paint of every shade is spattered over his shorts. His glasses are smudged, and his fro is misshapen like he hasn't picked it out in days. Amari's eyes are blood-shot, and his face is pinched like his carefree smile never existed. "Not you, too," he wails, backing away. *"Not my friends!"*

"It's us, bro! We're here!"

"I don't believe it. Y'all stay there. Stay right there."

I hold my hands out carefully. "How can we convince you? Ask me something only I would know."

"How long have you been here?" Leah asks.

"Amari?" This is bad. He's ignoring us, pretending like we're not even speaking.

"Clean you out. I'm going to clean you right out of here," Amari mutters. He digs in his pocket and yanks out a marker. Leah and I both freeze. My eyes fix on it like he's holding a hissing snake. We both know how much talent he can unleash. "Fake friends breaking into my school. Nope. You can't have it."

He uncaps the marker. His hand zips across the wall, drawing precise lines. Magic crackles along the edges as his creation solidifies. How do we convince him we're real before it's finished?

CHAPTER THREE

LEGENDARY PROBLEMS

"Amari, don't—"

He's drawn an . . . opening. The edges are rounded, with some kind of wheel in the middle instead of a knob or handle. He gives us a triumphant smirk and spins it. The weird door slaps open with a clang, revealing an inky blue beyond it. Water gushes through, the force of it knocking me and Leah off our feet. Amari flees, letting the dining-hall door slap shut behind him.

I rise up, spluttering, drenched, and shivering. Me and Leah grab each other for balance. Kinder's storm warning hops over the intercom. *"Proceed indoors immediately. A storm is approaching the school grounds. This is not a drill."*

"Good to know *that* still works!" Leah growls.

The water's up to our knees in seconds. Loose cans bob around the surface, bumping into tables. Rhyme Amari's door closed and we're good.

Time to dry out this sp-spout
be-before we raise a ruckus in the sch-school!

Leah squints at me, halfway to perching herself on a table. "What's wrong?"

My rhymes won't get past my own teeth chattering! "It's too cold!"

Leah sloshes over to me. "Maybe I can try to slow it down if—" She slips and nearly falls on her face. We're not ready for this. I gotta focus. The words won't let me down, I just gotta let them out. Dry ground is what we need. I take a deep breath, but the water's flow stops before I utter one rhyme.

"Keynan! What is that?"

A massive brown-and-blue blob blocks Amari's opening. The gushing water ceases. We both hop-slosh away in a panic—the thing is wriggling itself through!

This new creature spills into the dining hall with a fresh rush of water. Fuzzy tentacles as thick around as my neck break the surface, feeling against the dining hall walls and tables. The water level rises steadily. The strange creature latches itself to a lunch table, clamping down against the flow.

"Will this water ever run itself out?" I cry.

"It must be pouring in from some lake in the radiant waste!" Leah shouts. "The door is the only way out—come on or we'll get trapped!"

"Or eaten by that thing. Swim for it!"

We plunge into the freezing water. Cans and bags and dried food swirl all around us like we're in some gigantic pot of gumbo. I've never seen this much water in one place—let alone swum in it! The creek just outside of Bizzy Block has a few swimming holes, barely deep enough for diving. The slosh and slap tug me toward the door out. My shoulders are starting to burn from the effort. Along with my legs, my lungs, my face.

Wait. My face?

"Leah! The water's heating up!"

"I know. Keep swimming, we're almost there!"

We reach the way out at the same time. The doors have been pushed open by the water's flow, but some of the floating tables are jammed against the exit. We clasp our hands around the nearest one. "Pull!" It inches forward but floats back in place. A random wave dunks me under the water. I slap my way back up, coughing. "Leah, look out!"

One of those furry tentacles loops around Leah's leg. She squeals. "It—it *tickles!*" Laughter bursts out of her, until a wash of warm water makes her gag. "I can't stop laughing!"

I'm on the edge of panic—can you actually sweat underwater? I'm about to find out, because it's getting even warmer. Which means—I'm not shivering anymore. I could've been rhyming already!

Another tentacle zips for my leg. The fur is somehow *dry* despite the water. A laugh bubbles up from my throat. The grip is powerful but feels like a hundred butterfly wings wrapped around my leg. Leah cackles hysterically. "Do . . . something . . . Keynan!"

All of my kicking is useless. My arms feel like rubber, barely holding on to the table. Wait. That just gave me a half-decent idea. Another laugh bubbles out of me. More warm water slides in my mouth. I spit it out—why is our broth delicious? That's weird! I gotta focus on this rhyme—something quick and simple.

> *I'm rubber, you're glue*
> *Whatever I feel bounces outta me*
> *and sticks to you!*

The overwhelming tickles cease instantly. The water around the creature bubbles—boils, even—and the tentacles tug us even tighter. I groan in pain, but Leah shouts urgently. "Don't let go!"

The table is pulling loose! It twirls suddenly in a new eddy of water and bangs into my leg. "Ow!" The tentacle holding me goes limp and releases me. Another one snaps onto the table—it's dragging Leah back, too. I grab her leg and hold tight.

"I'm really sorry for this," she says.

"Sorry for—" She reaches down with her free hand and flicks my nose! "Hey! That hurt!"

A screech sounds from the water—the tentacle clutching Leah snakes away. More soupy water from the thrashing monster shoots us free. We rip down the hallway, flopping around. The water's speeding up. I flail for something to hold on to, anything! We sweep past the headmaster's office, the lights dark, then curve down the hall, banging into lockers along the way. Leah snags my hand. "Ride it!" she shouts. "The stairs to the second-year classes are coming up!"

A sucking sound grows steadily louder as the gumbo river pulls us along. Fear tremors through my body. "Good plan, but you forgot something!"

"What?"

"The water isn't going past the trophy case!"

Her eyes go wide. "Oh no."

The door secreted behind the trophy case first brought us to the hidden wing. We nearly got lost exploring up there, and found everything from Professor Touré's private tinkering room to these magic 3D printer rings and our first clues about Ratchet.

The problem with the stairs to the hidden wing? They lead down, too. So deep the bottom disappears in murkiness. None of us have gone that way, not even Ian. Too scary. Our little river is curving straight for it—this water doesn't flow like water should. I can imagine a whirlpool waiting for us in the impossible stairwell. If we get pulled in there . . .

"Keynan, get out of the way!"

I thrash my way through water-broth, ignoring my burning shoulders. A tumbleweed of flailing tentacles sweeps right past us, slapping desperately against the walls. It slips around the corner and disappears—and we're about to be next! My words spill over themselves as we cling to the edge of the closest lockers.

> *From the tip-top we need a quick mop—*
> *something to stop the drip drop and reverse*
> *the sop!*

Seal Amari's door too while I'm at it,
send that water back to its proper place
on the planet!

The water level drops steadily like it's sinking through the floor. We stand slowly to our feet. "We're actually okay! We're alive." I can't help but laugh. "Happy dance break?"

"There's no time for—oh geez. Fine!" Leah glares at me and does a little spin and shimmy. Water squelches out of our shoes. "I can't believe that baby-time rhyme of yours worked!"

"Sometimes simple is better. Let's check the dining hall, just to make sure."

The room is an absolute mess. Tables are jumbled up everywhere, with cans and other random food scattered underfoot. Most importantly, there's only puddles of water, and Amari's drawing is just a smudge of marker.

I whistle. "Soup's going to be mad."

"Not to mention Touré and Kinder."

If we ever see them again, I add silently. Leah's right. Peerless is literally flooded with busted magic. Maybe more than when Slickback and Disco almost pulled Ratchet inside. We're about to own some legendary problems—with no grown-ups in sight to fix them. "How are we going to dry this out?"

"With magic," Leah says reluctantly. "Peerless will rot apart from the inside out if we don't. And we won't be far behind."

Professor Touré warned us constantly about the dangers that just spilled all over Peerless. *Corrupt magic preys on your thoughts, uses them against you. Reality itself will trick you if you're not paying attention. Corrupt magic is difficult to purge—especially if you allow it inside.* I'm pretty sure I just swallowed a gallon of this tickle-monster gumbo while we were swimming for our lives! "When we find Amari and prove we're real, we'll all march straight to the oak tree," I say.

"And if that doesn't work, we'll . . . we'll tie up his hands and drag him there! He's constantly drawing stuff. Could be leaving surprises hidden all over the place."

"He's probably been here for days," I agree unhappily.

We trudge through Peerless, eyes peeled for drawings that could pop out and surprise us. Despite my nervousness, part of me is . . . elated. Amari's magic is even more incredible than I remember. I can't say this to Leah though, not after he just turned the dining hall into a giant vat of Soup's Soup—with us as the secret ingredient. But imagine what else he can do! What else could we all do if we worked together?

Leah groans. "I know that face. Something ridiculous is cooking in your brain. Whatever you're thinking, stop thinking it. Now isn't the time for a bigger mess, Keynan."

Like she knows somebody! "Pretty sure I just cleaned up that mess."

"You know we got lucky, right?"

"Whatever! It worked. Besides, I'm allowed to think things. You're thinking things, aren't you?"

"I'm trying not to, actually. That water just turned into soup for no reason, and our clothes are still soaked in it. Who knows what else it can do?"

"I'm sure we'll be fine if . . ." The words dry up in my mouth—I remember. What I'd thought when Amari's door first opened, how everything around us reminded me of *some gigantic pot of gumbo*. The water was bad enough. One careless thought from me had made the situation even worse. "You're right," I say faintly.

"Yeah. I know." Her gaze teeters between surprised and suspicious, but thankfully, she drops it.

"So what are we going to do when we find him?" I ask.

"Less swimming, I hope."

We agree that searching the first-year dorms is our best bet. The door to his room is wide open. I risk a peek in. "Amari?" I croak, swallowing a plum in my throat. "He's not here. It's empty."

Leah tilts her head, then places a finger to her lips. I pad after her, past the rest of the first-year rooms—silent and empty because the other students are still enjoying fall break, like I should be. Why, *why* did I have to mess with magic at home? Everything I know and love is turned inside out! But if I hadn't . . . I'd still believe in a lie, and I wouldn't be here to help my friends. Messed up as all of this is, I'm right where I should be.

Leah stops in the first-year lounge. Amari sits in one of the cozy chairs, knees squeezed to his chest and eyes closed. His marker is on a chessboard to the side. Leah's ready to pounce on it, but I grasp her arm. She shoots me an exasperated look.

"How do I know?" Amari mumbles suddenly, scrubbing at his face. *"They* said they were real, too! But they weren't! Nothing is! I keep turning it over in my brain. Why didn't I see it? How could I not know?"

I wince as he buries his face in his hands. We shuffle forward, and Leah rests a hand on his shoulder. *Say something,* she mouths. Amari's usually the one who sees answers to everything—most of the time before I've even thought to ask the right question. All of this must be hitting him extra hard.

"We're a crew." I bury him in a squeeze. "Your art. My rhymes. Leah's moves. We've got that, and we've got each other. If you don't believe in anything else, believe that!"

Leah joins in to make the group hug official. I didn't realize how much I needed it, and I hope Amari feels the same way. "I know how I feel when I'm dancing," she adds. "It reminds me I'm alive. I'd be doing it—"

"—even without magic," Amari finishes. He eyes his marker but doesn't pick it up. "We've combined art together. That means we're real, doesn't it?"

"Definitely," Leah says. "We can't be magic and make magic."

"Can't we?" I blurt out. "Tell that to Slickback and Disco."

"Not helping," Leah growls under her breath.

Amari taps his lip, lost in thought. "But what about the school? Where do we go if it's just one more illusion?"

"After everything we've gone through here?" I counter. "Those creepy little frosty bears? Ratchet? Peerless is probably the realest thing there is."

"How can you believe that?" Amari shudders. "The third floor is just as weird as the radiant waste!"

"No lies detected," Leah says with a frown.

Okay . . . now who's not helping? She shrugs when I give her the stink eye. "So fine. We test it and be sure. A rhyme will show us what's real."

Leah's eyebrows climb her forehead. "What? That's a *terrible* idea. Did you forget Touré's rules already? Don't. Do. Magic. In. Peerless!"

"Things have *kinda* changed since then! Just a little bit! What do the rules say about fake parents? Fake homes?"

"There you go leaving out the part where we were almost seafood. You are so brick-headed! I swear that—" Leah cuts off.

I scowl, folding my arms. She's always so dang difficult. The rules start as many problems as they stop! They only work for so long.

"Okay. You convinced me," Amari murmurs. "Nothing realer than a quintessential Leah and Keynan fight."

I roll my eyes—then see Leah doing the same thing, and try to stop midroll. Which just makes my eyes burn and water. Amari doesn't even try to hide his buster smile! And what does *quintessential* even mean? Who talks like that? Trying to out-vocabulary the crew's resident wordsmith? Rude.

I take a deep breath—I'll need some extra-long sentences to get Leah back on Team Keynan. But first things first. "My bad. You're right, and you're just trying to look out for us. As usual." There. That wasn't so bad. I even throw in a smile, although it hurts my face.

She purses her lips. "I can admit things are different this time. So maybe . . . you're right, too." Leah grimaces like she ate a bad plum, but it still counts.

"Okay . . . that was weird," Amari murmurs, but he's only cheesing harder now. "Apologies? Not convinced anymore." He clears his throat. "Sorry for back there, family. I was so scared."

"So were we. And don't worry—we'll fix it. Just glad you're okay." We trade our dap—*slap, bump, snap hook fly and dab*. We're back! Such a relief. The Peerless Crew is almost whole.

"Y'all couldn't have just done that? Instead of all this running? And swimming?" Leah throws up her hands when we both shrug. "Now what about the school?"

"How about we try something small, together?" I suggest.

"We could go room by room so it doesn't get too messy," Leah allows.

"Start with what we know and work our way out."

We both turn to Amari, and he nods uncertainly. I clear my throat, and Leah slips into a nice beat with her hands. Her skills make the rhymes more . . . connected, somehow. Stronger. I wish I could explain it, but they go together like peanut butter and jelly. The words practically leap from my tongue.

> *We're all here, pick me up, need a lil lift kit*
> *Feeling like a misfit, out to find a better fit*
> *Split away the fake skin with some of this*
> *real spit*
> *Feel our way forwards, more levels like*
> *some Braille lit*
> *Fly all day, soar words, revel in our orbit*
> *Sorcery, lore words, fade away—score it!*

Leah stops her beat, staring at me. No one breathes. Nothing happens. Amari lets out a relieved wheeze. "All real. That rhyme was incredible, Keynan. Like . . . forreal. I can't say I understood it all . . . but I felt it."

"Thanks," I mumble, aware of Leah's eyes on mine. My rhyme didn't stumble, but I can't meet her gaze. Does she know? The words came to me in a beautiful blaze. I wasn't in control. At. All. Our gumbo-saturated magic invaded me. And it felt *great*. Unreal, literally. Not the kind of thoughts to entertain about something so dangerous. Sometimes I really, *really* miss my notebook days. Things weren't always smooth, but I felt like

I could grab the rhymes easier. Now it feels like they grab me.

. "How about the rest of Peerless?" Amari asks. "We've got a lot of ground to cover."

Leah shakes her head. "First things first. We literally just got soaked in corrupt magic."

"Past time for the oak tree," I agree.

"Straight away." The worry in Leah's voice makes my skin tingle. "Who knows what it's doing to our insides?"

CHAPTER FOUR

WE TIRE OF YOUR GAMES

Only . . . I do know what corrupt magic is doing to my insides. That rhyme? Whew. Better than anything I spent a whole week writing. The words were nicer than my freestyle that stopped Ratchet. It flowed out of me as easily as breathing. I'm good, but . . . Professor Mendoza's warning comes back to me. *Children, children, children. You can't afford to be this naive. You'll know if it's inside you. You'll feel it. Like a color you've never seen before . . .*

Best advice ever—scared me into being a *little* more careful. Mendoza has to be real—she told me about magic. My fake parents couldn't even comprehend it.

Halfway down the walking path to the oak tree, skeins of green-and-purple whorls leap out of our skin. Corrupt magic. The leaves flutter as the tree's bark drinks it in urgently. A wave of dizziness rocks over me, and I sit hurriedly on the bench. Weird. That's never happened before.

"Guess we're stuck here for a while," Leah grumbles. We toss some questions around: Is there a safe way to uncover more illusion? Who's real, and how do we know for sure? What if something's happened to Kinder and the professors? Well, we try to toss questions around. Amari's still so distraught over drenching us that we spend most of the time reassuring him we're okay.

"Are you sure I can't at least fix y'all a sandwich?" he pleads as we leave the courtyard. "I've got a stash in my room—"

Leah rests her hands on his shoulders. "We. Are. Fine."

"Worse could have happened just getting back to Peerless," I add as we set down the path again.

"Speaking of which . . . what happened with you, Amari?" Leah asks. "During break? How did . . . you know . . ."

"I . . . I tried to draw up dinner for my granny my first night back. She's always cooking and deserved a break," he explains. "The tortillas parachuted off the table and chased us around the room. The peppers started yelling for more veggies and threw themselves on the skillet, and the beans . . ." He shudders. "My granny . . . she's

42

all like, 'Now, Amari, we don't waste a good meal.' But there's no way anyone can eat that many fajitas and be real. I just knew, and . . . I had to get out of there. I drew a Break—like in the radiant waste, it was easy!" Leah and I share an alarmed look. "Took me straight to the kitchen like it knew I was hungry."

"And umm . . . where is this Break now?" I venture.

"I erased it," he adds, a little miffed. "Give me *some* credit!"

"Seriously? After you just gave Peerless an indoor pool?" Leah teases. She's not mean with it, but he still winces.

"You did better than I did." I squeeze down the memory of my parents' shimmering hands until I'm sure my voice won't crack. "My rhyme didn't make a Break, but it did pull Jocelyn through for the rescue."

I nudge Leah, she's frowning in thought. "I . . . ran," she admits sheepishly. "It only took me a few steps. Like as soon as I set my mind to be here, my feet just made it happen."

"Weird," I say.

"Yeah," she agrees. "But we all knew to come back here somehow."

"Pretty sure I hate beans now," Amari mumbles to himself.

"Do you think Dez is okay?" I ask.

"Probably enjoying fall break just fine because he followed the rules," Leah says, her eyes twinkling. "I used to do that. You're rubbing off on me, Keynan."

My jaw drops—she's really trying to rewrite history? Hero status slander will not be tolerated!

"Actually . . ." Amari jumps in with proper facts. "Who's the one who snuck on Jocelyn's shuttle with all the third-years to rescue Keynan from the storm? Or talked us into the hidden wing so we could find a certain sister? Should I keep going?"

"What I meant was—I'm joking about—" Leah flushes, spluttering out excuses. Now I'm the one holding in a laugh for once! "We'll follow the first rule we see when we're out of this mess, deal?" Her glower means it's past time to change the subject. "Where to first?"

"How about the art supply closet?" Amari asks innocently. "Should be an easy place to start."

"I . . . okay. Sounds like a plan." Leah's lips squeeze together to hold in a grin—I keep my gaze down so I don't start *cackling*. If the whole school was on fire, Amari would wheelbarrow every last crayon, marker, and paintbrush from his precious closet before it burned down.

"You still got the key that Professor Touré gave you?" I ask.

"Not like we need it, but here." He pulls the looped cord over his neck and hands the key to me.

The supply closet is untouched and confirmed real when I test it with a rhyme. I'm just glad there's none of those pumpkin-headed centipede things lurking around after Amari opened the Break into the radiant waste.

"Not sure what's taking Jocelyn so long to get someone from Peerless back here," I say.

"Let's keep at it," Leah replies. "Past time we find our own answers, instead of trusting what everyone's been feeding us."

"You think they don't know?" Amari asks anxiously. "About our parents? Or that . . . they aren't real, either? The professors?"

Leah falters, then takes a deep breath. "I don't know what I don't know. But we've got to start somewhere."

Amari tugs my sleeve as Leah marches to the nearest classroom. "What about . . . Yo?" he whispers. "What if she's . . . you know . . ."

I shake my head. "We met her here, and here is real. Same as Jocelyn."

Amari tilts his head thoughtfully, but doesn't ask any more questions. Which is a relief—I can't handle anything else turned inside out, especially about Yolanda! Or the professors. Touré and Mendoza taught me the most about magic—stuff I'd have never figured out by myself. I'm seriously worried they're in trouble, too.

We spend the next hour combing through more student lounges and bathrooms, then back to the dining hall and auditorium, using rhymes to reveal hidden magic. Sometimes my freestyle creates the same orb of light I conjured back on Bizzy Block, and it's all I can do not to run back to the dorm and hide under my bed. My friends make it all right. Barely. I'm not the bravest, but I can be for them.

Thankfully, no busted magic pops up on our trek through the halls. There's no radiant waste hidden beneath the auditorium stage or stuffed behind the locker rooms. I'm convinced that Peerless is as real as it gets.

Our next room up is the teachers' lounge. The glass wall Slickback destroyed still isn't repaired—a tarp hangs over the open wall—but the ruined furniture has been removed. Amari wanders around curiously while Leah gives us a fresh beat. He tries the handle on a closet near the fridge. "Locked."

"Of course it's locked," I say. "Professors gotta know their snacks are safe, too. How are we going to—"

But Amari's already fiddling in his notebook. Drawing a key, I realize. "Y'all realize the only doors around here with good stuff behind them are locked, right? Or stuff they don't want us to find, which usually means magic."

Leah licks her lips. "If that's true, maybe using *your* magic around more magic isn't the best idea."

For an answer, he slides the key into the lock with a very convincing *click*. It turns easily. I whistle appreciatively. "Nice!" Leah's scowl sends me stammering. "But, uh, we gotta be careful. Follow the—"

Amari throws the door open. The room inside is dim and much larger than it should be. A flickering glow beckons us toward the shelves across from us.

"We tire of your games, children!" A voice bellows, but muffled and distant.

I groan—I *know* that voice. "We should have left the door closed. Throw the key away."

We stop in front of my bubble trap, a glowing, melon-size globe of magic. Slickback and Disco are both still inside. "Keep your delicious snacks! If everything is delicious, nothing is. Whatever you've done to invisibilize yourselves was clever—I'll give you that. But *oooh boy* you gonna get it when I crack the code!"

Reluctantly I edge closer. We can see inside the bubble, although the details are warped like peering into a fish bowl. The oversized, smart-mouthed gecko is marching through the fake Peerless halls, opening lockers at random and peering into classrooms. The fake Peerless we trapped him in—right before he almost destroyed the real one—is in shambles. Light fixtures dangle from the ceiling and half-eaten lockers line the hall. Every non-metal surface is blasted by Disco's color bombs.

"Where's the bird?" Leah asks nervously.

"They wouldn't leave each other," I say. "Gotta be in there somewhere."

"I heard you!" Slickback rumbles. "Where are you little brats hiding?"

Imagine if he had stayed loose in Peerless? I'm so relieved we caught this buster, I don't have the words.

"Look at this, y'all." Leah thumbs through a notebook beside the bubble. "Touré took notes." She squints, examining the precise handwriting. "Listen."

> Even though these beings are created entirely by a pair of gifted but irascible students, I can't ethically determine with certainty that they are any less alive than I am. Leaving them in the radiant waste or otherwise disposing of them would be cruel options, as is their current confinement. They deserve to be free—and yes, the irony stings.
>
> I'll need to discuss with the children when

they return. They should have a say in the fate of these beings.

Amari and I share the biggest grin. "You heard that, right?" I say to Leah. She's side-eyeing both of us extra hard. "What she called us? The word rhymes with—"

"Hassle?" she growls. "Is that it?"

"Actually, no. And those don't technically rhyme—"

She throws the notebook at me. Amari plucks it nimbly out of the air before it collides with my face. He flips through the pages, nodding thoughtfully. I feel bad for Slickback and Disco, especially after what happened on Bizzy Block. We were living—no, trapped—in a fake home. A fake life. They don't deserve that any more than we did.

"I need to think." We lock the closet back tight, leaving the pair stalking their artificial prison. I slide through the lounge's tarped-over wall. My friends follow me to the soccer field. Back where this whole mess started when I created that very first Break.

Clear skies are overhead, brilliant and blue. A perfect, beautiful day—if I didn't know better. "Our neighborhoods are the . . . fishbowls. Like what we made for Disco and Slickback. Just bigger, with better magic."

"Better lies," Leah mutters.

"If Peerless is the only thing we know is actually forreal . . ." Amari gestures at the soccer field and the woods beyond it. "Everything else is radiant waste? But why? Who made it?"

"I don't know, but I'm pretty sure who does."

"The headmaster? Professor Touré?" Leah squeezes her eyes shut. "But they could be as fake as our parents!"

I shake my head stubbornly. "They're real. Something's happened to them. You know they'd be here for us— even if it's just to make sure we don't mess up Peerless."

"True." Amari gives me a thoughtful nod. "Maybe we're all trapped in some Glory's experiment. Like . . . an ant farm."

"A Glory?" Leah folds her arms. "Ratchet's out there, spooking us with magic? I dunno."

Amari shivers. "Remember those old sorcerer battles Touré told us about? I'm pretty sure folks didn't call them the Wars of Illusion for nothing."

I swallow. A *war*. That's worse than a fight, or a battle. Like . . . dodgeball contests that last weeks instead of hours? But with awful magic flying back and forth instead? Too scary to imagine. If Ratchet's in some kind of war with Peerless—we've already lost without Headmaster Kinder and Professor Touré. We just didn't know it.

CHAPTER FIVE

BADDEST OF THE BAD

We sweep around the outside of Peerless, confirming at least one thing for truth with our beats and rhymes. The school itself is real. And really empty. No professors, no headmaster or staff. Jocelyn, or anything resembling a shuttle, is nowhere in sight. We're on our own.

Leah crosses her arms. "We've searched this school up and down. They're not *here*, Keynan."

"Then we need to get their attention, to be sure."

"We can't ignore the chance that something happened to them," Amari puts in. "If Ratchet can attack Peerless, our neighborhoods are on the menu, too."

"But what for?" Leah presses. "Why be so bothered about us?"

"I don't know—revenge for that L we served up last

time?" Amari holds up his hands. "Does a mad sorcerer need a reason to do anything?"

"I'm still not sure. Ratchet's never talked—unless you count roaring. Mainly tears up trees, or the school. Where's the rhymes? The magic?" They listen expectantly, like I've figured it all out. Great. "Me and Dez drove a Glory off—little old us?"

"Glories were supposed to be the baddest of the bad," Leah agrees. From what we've gleaned from exploring Peerless, Glories were the best to ever do it—and still got it all wrong. The fallout from their wars is what created the radiant waste.

"But if the waste cooked Ratchet's brain . . . maybe we just haven't seen full power yet," Amari persists.

We're going in circles. Leah and Amari are just as frustrated as I am. So many questions with no answers! We walk around the auditorium to Touré's greenhouse, hopeful for a snack. The raspberries there aren't ripe. That fits my mood perfectly. "My letter from Peerless was delivered by drone, and I'm pretty sure Ratchet tried to claw it out of the sky. Wouldn't that mean the drone traveled through the radiant waste to get to Bizzy Block?"

Leah claps excitedly. "If we can find out where they're sent from, we could view everywhere they go, too!"

"Say less!" Amari proclaims, marching off so quickly we have to scramble to keep up. "Ian found a few rooms full of old drones when we were exploring Peerless. You know, Hall Hop stuff. Why didn't I remember this until now?"

"Were you in the hidden wing?" I say anxiously.

"Yes and no. That's where they get fixed up—Touré's got workrooms stashed all over the place." He stops short. "But what we need is a tablet."

"I left mine at home," Leah moans.

"Me too," I add.

"Those wouldn't work anyway—we need one with admin privileges."

"Professor Mendoza hated her tablet, tossed it in the desk whenever she could."

"He's right," Leah says. "Good call."

We set off for Creative Writing. The room is dim and empty. Lifeless. Professor Mendoza's not my fave just because she teaches my fave subject or lives her best snack life every day. She pushed me in poetry and magic—even though she was petrified of the headmaster finding out. She saved the entire crew when we were stuck in the radiant waste.

"She never nagged us." Leah sighs, and I realize she's

thinking the same thing. "Except about raiding the berry bushes for her."

"Right? And making sure we sat under the oak tree to purge corrupt magic." I really, really hope she's okay.

"No tablet," Leah announces. "Some watermelon seeds though. Gross. Who keeps something like that in their desk?"

"Maybe she wanted to plant them herself someday," I say, hiding my disappointment. "I wish she was here to help explain all of this."

Leah closes the desk drawer. "Yeah, she always put her own sauce on magic—way different than Touré or Kinder. Too bad she was more afraid of getting in trouble than we were."

Amari taps his lip impatiently. "Let's go straight to the source. Headmaster Kinder will have a tablet, right?"

"If her office isn't locked," Leah observes.

"If that doesn't work, then . . ." I stop, about ready to kick myself. "Y'all. Why are we wasting all of this time when we could just *make* a tablet?"

Leah and Amari give each other a long look. "I don't know, Keynan," Amari says doubtfully. "I mean . . . electronics? Who can say it would even work if we got it right?"

Of all people, I'm surprised he's pushing back on this idea—when I'm mad I didn't think of it sooner.

"We've got to do something," Leah says softly. "Why not try?"

"Our last collabo didn't go too well," Amari points out.

"Well, we've never created something together, the three of us. Come on—it'll be amazing!"

Amari shakily agrees. We head to the dining hall—peering around anxiously for tentacles—and find some frozen Soup's Soup and pots for thawing and heating it. Some corn chowder feels like the best thing I've had in a long time while we figure out our next move. Amari comes up with the most detailed drawing I've ever seen—he's added everything that would go in a real tablet: CPU, motherboard, display, power supply. "Transparent for now," he murmurs defensively. "I'll add color when it's done."

Leah peers over it intently. "Wow, it's—quit giving me the stink eye! It's great, seriously. No notes. Keynan . . . ?"

Okay. My turn. Figuring out a new rhyme, with other people around? Too weird. My poems are usually private until they're perfect, but this is too important. I don't need to finish it before my friends see it because . . . well, they're my friends. We'll get it perfect together.

"Give yourself some wiggle to freestyle, too," Leah says, scooping out her last bit of Soup's Soup with a bit of cracker we dug up. "In case you need it."

"Good idea."

"And Amari, I still don't think he needs to rhyme something about every single piece inside of it."

"But if we get it wrong, it won't work," Amari argues.

"I'm with Leah on this one," I say. "It's about what it can do, not what it's made out of."

"Then why make it a tablet at all?" he asks.

"We don't know where the tech ends and the magic begins. But we agree on what it's supposed to do. Our magic will do the rest. Hopefully."

"Stuff we don't know the rules for yet," he murmurs, peering at his drawing. "Okay . . . but this could be worse than Slickback and Disco if it goes sideways."

Leah takes a deep breath. "Then let's make it count."

CHAPTER SIX

PAWPRINTS OF FIRE

I swallow—another magic mess, but tied up in our intranet? Like a magic computer virus? Imagining it gives me a headache. Can't worry about that right now. Definitely can't think about the last time we did this. Slickback and Disco. That one mistake cost us—

Stop that!

Crystal clear words. Intentional thought. Sublime rhymes. That's what we need. Leah wordlessly drums out a beat on the dining hall table. Amari sets his drawing before us—I'm still amazed at how he can draw such straight lines and sharp details. He's gifted. We're all agreed.

So, here we go. My time to shine. Again.

Sometimes felt and rarely seen, watch me seize behind the scenes

Between the screens and keys, manifest machineries

Activities and intellect that intersect, bring out the best

One tablet to connect the rest and pierce the Peerless internet

Oh . . . wow. Not the mess I expected at all! Buttery smooth even. My intent was clear and sharp. That's getting easier every time I freestyle.

"Nice," Leah murmurs. Amari gives me an approving fist bump.

The dining hall lights flicker. We edge away as Amari's drawing shimmers and crackles before us like hot grease on a skillet. "Here we go," he breathes.

"Was it like this with Slickback and Disco?" Leah asks.

"Nope. It was . . . messier." Also . . . I'm not afraid of what's about to happen this time.

The paper suddenly blurs and flashes a brilliant silver green. Rude! When I blink the spots out of my eyes, a whole tablet rests on the table. We did it! It worked!

"But does it *really* work?" Amari asks.

The other two stare like it might bite them, so I pick it up and turn it on. "See? It's even charged. Why all the doubt?" The plastic is warm to the touch. Just like we hoped, there's full access to the Peerless systems. Amari grins and I clap a hand on his shoulder. When we put our art together . . . anything can happen. Which is amazing and scary stuffed in the same box.

"Hey, this is something," Leah says, pointing. "The drones. The school can operate them!"

"We could use drones?" Amari gawks. "That could do . . . a lot. Wow."

"Imagine Kinder's face," I cackle. "When *she* gets a Peerless envelope from *us*!"

I hit a button that reads RETRIEVE out of curiosity. Nothing happens, so we keep peering over the tablet. There's commands for everything I can imagine.

A distant crash spins us around. A drone bursts through the doors and zooms to a stop before us. I gasp. "No way. Eli?" I haven't seen one in a while. The wings are bigger than I remember, with four spinning turbines paired on either side, humming like a big, happy beetle just wider than a classroom desk. I recognize the damage on Eli's belly—claw marks from Ratchet. "It's really you!" I exclaim. There's no doubt. A singe on one of the rear rotors where my Peerless letter got sucked in convinces me. Me and this drone been *through* some stuff!

"You . . . know this drone?" Leah asks dubiously.

"You *named* this drone?" Amari frowns.

"Yeah . . . short for reliable—"

Amari snorts. "Nicknames for everyone but me, that's how we're doing it?"

"Eli pulled me out of the storm when I rode my bike here, okay?" The doubt on their faces fades, hearing that. Somehow seeing Eli here, now, when we're floundering for answers, makes me feel like we're on the right track to getting some. Amari's all in, poking at the tablet. We agree to send a letter—but to Professor Touré, since Kinder's been ghost so far. Better to cover our bases.

Amari disappears for a supply run, returning with paper for an actual letter—even drawing a golden seal on the envelope. We decide to keep the message short and sweet.

Professor Touré,
Our neighborhoods are made of magic.
We're at Peerless and we need your help.
Unless you need our help. Then I guess
we'll come for you.
        —The Peerless Crew

We all sign our names. Amari gives the drone a thoughtful look, then paints *Eli* under one of the wings. He adds a pink-and-blue smiley face on the front, with Xs for the eyes. "So we can tell Eli apart from any others," he explains.

Leah snorts. "But those scratches already . . . oh." Yeah . . . if Ratchet's locked in on the school, other drones might end up with battle scars, too.

"It's perfect," I say.

A few taps on the tablet, and Eli zooms off, letter secured.

This is unbelievable. Our plan is working for a change! We'll even know when Eli reaches Professor Touré, thanks to the tablet.

"Keynan . . ." Amari says carefully. "What's that situation on your face about?"

"What situation?" I complain. "This is my face!" He and Leah exchange a glance that makes me scowl. "Fine . . . I was thinking how we just made a tablet. And gave a drone instructions with it. We could go even bigger."

"Fair enough." Amari purses his lips, tapping through screens. "I can see Peerless." His face scrunches up worriedly. "Also some kind of weird . . . alert. A notification maybe? From Kinder's office."

"Direct message?" I ask hopefully.

"Nope. I'm not sure what it is. We better check it out."

Fresh nervousness squeezes my ribs as we trudge to Kinder's office. We've sent out Jocelyn, and just now Eli. What if the headmaster and professors are all trapped in some conjured fall break vacation? Held hostage by a Glory or worse?

The admin area where Miss Molly, the headmaster's assistant, does her work is empty. Same with Kinder's office. Her gleaming desk still desperately needs a candy bowl. And a suggestion box. The enormous painting of Peerless swallows up the entire wall behind the desk.

"Maybe it's a bug with our tablet. Or not," I add hastily at Amari's glare. "Can you check on Eli?" I eye Kinder's painting mistrustfully. Peerless, surrounded by happy blue skies. Talk about an illusion! Maybe that's how Kinder hopes the school will look one day. Either way, the painting is different than I remember. Where's the hawk?

"Eli's still flying." Amari peers at the tablet, swiping to another app—he's practically mastered it already. "Our tablet's not busted . . . I think it's trying to sync with Peerless."

"But why here, instead of the IT room?" I press.

"Something's not right." Leah's eyes narrow. "Let's check for magic again. Maybe . . . change up your rhyme this time?"

I nod. "Good call."

Leah readies a beat and I slide into freestyle without thinking. The words just flow.

> *Sleuthing for the truth we got no time for*
> *headmaster lies,*
>> *no more surprises for these first-year eyes, time*
> *for the sun—*

An enraged shriek fills the air. The hawk I remembered soars back into the frame of Kinder's painting on crimson wings. The bird is big mad! We shy away as it swoops back and forth over the school, flashing as bright as Disco. The bird disappears off the canvas.

Leah spins in a wary circle, trying to look each way at once. "Did it . . . escape the painting? I don't need my ears pecked off!"

"Don't think so . . ." Some kind of guard. Like Buster, back on Bizzy Block?

"Figured out the sync," Amari announces. The entire painting melts away, revealing a hidden room. "Look.

At. This!" He prances in eagerly before we can grab him. Touch monitors swallow an entire curved wall, some hand-sized like our tablets, and others bigger than windows, but all fitting together perfectly like we're standing inside some massive segmented seashell.

A sharp lemon smell tickles my nose. Staircases and escalators and ladders and slides snake off in dozens of random directions, tangled up like a trapdoor spider's lair. My eyes water trying to follow where they go. Glowing transparent coils snake through everything, gurgling with pink and green hues.

"Wow," Leah marvels. "So this is how she pops up everywhere?"

I gawk at the biggest screens. "It's worse than that." There are controls for the season, the time of day. One screen is devoted entirely to Bizzy Block. My *home*. Leah and Amari crowd in, stunned.

"My apartment complex is here!" he exclaims. "The V."

"Mine, too . . . that's Concord Towers! Kinder's watching us? What is this?"

Words fail me. My brain barely accepts what my eyes are showing me. There's no Glory secretly capturing us in some fancy bubble trap. Our own headmaster can watch our every move from this hidden office.

"If I'm reading this right," Amari says with a frown, "she

can control *everything* from here. Any professor with admin privileges can track us with our tablets."

Another screen shows the worst yet, a long list of faces and names. "This looks like all the students at Peerless."

My mouth goes dry as I scan them, spotting students I know. Lacretia. Joey. Tasha. Akil. Some of the names are in red. The interface won't show their faces when I try to bring them up. I have no idea why. "I don't see our names yet—there's a lot, though." I swallow. "They . . . none of the students are real, either. Just like my neighbors. They have mood settings . . . conversation prompts . . ."

"What? No way. We said here is real." Leah bites her lip. "Peerless . . . the headmasters . . . she *controls* all of this?"

"Ian and Dez . . ." Amari cycles through the list breathlessly. "Where are they?"

"My sister?" Leah asks anxiously. Her voice is ready to split in half. Amari and I exchange a helpless look. This whole mess is bad enough with fake parents. Leah has a *sister*. If Yolanda's been fake this whole time, Leah might cave in on herself and never come back out. I couldn't blame her if she did.

Leah pushes forward. I stand aside so she can flick through the screen. She inhales sharply. "Oh, no."

There's no hiding from the very last name on the list: Yolanda Jameson.

She's not real. Just like our parents.

"Leah, I'm so sorry." Me and Amari sweep in for a hug. She's rigid as a concrete wall, jaw clenched.

"I don't believe it." She scrapes a knuckle across her eyes. "Some things you can't fake."

The pain in her voice makes my eyes wet. Why can't I think of decent words to say? None of this is fair, not a single thing that's happened! Everything about our lives is a hollow shell of pretend people and made-up places. Headmaster Kinder's perched in the center of it all, wrapping us up with lies too impossible to believe.

Amari steps away to examine the largest screen, wide enough to swallow up a whole section of wall. The display is covered with purple-and-orange swirls. Those patterns tug at my memory somehow.

"Y'all. Doesn't this look like my mural?" Amari asks. "Only finished?"

I squint at it. When Touré first brought us to the radiant waste, Amari got swept up in some kind of . . . artist inspiration fever? He painted a huge map on an old wall, and this screen definitely resembles it. All of the same landmarks are visible. Loop Land. The Pancake

Plains, the fiery tree. "He's right." I remember what it reminds me of—trying to read Eli's display, when the drone pulled me out of Bizzy Block.

The meaning of it all falls into place.

"Those swirls aren't storm clouds. That's radiant waste. Peerless is the only thing that's real," I whisper. Leah's head snaps up, and Amari stares at the picture with new, horrified eyes. There's no denying it. The gray block Amari didn't get to paint . . . that's the Peerless Academy. The breathing orchard beside it, where Touré gave us our very first magic lesson, is obvious. Loop Land—where those frosty bears attacked us—turns greener as we watch. A new season. There's more, too, places we haven't explored that twist and turn before our eyes on the map. We're completely surrounded by radiant waste—so much of it that the Peerless Academy feels like a leaf caught in a storm of corrupt magic. I press my hand to my belly. "I'm gonna be sick."

Leah covers her mouth with her hands. "It's everywhere. The whole map."

Amari fiddles with the controls and zooms in on Peerless itself. He points out shining lines worming through the radiant waste, connecting the school to glowing bubbles. "That's what I couldn't remember!" he exclaims.

"When I tried to redraw my map. No wonder Touré didn't want me to finish it." He can't hide the hurt in his voice. "She didn't want me to know the truth."

"Our neighborhoods?" I venture. "Those lines connecting them to Peerless must be the roads."

"Like tubes," Amari agrees. "Tunnels through the waste." I shiver at the thought of what might happen to Bizzy Block if those tunnels were broken.

"I count ten of them." Leah taps her lip. "If each one is a neighborhood . . . there's just ten whole kids for all of Peerless? And what about the professors?"

Hmm. Besides us, that would leave . . . Ian? Students we don't know? Professor Wiley? A sudden flash pulls my eye. "Hey! Did y'all see that? Can you make it go closer?"

"I think so." Amari nibbles on his tongue as he toggles the controls.

"Only a few real people in all of Peerless?" Leah laughs softly. "You'd think we all know each other."

"There!" I point out a white speck, surrounded by an angry crimson flare in some part of the radiant waste we haven't seen yet. A familiar shape stalks through what might be some upside-down mountains. My whole body tightens as Amari angles the view closer, revealing a glint of crystalline claws, pawprints of fire, and glittering shoulders. The new cracks along the monster's chest are easy to spot, too. I put those there—with a rhyme, when we battled in the courtyard—although I'm still not sure how.

Leah swallows. "Ratchet."

The monster freezes. Sniffs the air.

The display abruptly cuts off. Amari shrugs. "Sorry, y'all. Had to. Remember what happened when we got too close?"

"Good call," I say shakily. We tried to spy on the monster once, thanks to Amari's map and a pinch of magic. Ratchet *sensed* it somehow and set the map on fire. "I think you're right. Ratchet is a Glory."

I swallow. That's not scary. Not scary at all. Facing an actual sorcerer from the Wars of Illusion? Mad or not, Ratchet's probably forgotten more magic than we'll ever know.

"Definitely the smartest thing we've seen," Leah admits. "If a Glory wanted to hurt us, or Peerless, attacking our trees makes perfect sense. The saplings we tried to plant in the waste. And the oak tree would be gone if Keynan and Dez hadn't been there to save it."

"But why now?" Amari asks doubtfully.

"Because of us," I say guiltily. "Slickback and Disco weakened the school."

We go quiet after that—we all know we've just

repeated the same mistake. All that water from the radiant waste seeped into Peerless. The school is weak again, perfect timing if Ratchet is itching for a rematch.

"Don't get down." Leah squeezes my shoulder. "We've still got our art, and that means we can make anything happen."

"Our art and each other," Amari adds. "And . . . a block party. I want that more than my crew name."

"Can you focus for once? Please?"

"You said we can make *anything* happen—"

My friends are so strange. And I couldn't imagine any of this without them.

A thrumming vibration rattles Kinder's secret room. "That didn't sound good," I squeak.

"Maybe Ratchet felt us after all," Amari says breathlessly. "We need to protect the tree!"

We race out into the hall, my mind spinning and sliding for my best Ratchet-stopping rhyme. I barely know which end is up—but now we're fighting for Peerless all over again? Can't worry about that now—I best be ready to bring it!

CHAPTER SEVEN

QUESTIONS OF SENTIENCE

The air boils with light and heat as we race out. The hallway flails apart around us, walls and ceiling like spaghetti noodles circling a whirlpool. Ratchet's doing something I've never seen before. Can we stop it? A musical muttering ripples through my brain, as if every word I've ever said is getting yanked out of me. My teeth ache.

Professor Touré bursts into the hall before us. She does a double take, and her eyes flit between us and Kinder's office behind us. A brilliant purple wrap holds back her twists, but besides that she's wearing her same plain work clothes, like she just finished pulling up some weeds. The thrumming sound swallowing the hall dissipates. "Children? You're all back early." She eyes us warily and calls over her shoulder. "Come on out . . . it's safe. Relatively speaking."

Dez shuffles in, dazed. His clothes are rumpled—the same outfit he wore before break! A Peerless uniform with red shirt and dark pants. His cinnamon-colored eyes are bloodshot, and dirt splotches one of his cheeks. And his hair is a *mess*. That's the biggest sign that whatever's happened, Dez really went through it these past few days.

The wind fades as if the halls weren't just about to melt into puddles around our feet. I can't even imagine whatever magic Touré was about to unleash if she had decided we weren't us.

We rush forward to crush Dez in a hug. Amari reaches him first. "Glad you're okay," he whispers anxiously. "We were so worried."

"I'm fine," he says gruffly, like he's trying not to cry. "Thanks to Professor Touré. Ratchet . . . came after me at my home. I've been hiding from that thing since I got off the shuttle! It's . . . really good to see y'all."

A sudden whirring sound fills the air. Professor Touré lets out a surprised hiss as Eli zips around the corner. "Children, get behind me! I'll—"

Leah hops between Touré and the drone. I stretch

my hands out before the professor unleashes another rhyme. "No, wait! He's one of us."

"One of us?" she repeats slowly. "Keynan . . . do I even want to know?"

The drone inches closer to Touré—like Eli's afraid of getting cooked, too. Smoke is wafting from one of the turbines. Eli's more beat-up than Dez. A small mechanical grappling hook extends from the drone's body, holding the letter Amari crafted. Touré grabs it suspiciously, eyes narrowed at Eli like she's reading through the drone's programming—our programming.

"That wasn't there before," Amari murmurs worriedly, for my ear alone.

"What?" I whisper back. "Eli looks fine."

Amari gives me an *are you serious bro* look. "Drones don't have arms like that!"

Oh. *Ohhhh.* Somehow our magic has done a little bit more. Amari adjusts his pants, and I can only imagine that he's checking to make sure his tablet is secure. Touré's eyes flick over the note. "Y'all did all of this? Rhymed the conjuring?"

I swallow. "We did it together."

She traces the edges of the letter P on the envelope. "Not bad work at all, but this little tinkering of yours is . . .

off. There's a good reason people avoided mixing magic and machinery. Questions of sentience."

I stare at Eli with new eyes. "Like Slickback and Disco."

"Exactly. Another problem you've gifted me with. Better to be on the safe side and deactivate it."

"That can wait! We deserve some answers from you!"

"Take a deep breath." Professor Touré tries to fix me with a glare, but I'm not having it.

None of us are.

"You don't get to boss us around like we just got here." Leah's voice is steady, but her hands are squeezed into fists. She nods back at Kinder's office, the secret room. "Not anymore."

"I'm . . ." A heavy, defeated sigh escapes Professor Touré. "Sorry y'all found out about Peerless this way. Truly. It was never part of the plan."

"The plan?" Amari erupts. "What kind of plan needs fake neighborhoods for us to live in?"

Touré flinches. Dez turns to her, bewildered. "What? What is he saying?"

I cringe; he doesn't know. All of the helplessness and fear I tried to hide away are boiling right up again. My chest is tight—I'm shouting and I don't even care!

"The headmaster is using fake parents to raise us!

Made of magic. And she controls them from a secret room in her office."

"Not to mention my sister!" Leah snaps. "It's so wrong—how do we even know who we are if our family isn't our family?"

Touré won't meet her eyes. "I didn't create the faux parents," she says quietly. "And neither did Headmaster Kinder."

I stop short. "Then who—"

"Your *real* parents. They created Peerless." We all stare at her, too shocked to speak. "Hector. Alicia. And everyone else who gave input to their design. There are pieces of them everywhere in this place. I know you've felt it, even if you didn't understand what you're seeing."

"You're lying to us," I splutter. No. Absolutely no way. One of my parents' biggest lessons about being the best version of myself—being a Masters—is that we tell the truth. Always. And I can't imagine a bigger lie than what Touré just pulled. "They wouldn't do that!"

"Soup's burritos are exactly the same as my granny's." Amari's voice quivers. "That's not the only recipe, either. Come on—I've heard y'all say the same thing! It's not just me."

Tears bite at the corners of my eyes. The way the

courtyard gardens are planted, and the messy rows of tulips between buildings? Just like my mama does at home. Or how Professor Wiley's dap feels exactly like my baba's chunky fist? I can't believe it.

Leah folds her arms, scowling. Dez shakes his head, muttering like he's arguing with himself—and losing. "Why . . . why would they do this?"

A thoughtful expression overtakes Amari's face. "It's like they're talking to us. Through Peerless."

Touré smiles sadly. "That was the idea. I'm so sorry, y'all. This isn't fair to any of you, but it's what we had to do."

"You *knew* them?" I growl. "How long have they been gone?"

"Keynan—"

"How. Long."

"Three years."

Leah gasps. Touré's answer slams into my stomach like a hammer. Three years? That's a quarter of my life! Raised by—what did Touré call them? Faux parents! Amari has his eyes squeezed shut like he's trying to wake himself up from a nightmare. Dez pats his shoulder, but he looks just as sick as I feel.

Even with everything falling apart, I always thought we'd be okay—because we're a crew. My rhymes and my magic are better than they've ever been—we're creating together, incredible things. But all of this is too much. Our parents, the people I look up to the most, are just hollow copies? I can't even utter the obvious question— are any of our parents still alive? If they've been gone this long, I'm afraid the answer is obvious, too.

CHAPTER EIGHT

BUILT ON LOVE

None of us speak. The lie is too big to wrap my head around. Finally Leah's whisper cuts through the silence. "But why leave us here in the first place? What could be so important for them to build this gigantic lie around us?"

"They went to fight the Glories." For a while, no sound fills the hall except the gentle whir of Eli's turbines. My head is spinning. Did she really just say that? My parents, Heck and Alicia Masters, gardeners and community planners, are actually—what's the word? Sorcerers? Spellcasters? Conjurers? "They went to fight the Glories," she repeats. "And they lost. You were too young to go with them, and they didn't know how long they would be gone."

"I need to sit down," I wheeze.

Professor Touré strides over, and before I know it she's grabbed my head with both hands, thumbing open my eyelids and peering into my eyes. "You've been purging yourself of corruption?" she asks sharply. "How are you feeling?"

"Fine. Can you let go? I'm fine!" I only get away when she releases me, and I barely keep myself from stumbling. Sheesh, I can't wait to get my grown folks' strength!

She eyes each of us in turn. "Y'all been through the wringer. Came out better than anyone could expect of you."

Leah digs in. "But we need to know—"

"I don't know what happened to your parents, Leah. I'm sorry."

We all go quiet after that. A lump rises in my throat. She doesn't know if our parents are alive. The old grief in her voice leaves no doubt of what she believes.

"I'll answer your questions. But food first. Unless you put Soup back on duty?" She waits. "I thought not. Come on." She herds us all to the courtyard. The professor gives a grudging nod of approval when the oak tree doesn't pull corrupt magic out of us. She sweeps off for the kitchen.

Leah and I plop down together on the stone bench, the oak tree's branches creaking softly above us. Amari sits down cross-legged on a patch of grass while Dez paces. Leah wordlessly leans her shoulder into mine. For a moment, the peacefulness of the courtyard almost convinces me everything's normal.

Eli doesn't help. The drone whirs around the courtyard, shrinking back whenever Dez frowns at it. Boredom? Waiting for the next command? I want to talk more with Amari, but more important things are crashing down on our heads.

My stomach cheers when Touré returns with lunch. This actually might be the most decent meal I've had in—what? A day? Two? Times are seriously awful when we start forgetting snacks. We munch on grilled-cheese sandwiches and tart green apples slathered with peanut butter, washing it all down with cool water.

"Now . . . tell me everything. How you got here, what's happened since—all of it." Touré shivers. "The school feels off."

Leah goes first. I'm kind of relieved I'm not the only one wolfing down my food while I wait for my turn to talk—but feel extra guilty when I notice Dez picking the crumbs off his tray. He looks like he hasn't eaten in days. There's a hollowness to his face, like he's seen things that make his eyes try and squeeze themselves deeper into their sockets. "Glad you're here," I whisper. "Are you okay?"

"I don't know. This is . . . a lot. How are you so calm?"

"The crew is all together."

He brightens some. "I'm glad we turned out to be friends, Keynan. It'd be awful if we weren't."

Whew . . . is he ever right about that. I offer some dap in agreement. By the time Touré finishes grilling us with questions, the courtyard lights are flickering on, and the sky is turning a pinkish purple. "I know you have a million things to ask me," she says quietly. "But I need you to wait a little longer. And you all need sleep, you've been through a lot."

I open my mouth to protest, but a yawn comes out instead. "Tomorrow," I agree reluctantly. No one else pushes back, either. We're all exhausted.

Professor Touré jabs a finger at Eli. "You . . . come with me."

The drone dips behind the raspberry bushes. Touré kisses her teeth.

"It's okay!" I call out. Eli hovers closer to me, nudging at my legs. Acting . . . nervous. I'd feel the same way in the drone's place. I scoot away from the buzzing turbines— and I swear Eli whines. Like a big metal puppy. "She won't hurt you. Promise."

Eli zips out, gliding in a circle around Touré's heels. She blinks and strides off, Eli whirring beside her.

81

"Wow, Keynan," Leah murmurs. "That one listens to you. Rhymes are definitely improving."

"Listens to *all* of us, hopefully. Or trusts us." Something Slickback said bubbles out of my memory. *Here's some free schooling: name everything you create, or someone else will steal it.* Eli's been nothing but *reliable*, that's been true. I better remember Slickback's words for all of my rhymes. Never thought I'd hear solid advice from a talking lizard. Hmph.

As we tramp off to the first-year dorm, Amari clears his throat. "Anyone up for a . . . sleepover? I'm not in love with the idea of being alone in my room."

"Same!" Dez agrees immediately. We haul blankets and pillows from our rooms through the hallway and into the common room, building up a cozy nest with couch cushions and throw pillows. All of us try to chatter about something while we brush our teeth, but conversation shrivels up every single time. I can barely believe this is the same room where we all hung out together on the last day before break. Inhaling snacks, playing games, laughing until the sun came up. Now everything's turned inside out.

Leah's hand hovers near the light switch. "They could have just told us the truth about the radiant waste, the Glories, and everything!" she erupts. "So what if we're first-years? We still could've been getting ready to fight them! We could have helped."

That thought echoes in my brain long after everyone's asleep. My dreams are full of me riding Ratchet around the radiant waste, planting saplings, only to turn around and discover a saddle on *my* back! *Just a little while longer,* a voice urges. When I crane my neck to see who holds my reins, musical laughter jolts me awake.

The next morning, a tablet notification tells us that Professor Touré's waiting for us in the dining hall. We all head down together. Finally, it's our turn to ask the questions.

Touré directs us to a table. "Ask," she says simply. Soup is nowhere in sight, and she spoons out a simple break-fast of cheesy grits as she listens to Leah's questions. Well, Leah's rant.

The professor waits for her to finish. "Help your parents *fight* the Glories?" Her lips purse in an almost-smile. "I can't speak for them, but I'd bet a spa weekend your par-ents would say that's *exactly* why they created Peerless.

"Oh, they argued about it, believe you me. But they needed y'all grounded in their best, not their hate for the sorcerers who turned the world inside out. Broke magic itself. They wanted you to be kids, not . . . soldiers. Every neighborhood holds memories of what made your parents love the world before the radiant waste swallowed it up. People they knew, ideas they cherished, food they loved to eat. If y'all were brought up just training to defeat the Glories, they were afraid you wouldn't have anything else in you. There wouldn't be anything to go back to once the fight was over, anything to love."

Amari nods slowly. "People with no love would just screw the world up again."

I blink. Leah and Dez go quiet, too—although they both looked ready to argue. As much as everything Professor Touré is saying has my insides twisted up, hearing it from Amari hits different. He's right. I may hate what our parents decided—leaving us. How am I supposed to feel any other way? But I can admit to just the tiniest bit of reason behind it. They had to pick between two ways to hurt us. They just picked wrong.

Maybe that's the whole point. There was no right choice.

Professor Touré twists a ring around her finger. "Peerless is a lie, and lies are never good. But it was built on love. If your crew can see the love behind the lie, then that's something. A start."

"That doesn't make me feel a whole lot better—my home is still fake," Dez mumbles. "But knowing my parents put everything there just for me helps. A little."

"Why bother with a whole fake school?" I ask. "That seems like a lot of trouble."

Touré snorts. "Don't I know it. But what better place for y'all to learn while they were gone?"

Amari cuts in with a question. "So our drones, *Build-A-Scholar* . . . that's all Peerless and nothing else?"

"Yes and no. Other schools followed the Peerless example."

Leah and I share an excited grin—we're thinking the exact same thing. When Touré took us into the radiant waste for the first time, we stumbled across a camp. A little pocket of the old world, with some supplies, raggedy blankets, and just enough room for someone to sleep. But it was completely free of corrupt magic. "So what we found in the radiant waste was from another school?"

"What was left of it, maybe." Professor Touré eyes us suspiciously. Whatever she sees on my face, she doesn't like—so I give her my most innocent smile. *Nothing to worry about!* Her frown deepens. "These dishes won't wash themselves. And I need some help in the greenhouse."

Amari mutters something about how break shouldn't feel like detention, but I'm almost grateful for the chores. So much to marinate on—other schools! A small hope is worming up inside me, just as fragile as the sprouts we transplant. Restoring the radiant waste, healing broken magic, felt like an impossible task before. Now? It's even bigger than we imagined. But if there are other schools . . . who knows what we could do together?

Across from me, Amari nudges Leah. "He's making the face again. It's your turn."

"What's the face?" Dez asks curiously.

Leah sighs. "It's like . . ." She tilts her head to the side, bites her lip, and squints off at something past my shoulder. "This?"

"Oh!" Dez nods. "I've definitely seen that. When he dunked my circuit board in the water in physics, and . . . right before he dragged me off after Ratchet. That face is never a good sign."

"I don't look anything like that!" I splutter. Seriously? Dez? He's said two words since we've all been back, but now he's suddenly extra generous when it's time to chatter about me? "And my ideas have done plenty for us. Like saving the school?"

Amari chimes in as if I didn't say anything. "Yeah, the face usually means he's thinking about something that's going to get us all into trouble."

Leah winks at me. "And this is the part where we say . . ."

"Fine!" I grumble. "I'm not thinking it."

"But say what it is so we can tell you it's a bad idea."

I'm so tempted to throw a dirt clod right at Leah's nose, but Touré peeks into the greenhouse just then. "All wrapped up?" She takes in the sprout I hastily set down, and her eyes narrow. "Keynan . . . what are you thinking?"

My face is hot enough to catch fire as my friends explode into laughter.

That evening we break for dinner in Touré's workshop, a platter piled high with sambusas, filled to bursting with savory meat, garlic, and onions. Touré's been examining Eli all day. Actual wonder seeps into her voice. "I want to get some more repairs done and compare Eli with the others in storage." She's almost . . . affectionate about the drone, as she relays how the batteries apparently charged themselves with movement, and how there's new code in Eli's programming every time she checks.

"That's great and all," Dez pipes up. "But can we go back to the part about other schools? How many are there besides Peerless?"

"We don't know. But Peerless was the first model." Touré fixes me with her steady brown eyes. "Your parents' model, Keynan. They rhymed together every brick. For those other schools, who knows? Probably swallowed by the radiant waste or worse. I barely keep Peerless from falling apart as it is. None of it was meant to last this long."

One thing at least isn't a lie—my family is made of strong stuff. But that smothering ache has slipped back into Touré's voice. She lost it for a moment, discussing Eli. It's been there the whole time: She's given up. A long time ago, maybe.

"Peerless isn't in that bad a shape, is it?" Leah asks.

"I had enough tricks to keep things up and running awhile longer." Touré shakes her head sadly. "But whatever y'all did here since returning . . . things are way off. I'm not sure if I can fix it."

"Maybe we can find another school," Amari ventures. "Ask if they'll take us in."

"That might work." Touré looks doubtful. "More people, working together? More complicated but better than being ground up by the radiant waste. It never stops trying to find a way in. It's relentless."

"Peerless belongs to us," I say, surprised at the stubbornness in my voice. "We can't just leave it, not after everything we've seen!"

"But Keynan . . ."

"No, Leah! Finding the camp, and the museum." I turn to Amari. "And what about your map? They could all be clues to help us heal the radiant waste. Maybe even . . .

find our parents." There. I said it out loud. I glare at Touré, daring her to say different. Someone's got to hope they're still out there. Still alive. "All I know is that if any of that's going to happen, this is the crew who will make it happen."

They trade scared looks, nobody willing to speak up. I'm afraid, too, but I believe in us. I don't want them to agree because I gassed them up. *Moving people around with my words,* like Leah said. That's not how a crew should work. So I wait.

Dez nods first. "I'm with you, Keynan. We didn't go through all of this for nothing. Our parents were probably all friends. We should be, too."

"Best friends," I agree. Leah tilts her head at me. I already know. Amari takes a deep breath and nods, too.

"Looks like we're staying," I say to Professor Touré.

"Looks like," she says quietly and stands.

Things are different. We all feel it. Touré's still the grown-up, still a professor—but not *quite* as in charge as before. *She's given up,* I realize, *and she knows we haven't.* But if she's willing to see this through, trust us a tiny bit more . . . maybe we can give her some hope, too. "Let's call it a night," she says. "Get to your rooms, and I'll wrangle up some fresh uniforms for the week."

"Uniforms?" Amari croaks. "But what about fall break?"

"No break for anyone now," Touré replies. "No more games."

We set off, but Touré's hand on my shoulder stops me. "They believe in you, Keynan Masters."

I search her face. There's a seriousness there that's disarming, makes me feel like I'm on a stage with the whole world watching. "I know . . . I wish I knew why."

"Everything you say is a life raft for your friends, Keynan. Even without the magic. They listen to you. And you try to do what's right even if you're wrongheaded about it." Her serious expression softens. "I know what that's like. The weight of it. Are you ready to keep them safe?"

"I am," I reply.

"Good. The first thing we need is—"

The ceiling above her splinters apart. A set of freakishly sharp glittering teeth rips away drywall, metal, and wiring. We scramble back from the falling chunks of ceiling. A hole the size of a classroom reveals Ratchet's snarling face, glaring straight at me.

CHAPTER NINE

ALWAYS HUNGRY

An immense groaning shivers through the building, so loud I feel it in my bones. Ratchet pads forward through the hole. But I ain't scared. We're all together this time, not scattered around Peerless trying to hold everything together. Ratchet picked the wrong day! The lockers rattle with the Glory's menacing growl.

"Not you," Touré whispers to my left. "Not now!"

"Keynan!" Leah shouts from the other side of the rubble filling the hallway. We're cut off from each other.

Ratchet seems . . . bigger. Working out? A sudden image of Ratchet doing jumping jacks in the radiant waste pops into my head. Nope. That's ridiculous. Doubling up on snacks? If there are more magic schools hidden in the waste, the thought of extra snacks makes me extra nervous. Ratchet's whiskers glitter like threads of diamond, and brilliant purple-black horns curl around those catlike ears. The air around them ripples as if they're hot as lava. Ratchet definitely didn't have sizzle horns before! The last time we clashed, my rhyme shot spiraling cracks all across the creature's chest. They're still there, but sealed up like brilliant turquoise veins glittering in the sapphire muscle.

Another roar shakes the ground. Touré and I both clap our hands over our ears. Through the gaping hole in the ceiling, clear blue sky splits apart, revealing the roiling purple and orange of the radiant waste. Wind pours into the hall. Corrupt magic prickles my skin.

Ratchet is more powerful than ever—back to finish the job.

"Ratchet's tearing down the illusion, just like at my house!" Dez's frantic shout reaches us from behind Ratchet. "We need to run!"

"No! We've got to seal it or we'll lose Peerless!" Professor Touré pulls herself to her feet. "Keynan! I can't do it alone!"

I freeze, doubt rushing in. This is the same kind of mad sorcerer my parents fought and lost. Hunting *us*. Can we even stop Ratchet? Did luck carry me through last time?

I want to squeal and hide. My friends' panicked shouts won't allow it. I can't let them down.

Ratchet's entirely focused on Touré now. I edge to the side. My eyes lock on Leah, climbing over the mini mountain of rubble. We clasp hands and I hoist her up. "Dez is stuck, I need help to get him! What's the plan?"

"Professor! What—what do you want us to do?" I cry.

"Make a distraction!" Touré calls. "Anything will help!"

"We got you!" Leah springs forward, waving up at Ratchet. "You want our school? Try and take it!"

The Glory's blazing eyes swing around, fixing on Leah as though nothing else exists. A six-clawed paw flashes forward faster than I can cry out. Leah leaps out of the way as debris goes flying. She flips and spins out of Ratchet's reach. The air around her quivers. Everything around her moves . . . slower. Grit drifts from the broken ceiling like snowflakes. Sparks from a broken light shoot lazily behind Professor Touré. She's down on one knee, whispering fiercely to herself. The cloud of dust from Ratchet's attack expands sluggishly. Like the whole space is stopping to bear witness. The air ignites in a rippling wave of gold and red. Ratchet roars in confusion, twisting away.

Leah's moves and magic—I don't understand any of

it. Do I really need to, though? She's amazing. The sky above us boils like it's resisting her will. I finally remember I'm supposed to be helping. "Amari! Your time to shine!"

Amari flinches in his hiding spot behind a bank of crumpled lockers. He scoops up a chunk of plaster and scrawls furiously on the shattered brick beside him. From somewhere behind him through the tumult, I hear Dez beatboxing. He peeks out from behind a shattered piece of wall and gives me a thumbs-up. Between Leah's moves and Dez's beats, the entire space is vibrating with energy and waves of light. I'm up!

When the Peerless crew is under attack
We draw up friends to fight back—

"Fight back!" Professor Touré responds.

Fight back!
Our rhythm and rhymes about to send you back
Because we fight back—

The others join in too. "Fight back!"

Fight back!

Amari's drawing ripples and plucks itself out of the broken wall. Spiders. Clumsy, chunky, brick-sized spiders with knobby knees. Dozens of them! Ratchet swats at them scornfully, still circling Touré. She gestures me off, never taking her eyes from the Glory. "Go."

"Help me! I'm stuck!" Dez squeals over the gusting wind. "I hate magic. All of it!"

"Amari!" I screech. "We said no bugs!"

"I know! I'm sorry!"

The spiders spin and step and flip through the rubble, clattering and crackling and cartwheeling in every direction. My rhymes are gone—too busy squealing.

"Are those on our side?" Leah's entire dance flow shatters. She's hopping around on her tiptoes. "Tell me they're on our side!"

"I think so!" Amari cries. We rush over to help; he's frantically clawing away the chunks of concrete where Dez's leg is wedged. "Why didn't you finish the rhyme and tell them what to do?"

I should have—he's right. But I freaked out. It's like Slickback and Disco all over again. We tried to make something and didn't plan it through. Now there are terrifying bugs scattered all over the hall.

Ratchet slaps down on one. Bricks explode under the Glory's monstrous palm. The rest of the spiders drum their legs on the debris, a clatter that makes the hair on the back of my neck stand up. Dozens of brick spiders swarm Ratchet, scurrying up crystalline paws and clinging to its shoulders and back. One by one they burrow into the crystal skin. Yellow-and-white flowers burst out of each hole. Ratchet twists around, slamming into walls and lockers as we scramble away. An enraged roar chokes off as the Glory bellows out clouds of golden glitter. The wind scatters it.

"Pollen," I gawk in wonder. What in the world is happening?

"We need walls with a quickness, magic be my witness, bricks please help me fix this!" Professor Touré's effortless rhyme washes over the space. Chunks of broken brick tumble up the wall, stuffing themselves into the ragged hole. The brick spiders that Ratchet smashed sprout new legs. Me and Leah scramble into each other as they scurry past. So creepy! They cocoon themselves into the breach, sealing the hole.

Ratchet's tails lash out, swiping away spiders on every side. Amari had it right the whole time—the Glory hates spiders, too! Ratchet's legs are covered with them!

"Nice!" Dez shouts as we finally pull him free. His pant leg is ripped but he's okay. "Doesn't feel good being pinned, does it?"

Ratchet's tails zing straight at us. Leah dodges out of the way, but Amari screams as sharp crystal blurs past him. He collapses, clutching his shoulder. We all encircle him, eyes wide with fear.

"Professor!" I shout. "He's hurt bad!"

"Get him out of here! All of you, I mean it!" Professor Touré's rhymes repair Peerless around us—cracks reseal in the floor and walls, broken doors glide to their hinges. Ratchet is untouched—Amari's spiders gave the monster more trouble!

Why is the professor holding back?

The brick spiders spin silvery webs now. Ratchet's swallowed by flowers and vines, but ripping them free. It's up to me. The corrupt magic in the air ripples and shimmers as Dez starts beatboxing, nodding at me hopefully. I get an idea and turn it loose.

I'm here to turn back time, or really flip the page
Pretend like things don't fall apart and it's a
brand-new age.
Set the walls up new, reverse the Glory away
Start a fresh chapter, same day, new plaster new
brick
Get Amari patched up faster, fix this whole
thing quick!

Sudden tightness slithers through the space. The air presses on my skin. Pieces of the ceiling shiver around my feet, then leap up. Some of the brick spiders twitch and stop attacking Ratchet. They shrivel smaller, down into spider eggs, and wink out of existence. Something's wrong. Leah takes two lurching steps back, away from Amari. "Keynan! What did you do?"

Amari jerks awkwardly to his feet. A flash of red— one of the Glory's tails glances against his arm again. His wound is gone. The brick spiders that didn't disappear march back into the wall, becoming drawings again. The ones that aren't trapped by my freestyle swarm Ratchet, but the rest of them flee.

Ratchet bites and tears at the blooming flowers, completely ignoring us. Petals rip past on another gust of wind. Ratchet chomps at a paw, too. I squint. Are roots sliding under the Glory's crystal scales?

My rhyme. I wanted it to fix Amari—and it got that part at least, going back to before he was hurt. But nothing else worked out quite how I expected.

We cluster by Touré as Ratchet rolls and snarls down the hall, away from us. "You poor thing," Touré whispers. Leah and I exchange disbelieving stares. That monster nearly took down the school—again! Hurt Amari worse than I've ever seen. How can she show Ratchet one scrap of pity?

The Glory howls and springs back through the ragged hole in the ceiling. Touré unleashes a flurry of rhymes, sealing up the opening just as Ratchet's three tails clear it. The wind immediately stills. A crumpled bank of lockers beside me groans and heaves back into place on the wall. Dez claps me on the shoulder. "Nice job. And not to call anyone out"—his eyes slide over to Amari, plucking grit from his fro—"but can we maybe not do battles with creepy-crawlies that *we* made?"

Leah snorts. "I know you're new to this, but this crew doesn't exactly do the reasonable thing."

Touré sighs in relief as she examines Amari's arm. "Keynan . . . your rhyme was more about *time* than anything else."

"Just like back at the museum," Leah says, giving me a fearful glance.

"Yeah." Amari swallows. "That was the worst."

My face flushes. The weird museum we encountered in the radiant waste trapped Leah and Amari in a strange, scary time loop. For me, just a few minutes passed before I freed them with a rhyme. For my friends it felt like hours, trapped running, afraid they would be stuck like that forever. I wasn't there in time. I wasn't careful. My mistake almost broke apart our crew. That same fear and doubt back on their faces makes me sick.

"I'm . . . so sorry, y'all. I've got to do better." I hang my head, peering at my shoes. "I shouldn't have let the rhyme take me there. I just . . . didn't want Amari hurt, and I almost made it worse."

"You have a gift, Keynan." Professor Touré eyes me like she's never seen me before. I'm a little proud at that—she's recognizing the skills, finally! And I'm not being scolded or put in detention for doing what I do best. But I can admit I'm plenty afraid, too, because I can't tell if she likes what she sees. "I should have steered you sooner. Messing with time, the laws of physics . . . directly? It's never going to be perfect. There's too many things that could go wrong. Too many variables to account for. Too much we don't know yet."

"Maybe it could work . . . but the rhyme might take days to finish. Weeks." Amari taps his lip thoughtfully. "That's why the spiders didn't all turn back into my drawings."

"And why I'm the only one who moonwalked back across the floor," Leah adds.

"Exactly. Broken time will open us up to all kinds of nastiness." Professor Touré peers up at the ceiling. "There are legends of an old-school sorcerer trying to reverse time, rhyme herself younger. The conjuring half worked."

"Halfway how? Grown body? Baby arms?" Amari sounds mystified and horrified at the same time.

"Worse. Body stayed the same, with the mind of an infant within."

Dez looks like he's trying to decide whether Touré is joking or not, but her face is stone serious.

"We're all okay, so who cares?" Leah cuts in. "He got it done!"

"Words matter. *How* we get things done is just as important. Shortcuts and half measures are how the Glories were first seduced by magic in the first place!"

That definitely shuts us all up. Turning out like Ratchet? Hard pass. "I'm sick of being chased," I declare. "Why not try to trap Ratchet for good this time?"

Leah's eyes flash. "Now that's what I'm talking about!"

Touré shakes her head. "You sweet, first-year, just-learned-magic children. Do you think Kinder and I haven't spent every waking moment trying to deal with . . . Ratchet? Half the time we can barely track the creature's movement through the waste. Needing help is an understatement!"

"We're your help!" I exclaim.

"Where is she, anyway?" Dez asks. "The headmaster?"

Professor Touré flashes him a hooded look. "Scouring the radiant waste for resources. Clues on how . . . Ratchet draws power from corrupt magic."

"You tell us all the time about working together as a

crew," I persist. "If all of us—professors and kids—were working together, we'd have Ratchet taken care of in a week. Easy! We can keep up with you!"

"Bet on it," Leah agrees firmly.

Professor Touré rubs her temples. Pretty standard for most times we talk, for some reason. I'll have to ask her why she does it. We follow as she strides back toward Kinder's office. "Every encounter, Ratchet grows stronger. Don't you understand? I need you to do more than keep up—I need you to plan ahead."

I open my mouth and close it again, remembering the new turquoise veins where I'd cracked through Ratchet's crystal skin. The scales *did* look tougher than the last time.

"She's right, Keynan," Dez says with a shudder. "Those horns weren't there back at my house. I saw Ratchet up close—I know!"

"Y'all, remember the desk. How small that first paw-print was?" Amari asks. "Every time we use magic, Ratchet changes."

"Finally, some wisdom. There's hope for you yet." Touré takes a deep breath. "Yes, Ratchet comes back stronger, or faster. Weirder. Every escape, every time we fight and lose, the monster remixes itself."

The problem numbs my brain. I thought I had won,

driving Ratchet off the last time—but all I did was make the Glory stronger. How do I beat a remixed monster that changes faster than I can rhyme? We return to the monitoring room, only to find half the screens gone dark—including the one with the largest map of the radiant waste. I wince. "Oh no. Did my rhyme screw this up, too?"

"Peerless runs on magic, and this attack seriously stole from the flow." Touré rubs her temples. "The headmaster will be thrilled."

"So Kinder's real." Leah nods to herself. "No doubts about it."

"Yes. The two of us run Peerless." Touré arches her eyebrow. "Not that a full complement of staff could ever hope to contain the four of you."

I brush some dust off my pants, trying to hide my surprise and disappointment. Just two real people out of all of the grown-ups? Jocelyn isn't real? She sure had me fooled. Soup, Nurse Manny, my professors—Professor Mendoza? That one stings most of all. How is she not real? She slid me hints about magic, even when it could've got her in trouble. One wrong rhyme could have made her unravel . . . just like my faux parents. Did she know that, and trust me anyway?

My head is spinning, and I'm not alone. Amari and

Leah are frowning. It's one thing to wonder if your people are real. Another completely to find out they're not. Dez bites his lip. "Professor Wylie helped me figure things out," he whispers. "No way."

"I'm sorry." Professor Touré sighs. "Get yourselves straight to the oak tree for purging. Rest. You deserve to grieve, but we've got a ton of work to do and no time to do it."

"What work?" I ask in bewilderment. Did we not just chase off a Glory?

"Keeping the corruption from swallowing Peerless, of course. Can't you feel it?"

I stop then, and try. I feel . . . something. A thousand wispy hairs tickling the soles of my feet. The air wavers around me like I'm in the creek back home and spun around in our swimming hole's current. Leah rubs her arms, while Dez and Amari exchange anxious whispers. They feel it, too.

"It's not just Ratchet coming for us now." Professor Touré shudders before she hurries off. "The waste is always hungry."

CHAPTER TEN

ROUGH SHAPE

After all the chaos we just survived, I'm actually looking forward to a quiet, boring afternoon in the courtyard. Of course, it doesn't start that way. When the motes of busted magic start floating out of our skin, Dez leaps up and sprints around the oak tree, flapping his arms. We finally drag him to a stop and Amari assures him this is a good thing. Guess we left out some important details.

Once Dez is calm again and Touré pronounces each of us purged, we all find quiet nooks to be by ourselves. The professor strides off to inspect Peerless's damage.

So much has happened, it's enough to make anyone dizzy. My freestyling, for example? It's nice. *Nice.* My words can stop time. Give heart and soul to drones. Shatter monster skin. I could go even bigger, too. Like getting

Ratchet off our backs. Or finding out what happened to our parents after they left us to fight the Glories. They've got to be out there. Somewhere.

I'm more than a little worried about that part. The waste is bigger than any of us ever imagined. Not just a place we go to. It's all around us. Creeping into the school, my head. If I stop to think about it too hard, my chest feels like a cage, with my heart trying to beat its way free. Peerless is a ship trapped in some stormy sea, constantly needing to be patched up so we don't sink. Touré has never mentioned where the waste ends, either. Does it stop? Or did it cover the whole world?

Me, thinking I could fix all of that? As embarrassing as it gets! Kinder and Touré must have been howling in laughter at us, real tears and all. The first-years who really thought that planting a few saplings in the waste would change everything. Those trees we tried to plant never had a chance. Ratchet just finished the job early.

There's a whole other problem. How many Glories are prowling around the radiant waste, anyway? A handful? A hundred? Are they all as terrifying as Ratchet? Or are some twisted in a whole other direction, like the rhyming voice that taunted me in that strange museum? They could all be as different from each other as I am from Disco. No wonder our parents never came back.

No . . . nope. Can't worry about that right now. Hurts too much. This isn't the time to get sad, no matter how much I deserve it. I gotta stick with what we know, especially with illusions and lies all over the place.

We haven't even seen the worst that Ratchet can do. The idea of a Glory toying with us, testing Peerless? That scares me plenty. I trust my rhymes, though—the more I lean on them, the more they come through when I need them. And I trust my crew. If Ratchet can remix . . . well, we'll just have to level up together, too.

Leah is already snoring softly in a hammock by the time I get comfortable; trails of glitter drift from her skin. I feel awful for her, trying so hard to fix things with her sister only to find out she was never real. I doubt she's accepted it—I couldn't, either. I forgot to give her back Yolanda's heart-shaped necklace before we left for fall break, and it doesn't seem like a good idea now. Who would want a reminder like that of their fake sister?

Amari and Dez are both bleary-eyed and exhausted. Amari's giving Dez a crash course in busted magic. The two of them are still whispering together beneath the oak tree when I finally fall asleep.

I wake to Professor Touré's hand on my shoulder. "Wake them up. I've got good news."

After some nudges and yawning, I gather the crew in so we can all hear it together. Touré's eyes are on me the whole time. She keeps telling me I'm the leader, but then sits back and watches me like she's not sure if she made the right call. I fight down a shiver.

"Listen up," she says. "The headmaster has returned." We all stir uneasily. That is good news, but why doesn't it feel that way? "We've repaired the power loss together. Peerless can be saved."

The four of us let out a collective sigh of relief. "I knew it would hold up," I whisper. Masters are made of strong stuff, so that means we should *make* strong stuff, too.

Touré's not done yet. "But we need—"

"Can't we get one easy thing?" Leah groans.

"—raw magic to keep things running. Which means classes resume next week."

"What?" Dez exclaims. "That's in three days! What about break?"

"You expect us to just go back to class?" I splutter. "After all of this, really? Fake class?"

"I do. Don't try me, either!" Touré fires back. "Art conjures our magic. Yes, Amari—even your stick figures! That magic keeps your neighborhoods from falling apart. It holds Peerless together."

"But the way things were before wasn't exactly working!" Leah snaps.

"If you have a foolproof way forward, I'm ready! No? That's what I thought. So we keep the walls strong, in case Ratchet goes after us again. You'll do classes—and some extra to build up what we lost! That means extra credit, homework, whatever I say. Clear? Then show me."

We grumble, but one by one we nod our heads. This is all the way wrong. But I'll never forget the fear on my faux parents' faces when my rhymes disintegrated their hands. Or how afraid I was to see radiant waste bubbling under Bizzy Block. No way I'm letting anything like that happen to Peerless. It's all we have left. If the school needs us to go to class . . . what choice is there?

"The faculty and students might act . . . off," Professor Touré advises. "We've never had to shake up Peerless like this before. Their conjuring will work well enough to give you basic curriculum. Go ahead and turn in early tonight. Rest. If I can't dig up Soup to fix some proper meals, I'll feed you myself."

As we trudge off toward the dorms, Amari tugs my arm. "If we're really going to pretend like nothing happened . . . we can at least do things different."

I stare at him. "How, bro?"

109

"I don't know. But it'd be cool if Peerless was on our side."

The next few days go by in a daze. Amari plays chess by himself; Leah disappears in the dance studio for hours at a time. Me and Dez actually spend more time together, trying out rhymes and beatboxing, really getting an idea of each other's flow—out on the soccer field, of course, far away from Peerless itself in case we mess things up.

That's the thing, though. We're not even trying to do magic—we're just having fun with the music, the creativity of it. A salty rhyme from Professor Okoro's perspective of how we used to fight all the time. Another rhyme about Soup and Kinder arguing over her botched smoothie. That one leaves us in tears. This is what I imagine things were like before the Wars of Illusion. Not looking over your shoulder for a storm, not checking underfoot for the radiant waste. I really *do* peek over my shoulder for Headmaster Kinder out of habit, every time we rhyme. Can never be too safe! Whatever she's doing, she's too busy to bother with us.

Peerless is in rough shape. Between our gumbo pool and Ratchet's attack, corrupt magic is everywhere. My reflection tries to freestyle with me in the bathroom.

Fireflies on the soccer field flash new beats my way. There's so much weirdness happening that Kinder's storm warning doesn't even go off anymore.

Professor Touré checks on all of us often, whether it's bringing by meals or making sure we're sitting under the oak tree—daily—in case some lingering busted magic is hiding in Peerless. She's cheerful as can be, but more than once I catch her hiding a yawn behind a fist.

"Where's Headmaster Kinder?" I demand on one occasion. "It's not fair that you're stuck looking after us by yourself."

She smiles softly. "You're not the only ones who need looking out for."

If I didn't have my rhymes, I'd be absolutely out of my mind with boredom and nervousness over what comes next. Will Ratchet pop in and surprise us again with another remix? Or some new awfulness that pours out of the radiant waste? I can't stand the sitting and waiting. Touré won't let us help check the school even though we pretty much did that on our own already.

"Okay, I need a break!" Dez puffs out his cheeks after our latest beats-and-rhymes session. "I know I make this look easy—and good—but my lips feel like Leah's been dancing on my face."

"Sorry," I manage. "This has just been . . . fun, you

know? Nice to do it and not worry so much. Have you seen Leah today? She's been quiet."

"Nope. Probably just enjoying what time she has left. Could you imagine? I'd always wanted a big brother, but I'd rather be raised by Headmaster Kinder than find out my sibling was fake."

"Heard that," I say with a shudder. "In a way, Headmaster Kinder *did* raise us these past few years." I recall the creepy acceptance letter I first got from Peerless, with the flashing golden seal. Dez gags when I describe how it completely flipped my faux parents' opinion about me attending. I thought Kinder had used magic on them. The truth turned out to be even worse. "Their voice, her words."

"Don't say that. Great. Now I can't unthink it."

Something bothers me about that, though. My faux parents *resisted* what Kinder's letter told them to do. All after I spit that awful rhyme. If my real parents created the magic of Bizzy Block, why would they allow my faux parents to disagree with Kinder, the person running the whole thing? Maybe the faux parents can reason for themselves, like Slickback and Disco. What if the professors can all slide over to Team Keynan, too—same as Jocelyn? Or Professor Mendoza? "She can't be the only person who moves them around with magic, right?"

"You and your questions, just like we're back in Professor Okoro's class," Dez grumbles.

"Sorry." I put the thought out of mind for now. Dez is right, our friends need us. "I'm with you about Leah, though. It's not fair to make her go back to school like nothing happened. She needs someone to talk to about all of this."

"Seriously. I still can't believe school is starting tomorrow." Dez shakes his head. "It's all upside down. What if we just said no?"

I purse my lips. "Then everything our parents built would fall apart."

Dez sighs. "True. Let's head back. I don't want Professor Wiley starting us off tomorrow like how the year started," he teases. "Digging Wiley Squad out of negative points! Feels like forever ago."

I groan. "Don't remind me!"

Back in the first-year dorms, we reluctantly part ways. We've spent most of our time in the common lounge or the courtyard—my room alone by myself felt too weird. The space feels even more barren without Ian there. Somehow I doubt his return will make it feel better, now that I know that he's not real.

A whole new set of clothes is back in my room's closet. As if we're back after a refreshing break. Another illusion, just like everything else in our lives. Whatever we do next, we'll need to help Touré and Kinder stop Ratchet. Somehow I know that Glory is coming back for us. Back for me. I fall asleep cooking up rhymes that will flip those diamond scales to glass. Or conjure up a magical trap, just like we did with Slickback and Disco. In my dreams, the monster's glass remixes to molten steel. The vines that snared Buster so easily burst into flames. The teardrop prison that held Slickback and Disco boils away. None of my rhymes work.

CHAPTER ELEVEN

THIS USELESS CHARADE

That morning I wake to a pinging alarm. A new tablet rests on my nightstand. This is really happening. Going to school like our world hasn't been turned inside out. I get up. Groggy. Almost slip in the shower. Shea-buttered up. Dressed—fix my backward shirt. I keep expecting someone to pop out and point at me, laughing, and announce that I just fell for the biggest prank in the history of pranks.

A knock on my door reveals Amari, a huge yawn cracking his jaws. "You look like I feel," he announces.

Leah and Dez join him, both with sleepy eyes, too. Guess I'm not the only one who didn't get any rest. I hope they at least didn't deal with nightmares of their own. "Y'all ready for this?" Dez asks. "It's about to get weirder."

"The fake ones are all back," Leah murmurs. "Touré called them constructs."

"I think I liked it better when it was just us," Amari adds unhappily.

We reluctantly set off to breakfast—and Dez is so right. The hall is packed with faux students. Greeting each other like old friends. Telling fake stories about their fake fall break. Some of them are . . . off, too. Eyes and mouth and nose scrambled around on their faces. Like someone put a jigsaw puzzle together wrong. Others walk backward or stare at blank walls. Corrupt magic is latching onto faux students like they are free snacks. I ignore the ones who recognize me as we hurry to the dining hall.

Soup welcomes us back with piping-hot waffles. He's standing in the same place where the tickle monster tried to swallow us just a few days ago.

"Well, look who it is!" he exclaims. He wears his trademark white chef's apron and a hairnet over his immaculate cornrows. "The feistiest first-years to ever do it! Y'all missed my cooking, huh? Go ahead, admit it—I won't tell your parents!"

I wince. The waffles smell delicious, but my stomach isn't rumbling. Amari pokes at his food suspiciously as we scope out a place to sit. The dining hall is full of noise and energy and life. First-years on every side embrace and trade stories about what they did during break. Faux students. Welcoming us cheerfully. Their greetings slide right past me. Their hugs slip off my shoulders and their dap oozes off my knuckles. It's all more than I can stand.

"I'm going to head to homeroom," I say, glancing at Leah. "You okay?"

"Never better." She laughs softly.

Amari and Dez dart worried glances after me, but I make a calming gesture as I dip out. They shouldn't miss out on a delicious breakfast just because I'm not in the mood.

In Professor Wiley's classroom, half the first-years are already chattering away. Lacretia beams at me from the front row. "Hey you! How was break?" She's just like I remember—an eager, bright smile and a cheerful attitude that never stops, with her hair pulled back into a ponytail, always peering around like a curious bird. She's not real, but it would be awkward to ignore her just because of that.

"Fine," I lie, sliding into the seat beside her.

"So splendid to hear that."

Every student turns at the cold voice behind us. The room falls silent as Headmaster Kinder sweeps to the front. She's wearing a deep coral pantsuit, with vivid magenta heels and a checkered sash that pulls it all together. Long microbraids spill over her shoulders. Her sparkling earrings reflect shimmers across the rose-colored blush on her deep brown skin. She glances distastefully at Professor Wiley's desk and sits on it. "Who wants to ask me how my fall break was?"

I bite my lip as her brown eyes bore into mine. For once, I'm speechless. I kinda thought we bonded after joining forces, running Ratchet out of Peerless—the first time—and trapping Slickback and Disco. Our teamwork saved the school. But from the expression on her face, that's all old stuff. Like expired extra credit. I'm pretty sure I can turn things around, though. It'll just take a bit longer than I'd expected. Another week or two. Tops.

The question is . . . do I really want to be friends? After everything we've learned in the past few days? Not without some serious explaining.

More first-years bottleneck at the door before sitting nervously. Dez and Amari are the last to enter, cradling their tablets, eyes fixed on the headmaster. A second later, Leah walks in uncertainly and plops into the last open seat.

"We're finally free of this useless charade, aren't we?" Headmaster Kinder says. *"Leave class, fancy fast."*

Lacretia stands, face blank. My stomach heaves.

I've seen that same expression before, eyes full of nothingness—back on Bizzy Block, when the storm twisted my faux mama up. "Hey, are you—"

Lacretia abruptly cartwheels around the desks and through the open door. Every single faux student stands, one after another, cradling tablets or backpacks or books. They file out of the desks, one by one, cartwheeling in perfect sync just like Lacretia! Even Leah's jaw falls open.

I gape at Kinder. "That was barely a rhyme," I croak. "And you didn't even have a beat!"

"Which should show you how much you still need to learn," she retorts. "I'll be honest. You three are a pain. I don't have time for your nonsense. But if you're serious about keeping Peerless safe from—"

"The Glory?" Amari offers.

She regards him for a moment, eyes glittering. "I imagine you'd know a Glory straightaway if you ever saw one. As I was saying. If you don't want Peerless consumed by the radiant waste, we need to build it back up, brick by brick. Keep feeding it bland, basic art. I don't care if it's boring. I don't care if you repeat assignments. Do. It. In time, I'll fix the damage you've all caused and protect you from another attack. With some help."

I can't help but share an eager grin with the others. We're doing more stuff to help Peerless, just like I knew we could! The limits are endless. Professor Masters! I like the sound of that.

Five professors file in wordlessly to stand behind Headmaster Kinder, all cohort professors. Wiley—me, Dez, and Amari's homeroom professor—folds his arms and regards me skeptically. There's no smile in his eyes. And he's . . . bigger. Beefy, like he spent fall break doing pull-ups in the gym. His shirtsleeves are squeezing his arms.

"What's wrong with him?" Amari murmurs. "He's actually wearing his tie."

Leah frowns at Professor Valiant, a lean person with curly brown hair, who stares at us like we're a smudge on the wall. Qadira and Osana I don't know, but I'm pretty sure that Professor Guerrero is Yolanda's old homeroom professor.

"With all of the . . . danger Peerless is in, they've been . . . reconstructed to better defend the school from the radiant waste." Kinder's eyes focus past us, like she's deciding what she wants to say next. "You'll need to prepare yourselves for the changes. I'm reconjuring Peerless."

The four of us steal bewildered glances among each other. "That means . . . fixing it?" Amari asks carefully.

"Yes. The conjurings holding everything together are very complex, and very much falling apart." Kinder grimaces. "Literally falling apart, in some instances. You've likely seen constructs that are . . . less themselves since day one." Spooky flashes of my old faux student encounters pop into my head. Taffy fingers in a study room. Flip-flopped arms and legs running late for dance class. Not to mention the scramble-faced faux students we saw at breakfast. "That will all change shortly. It will be as if you've never been here. None of the constructs will know you. Tomorrow will be a fresh start. Introductions. Classes. Everything. So Peerless can run smoothly again."

I open my mouth and close it again. This is even worse than what Touré told us!

"No clapback, Keynan? I'm amazed." Her gaze lands on Leah, and for some reason her voice softens. "You'll all stay with Professor Wiley's cohort. It doesn't make sense to keep you apart any longer, since you've found each other. You are . . . a crew, after all."

We exchange sullen glances. "But we stopped Ratchet before," Dez complains. "Doesn't that count for something?"

"The school is weak. Weak as it's ever been, thanks to your shenanigans. It's only a matter of time before Peerless fails if I don't do something drastic." Her expression hardens. "And I won't let Peerless fail."

My head is spinning. *Again.* It hasn't stopped since my freestyle peeled my room apart! Everything we've known about Peerless is just going to get wiped out?

Professor Mendoza's made of magic—so she won't even remember me? All the stuff I've learned, the time we've shared together? That's not fair. And not just her... Ian! He's the one who warned me about magic in the first place! And Jocelyn... she saved me from my home when the radiant waste gobbled it up. Magic-made or not, these are my folks, and Peerless won't be the same without them. I won't be the same. "Can we . . . at least have our same classes?" I choke out.

Professor Wiley glares at us all. A vein stands out on his neck, just above his too-tight collar. "You should be grateful for Headmaster Kinder's sacrifices," he says gruffly. "Peerless won't survive without a whole new set of rules." Yikes. I share alarmed glances with Amari and Dez. They're staring at Wiley like he's grown spines and fangs. What happened to the professor who told me we're all a family, especially when we mess up? Is this a sneak peek of the rest of Peerless for when it changes, too?

"Disobedience will not be tolerated," Professor Valiant adds in a spooky-quiet whisper. "A clean slate is needed. For the good of us all."

Kinder smiles. "Couldn't have said it better myself."

My friends are quiet, too, just as stunned as I am. It's not like we're turning a tablet off and on again. Everything that makes Peerless feel like home away from home will be wiped out.

"Keeping to the same routine would help us," Dez offers shakily. "After everything that's happened."

Amari bobs his head in agreement, staring miserably at his tablet.

Kinder studies us. "I'll allow it."

"Could we have Professor Touré for homeroom instead?" Leah asks hopefully.

Headmaster Kinder's face goes perfectly still, like the slightest whisper might crack it. "Professor Touré . . . is needed elsewhere." She inhales sharply. "Now go." Her eyes fix on each of us in turn as our tablets chime for the next class.

"And if I hear one *hint* of you all endangering Peerless any further . . ." Behind Kinder, all of the faux professors mirror her exact expression. Their necks swivel to each of us so her glare is quadruple strength. A chill wiggles down my spine. "Constructs aren't the only students who can be taught to cartwheel when I command."

CHAPTER TWELVE

THIS ONE HURTS

We all jump as our tablets ping. Kinder's threat hangs in the air as we hurry out.

"She's scarier than before," Leah manages. "And the homeroom professors! They're acting ready to take on the radiant waste by themselves!"

My knees are wobbly. "I didn't even remember to ask about our parents."

Amari and Dez duck their heads together, whispering urgently. Leah and I give each other a quizzical look. What are they cooking?

"I have thoughts," Amari announces. "But I need time to map them out. See y'all at lunch." He nudges me, and I halfheartedly do our dap—*slap, bump, snap hook fly and dab*—before he sets off. I'm glad someone is feeling good about Kinder's plan, because it sure ain't me. Dez shrugs and shuffles off. I'm sure he realizes how awful this will turn out.

Leah falls in beside me as we head to Creative Writing. "Hey, you're usually the one who's supposed to cheer me up, remember?"

I offer her a shrug. It's all I've got. "None of this is going the way I hoped. I mean . . . we're heroes! We saved this place. And none of it even matters. We're right back where we started."

"Only if you frame it that way," she says. "We know more than we did before. We know the truth about our parents. Now we can—"

She goes dead quiet. Ahead of us in the hall, we spot Joey—a second-year who stays on everyone's nerves—bragging loudly about all the sleeping in and gaming he did over fall break. His attitude and first-year slander absolutely made me itch. But he's a faux student. A construct, as Headmaster Kinder called the students around us who are part of Peerless's magic. His smug sneer doesn't hit the same.

Joey's not the reason Leah's standing stiff as a fence post, though. He's strolling beside Yolanda. She's Leah's sister in every way imaginable. Same challenging brown eyes, round cheeks, and brown skin—Yo's just older and taller and tougher, with a pixie cut instead of Leah's locs.

Yolanda approaches. She hasn't seen us. Leah is rigid, but fear and hope play tag on her face. Her lips part, ready for the biggest smile. But Yolanda turns down a different hall, high-fiving Joey. Their laughter echoes around the corner. She didn't even glance our way.

"No wonder she ignores me," Leah murmurs to herself. "It all makes sense now."

"What do you—"

She strides into the room, leaving me to puzzle over whatever she just figured out.

We settle into class, even taking our usual seats. Professor Mendoza isn't nestled behind her desk, where she's usually munching on whatever fresh fruit she's managed to snag from Soup. Everyone who isn't straggling in is jabbering excitedly. Lacretia is in her normal seat beside me. One look at her face roils my stomach. She's dazed, blinking like she doesn't understand how she got here after Kinder's rhyme. Professor Mendoza used magic on me like that—to keep me out of a fight with Dez. I remember how wobbly I felt afterward. I don't care if Lacretia's a faux student or not. She cares and thinks and acts, doesn't she? Doesn't that make her real?

"Hey, you okay?" I ask, offering her a friendly smile.

"Oh hey, Keynan." She smiles back, but uncertainty still lingers behind her eyes. "Sorry. I just haven't felt like myself lately. Feel like I caught a bug over fall break. I'll be fine, I'm sure!"

"Glad to hear it," I hear myself saying. It's weird . . . talking with Lacretia is like, well—talking to Peerless. The school itself. She's a part of it, after all. She smiles at me and busies herself in her tablet.

I turn back to Leah, already hunkered over her tablet. This isn't fair. Diving back into classes after our whole world just got flipped inside out? Right as I drag out something encouraging to say, Professor Mendoza saunters into the class.

Seeing her again is a joy. She's exactly as I remember, a pinch taller than me, wearing a plain brown tube dress with a crinkled scarf of ruby and pink. Her hair is pulled back in a messy bun and she's balancing a handful of cherries with her tablet. *Yep, still about her snacks.* Even Leah can't help but smile.

"So sorry, class!" she says, flashing her teeth. She gives me a wink. Just that small thing—someone actually happy to see me—and Peerless suddenly feels bearable again. We're gonna be okay. Mendoza's light brown eyes twinkle hungrily, flicking back to her tablet. "Good to see you back and flourishing, I trust? Yes? Tell me every-thing you've—actually, no. I don't care. I trust your time at break was productive. If you'll check your tablets . . ."

I glance down, eager for a new assignment. Creative Writing was always my best class, even if the homework was boring, and especially when I wasn't getting in trouble over—

"Keynan?" Leah gasps. "Are you seeing this?"

"One sec, my tablet hasn't loaded the—"

"Keynan." Leah's urgent whisper makes me glance up.

Professor Mendoza is frozen in place. The overhead lights flicker off. Our tablets wink out. The cheerful chat-ter around us cuts off. Cherries spill from the professor's napkin one by one and roll around on the floor.

No. Not this again. I'm back on Bizzy Block all over—when I survived a storm, but it took a piece of my mama with it. That's how Professor Mendoza's face looks right now. Empty. I clasp a hand to my mouth. The only sound is me and Leah's breathing in the murky red glow of the emergency light above the classroom door.

No one else is moving. The entire class is sitting silently, just as frozen as Mendoza. "What's happening?" I cry.

"It's not a storm," Leah says. "Or Ratchet. There's usu-ally screaming for that."

The lights and our tablets snap on at the same time.

Chortles and teasing suddenly leap out of the first-years around us. Me and Leah flinch, staring around in shock.

Lacretia's frown is gone. She cheeses extra hard, leaning all the way into my personal space. "Hi! I'm Lacretia. Looks like you finally figured out where you're supposed to be."

I wince. "Oh, no."

"You feeling good? Refreshed? Confident?"

Every question feels like a slap to the face, because I've heard all of this before. I knew the reset was coming, but this really stings. "You still feeling sick?" I ask Lacretia carefully.

Her smile breaks, but just for an instant. "I'm studying dance."

Leah swallows. "Kinder didn't waste any time with her reconjuring."

I risk a look back at Professor Mendoza. Her shoulders jerk toward her desk. She opens her lips and hesitates, as if Kinder's magic is rewriting whatever she meant to say on the spot. I don't know if I can take this. I stand up and go to her. "You can hear us," I plead, my face suddenly hot. "I know you're in there!"

A lone tear trails down Mendoza's cheek. Her glazed eyes focus on me, and she smiles unsteadily. "Keynan, is it?"

I let out a gasp and search her face, peering for a sliver of recognition. *Anything. Please.* I force out a laugh, spinning back to Leah. "You saw that, didn't you?"

She bites her lip, eyes brimming with tears. "I . . . yes, Keynan. I saw it."

Professor Mendoza continues on behind me. "The one who thought he was too good for this place. How fascinating. There's nothing I love better than a fresh new voice to mentor. Let's see what you're made of."

No. I cringe, suddenly aware of the rest of the first-years staring at me curiously. I remember *all* of this—she's said it before. Back on my first day at Peerless. I return to my seat in disbelief. Leah squeezes my hand as I plop down.

"She's gone," Leah murmurs sadly. "Oh. Her cherries."

The professor is starting her lecture, and she's smashed one of them under a sandal. The Mendoza I loved, the one who gave me extra credit in exchange for snack bribes, would weep plump tears over such a waste. "Not you too," I whisper, half to myself. "I needed *someone* on Team Keynan."

Leah sighs. "Sorry, Keynan. I know this one hurts."

"I . . . I could rhyme her out of it, bring her back to the way she was . . ."

Leah shakes her head sadly. "It's what's best for Peerless. You know this."

Do I though? Can Headmaster Kinder be believed? Everything is so messed up. All I want to do is run out of here, hop on my baba's old bike, and ride until I'm back home at Bizzy Block. Forget this nightmare in one of my baba's hugs and groan over his terrible jokes, and laugh everything away while I help my mama cook dinner.

That's the worst part of all. Everything I'm yearning for is built on lies. I don't know if I could admit this to any of my friends, but I almost wish I'd never uncovered the illusion.

"Lacretia?" Mendoza calls. "Recite today's reading. Class, follow along on your tablets."

Mendoza drones the class through a lesson and leaves us to study on our own. She weaves through the rows, making sure we're all on task. I can hardly believe it. The old Mendoza would be napping at her desk. She stops beside me. "Keep doing well, Keynan." She blinks and gives me a hesitant frown. "Extra credit is always possible for hard workers. Perhaps the headmaster will approve."

I slump back in my seat as a stranger smiles down at me. If this is the new Peerless, I don't know how long I can stand it.

CHAPTER THIRTEEN

SCREAMING ON THE INSIDE

We meet up with Dez and Amari at lunch. Judging from their faces, the reconjuring flipped classes around for them, too. In the dining hall, Soup introduces himself like we've never met. He just served up breakfast this morning. "Five different kinds of salsa today," he exclaims proudly. "Handcrafted for today's Welcome to Peerless tacos! I recommend the mango—it has a kick!"

"At least reconjuring Peerless didn't ruin everything," I say around a mouthful of deliciousness.

Dez slides his tray away a few minutes after we sit down. The others barely pick at their food.

"What's wrong?" I ask. "These are amazing."

"You weren't here yet," Dez mutters. "This was the

exact same thing he made for our first day. Same Welcome to Peerless speech, all of it."

Amari shudders. "Same first-year conversations. Same lessons. Same stick figures! This place felt so strange until I met y'all—I just didn't understand why until we heard the truth. I couldn't imagine it without us."

Suddenly I'm not so hungry anymore, either. "So what were these thoughts you wanted to tell us about?"

"Only if it's good news," Leah puts in glumly. "The more we learn about Peerless, the worse it gets."

Amari glances around furtively, then pulls a tablet from his backpack.

I sit straight up. "That's the one you made!"

"*We* made. Crew effort. Go ahead and say it. You love me."

"We love you!" Leah eyes it curiously. "So . . . we can dig into everything Kinder's been hiding from us?"

"Yup!"

She nibbles her lip. "Part of me thinks we should just chuck it."

"It will take some freestyling," Amari adds carefully, "but I'm pretty sure we can tweak what Kinder did with her reconjuring."

I let out a long breath. After a string of awful days, this

is definitely a step back to winning. Kinder means well, and she cares about us in her own super-grumpy way. Sometimes she just needs some help to get things right.

"But why?" Dez asks anxiously. "Why mess with any of it?"

"We lost so much," I say. "Kinder's treating Peerless like a machine. But it's more than that. It's just as alive as the oak tree. The professors grew with us—we can get a handful to act like themselves again. We've gotta show her how it could be if it's . . . well, what I'm guessing my parents imagined."

My friends nod in agreement, but Leah and Dez definitely don't share Amari's eagerness. I can't blame them. No one wants to cartwheel from class to class because Kinder decided detention wasn't teaching us anything.

When classes wrap for the day, I trudge back to the first-year dorm, mulling over our next move. The door to my room is cracked open, and I peer in cautiously. Ian's back, grumpily stuffing clothes in his closet! He's taller than me and lean as a stalk of corn, but we share the same shade of brown skin. His scowl disappears when he spots me. "Oh, hey! You must be Keynan. I'm Ian."

Ugh. Another friend reset. I can't do this again. "Why weren't you in classes today?"

A bewildered look dances across his face, somewhere between Lacretia's blank stare and Mendoza's confusion. "The headmaster needed me for . . . something. I'm not sure, actually!" He laughs unsteadily. "Did I miss a lot?"

"Nope, not a thing." I plop onto my bed before he sees my eyes leak. "You're here now. That's all that matters."

He goes back to sorting his things, chattering about engineering and which classes are his favorites. Ian. Excited about homework? Lasting an entire conversation with zero mentions of snacks? No exploring the school, no Hall Hop? When it's bedtime, he wraps up the night with snoring—the one part that stayed the same.

I think I hate it here.

We slog through the first week of classes, screaming on the inside. I try not to bug Amari every day about using the tablet to give Peerless back some flavor. Leah and Dez are all about being careful, especially Dez. He irritates me whenever we debate about it, but Amari and Leah both remind me he's seen the least magic of any of us. But we've already got a list of faux students and professors we want to free from Kinder's conjuring—which Amari constantly reminds us isn't a guaranteed thing.

"We've got to take our time," he urges one night, after

Dez and Leah have dragged themselves off to bed. It's just the two of us, wrapping up a game of dominoes. He's taken two straight against the three of us, but I can beat him one-on-one.

"If Ratchet's out there remixing into something stronger, shouldn't we be, too?" I fire back.

"Trust me on this one, Keynan," he says, frowning as I set down my next domino. I'm kind of relieved he's so bossy about how we use the tablet. For once, everyone's not looking to me for the final say on a huge decision for the crew. "Hey. You just locked up the board."

I blink, staring at the game—he's right. All the sixes are out. Neither of us can go. We show our dominoes. Mine add up to the least amount, which means I get his points. "Nice. Give 'em up!"

He arches an eyebrow and slides over his bones. "You didn't plan that!"

"I did. My middle name is strategy. Don't hate."

"Okay, Keymaster," he says with a smirk. He has mostly blanks left—I didn't get a lot of points. That win might not come tonight. "Glad your feel for magic is better than your skills playing bones!"

I shrug and wash the dominoes for the next round, losing myself in the clack of the bones as I mix them up. The set is really old—a gift from Old Zeph back on Bizzy

Block. From before the Wars of Illusion maybe? That would be something.

The good news is, Kinder's plan is working. Another week passes. The telltale signs of magic leaching through the school are shored up one by one. Touré and Kinder constantly stalk the halls, tablets in hand, a little less stressed with each new day. One morning as I'm plodding into the dining hall for breakfast, they're already striding out, debating about reopening the hidden wing between bites of breakfast burrito.

"Maybe we need to just . . . wait." I bring up my doubts with the crew one evening after classes, during our free time in the courtyard. We spend time there out of habit now, just to make sure corrupt magic isn't sinking claws into us when we least expect it. "The school is less weird. We should trust Kinder's plan."

Amari chokes on his mug of cider and squints at me. "Okay, we need to get him to Nurse Manny. Who are you?"

"If the school is doing better, this is the best time to try something new," Leah counters.

Amari's head swivels to her. "Okay, now who are *you*? Are y'all flip-flopping sides just to mess with me?"

"I know, I know! But we see Mendoza every day. It's like . . . there are pieces of her left, trying to get out."

"Some strategically located snacks might help her

remember herself." Dez purses his lips thoughtfully. "I'll bet she's not the only one resisting Kinder's magic."

As much as I want Mendoza back to her old self, something still doesn't sit right with this move. But Amari's so eager to try, I give in and promise myself I'll follow through on it no matter what. "If I'm right about this, we could stop Ian's snoring for you!" he chortles, scampering off to the lounge. "I just need to find the student directory again. Tomorrow we'll try."

Two pillows wrapped around my head that night barely keep Ian's trumpeting nose out of my dreams. The next morning, I'm all in on whatever Ian's cooking. An insistent knocking comes before my alarm goes off. I eagerly throw open the door and Amari bursts in, completely distraught.

"Keynan! The tablet's gone!"

"What?"

"I fell asleep in the study lounge. Someone took it!"

We're all panicked over breakfast, waiting for Kinder and Touré to march in. But no intercom announcement, no classroom visit, no detention. Nothing.

We retrace our steps, even carefully ask Ian, Joey, and other faux students known for pranks if they've seen it. We manage to slip back into the teachers' lounge to check if Slickback and Disco are somehow loose and out to make us miserable—but they're still trapped in their magic bubble.

Three days of this and nothing—not a trace of the tablet, and not a sign of trouble. "If Touré and the headmaster don't have it," Dez muses during another afternoon in the courtyard, "who does?"

"I don't know, but our plan is over before it started," Amari groans. "Should we . . . make another one?"

"Y'all, we don't need the tablet," I say suddenly. "*We're* the magic!"

Amari shakes his head. "But there's a whole system here that—"

"Their system," I cut in. "We gotta do our own thing. Besides, what other choice do we have?"

What kind of rhyming skills will it take to impact our faux students at all? Headmaster Kinder made it look easy, and barely used a whole line to do it. All those cartwheels and the coordination would take me pages! I can't even get my parents' jambalaya recipe right. Now I'm trying to tinker with their magic? It's got me more nervous than I want to admit.

But I've got to do something.

So I start working at it, the next day in Creative Writing. Professor Mendoza gives us a new assignment to memorize and it's bad—so basic I've got it done in a few minutes, and half the class is drifting off. She sits at her desk, merrily rummaging through her desk drawers like she lost something.

"Not sure how much more of this I can deal with," Leah mutters, staring at her tablet.

"No worries," I say absently. "This one is rough."

"You gonna be okay? You're quiet today."

I barely look up as she stands. "I'm good."

She plucks the hall pass from the classroom door and steps out. I can't blame her one bit. She still ain't over the sting of learning about Yo. Can I help somehow? Oh! I keep forgetting to give her back that necklace—her sister's necklace. But I'm not sure if that would just make her feel worse.

I set about composing a new rhyme. Flipping the script could bring Mendoza back quick. I'm absorbed in the joy of writing again—and terrified of getting this one wrong. Professor Mendoza's advice sure could help my whole crew right now.

My tablet chirps the end of class. That was fast. "Hey, I think I've got a good start for—" I stop, realizing I'm talking to myself. Leah's desk is still empty. She never came back to class.

CHAPTER FOURTEEN

NO OTHER CHOICE

I hustle through Peerless, searching all of the obvious places. Leah's favorite study nook. The dance studio, full of mirrors and shadows. Her hidden hammock in the courtyard, near the burbling little creek. The student lounge in the first-year dorms where we play spades. Nothing.

I end up in the dining hall just as lunch is starting. Leah's not in either food line or sitting at one of the long tables. This is just weird. Amari and Dez saunter up, debating over baked potatoes or the nacho bar, and latch on to my worry when I explain. "I've checked bathrooms, dorms, courtyard, homeroom . . . I can't find her anywhere!"

"Let's look again," Amari offers. "It's a big school. And

leave a message in Mirror Maze Castle so she knows we're looking for her."

Why didn't I come up with that? Amari's clear head is a relief. Dez suggests we go to Nurse Manny in case Leah's sick. A sign on the office door says they are out for lunch, and no one's in the exam room. We pass back through the courtyard one more time, calling Leah's name. More nothing.

"Gotta be in her room," Amari says, but he doesn't sound convinced. "That's where she'd go back to, right?"

"No answer in Mirror Maze," Dez adds.

I double-check mine, too. New notification on the tablet! I swipe it open eagerly and read:

The start of a new semester can be a lot to take
in. You've got this.
Love you and miss you!
—Mama and Baba

Big sigh. I got this exact same message when I first started at Peerless. Fake encouragement is the last thing we need right now. "Nothing for me either," I grumble.

"Maybe she linked up with her sister finally?" I venture. "If she's in the third-year dorms—"

Dez nods ahead. "The way these busters stomp around? I doubt it."

Professor Wiley and Professor Guerrero march in lock-step along the courtyard's outer walkway. They stop as we emerge from the garden path. Their heads swivel, watching us like eagles.

"Act normal!" Amari whispers.

"How?" Dez demands. "They're freaking me out!"

The reconjured cohort professors always make me shiver—especially Wiley. He used to be so cool, and now he just looks hungry for a fight. But I'm really worried, and this is worth getting on their bad side. I clear my throat. "Professors? We might have an emergency with Leah. Can Headmaster Kinder find—"

They both stiffen at mention of her name. "The head-master isn't to be disturbed," Wiley barks.

"But we need—"

"Under any circumstances! Or we'll deduct cohort points."

I blink. Professor Wiley will take points from *himself*? "Then Professor Touré—"

This time it's Professor Guerrero. "Professor Touré isn't to be disturbed under any . . ."

I don't need Dez's prodding to leave the cohort

professors alone. They are doing way too much. We head straight to the dorm and I knock on Leah's door again. No answer, but a shadow flickers under the door— *someone's* inside. "Leah, are you okay? I saw you."

Still nothing. "Does anyone remember her roommate's name?" Amari and Dez both shrug. The door's unlocked, I crack it slowly. "You got us worried—"

No one is in the room. The dull glow of a Break flickers between both beds, hovering silently. My heartbeat slaps my ribs so hard I'm surprised it doesn't echo off the walls.

"Oh no," Dez groans. "We're not supposed to use magic in the school!"

"She's gone into the waste by herself!" Amari wails. "Why, fam? Now?"

I finally pull free of the shock. "Close the door! Get inside before someone sees."

We curl around the Break warily, like a snake coiled in the center of the room. "Magic right in the middle of Peerless," Dez murmurs. "Those cohort professors aren't great at their new jobs."

"And why hasn't it set off Kinder's storm warning?" Amari adds.

"Good question." I spot a folded piece of paper on Leah's desk; a note written in elegant, flowing curves.

That bothers me somehow, tickles my memory as wrong. But I quickly push that aside as I read out loud.

> Don't follow me, Keymaster. That thing at Peerless isn't my sister, I don't care what Kinder or Touré says. Yolanda is real. We grew up together, and she's lost out there in the waste somewhere. That's the only thing that makes sense. I won't give up on her.
>
> —Starbreaker

As soon as I finish saying her name, the Break wobbles and flickers—then abruptly snaps shut. We're all quiet for a moment, just staring at the space where it used to be.

"She . . . she made a Break so it would close by itself?" Amari whistles. "Can you do that, Keynan?"

My face goes hot. "Sure I can! Just, um—"

"Make it make sense!" Dez exclaims. "Yo's name was on the faux-student list. Y'all saw it!"

Me and Amari exchange a long look.

"But we also saw Yolanda's old homework recording," he murmurs. "Where she wanted to warn all of us about magic. Tell us the truth about Peerless. She sure is *acting* like a real big sister."

I nod slowly. "If Leah believes it, that's good enough for

me. Remember this?" I edge over to Leah's bunk bed. This was her sister's room when she was a first-year—before any of us got here—and Yo had scratched a message into one of the wooden slats. I imagine it would be the last thing she saw every night before falling asleep.

something's wrong with them, not you

"Okay, my bad. Can't imagine a faux student doing that." Dez shudders. "I feel awful for her now. Can you imagine being the only one in your class who's real? I can't. No wonder she was so mean."

"Touré and Kinder are going to stuff us in a closet after this," Amari mumbles. "And not the one I want."

"Yep," I agree. "But it's not like we didn't try. The cohort professors are the worst."

"Wait, what?" Dez asks anxiously. "We're going out there? After what happened to y'all last time?"

An awful flutter in the pit of my stomach gets ten times worse. Memories of our time in the radiant waste flood back. The constant wrongness of it, like wearing all my clothes inside out. Not one thing went how we planned, and corrupt magic trickled into my rhymes—made them ten times better.

And worst of all? I loved that part the most.

Amari looks exactly how I feel. But he's waiting for me to say something first. "This is what Peerless Pact is all about," I say. Me and Leah started the Pact, a promise that we would always have our crew's back, no matter what.

We quiz Dez on what he knows about the radiant waste. The basics are easy: don't touch anything, don't trust anything, stick together. Touré beat the important stuff into his head, at least.

"Dez, it's a lot out there," Amari says worriedly. "We'll fall apart with no beat."

"I'll be fine," Dez grunts.

"And I trust him," I say firmly, offering Dez a fist bump. "We dealt with Ratchet the first time. Me and you. That's gotta be like a third-year-level lab assignment. You'll be ready."

"So last question," Dez says. "When do I get a nickname?"

Amari quirks his eyebrow. "I've been waiting for one of those, too."

I'm grateful for their good energy. They're keeping my own nervousness from boiling over. Something awful happens whenever we enter the waste. Every. Single. Time. We're down crew, and Dez is brand-new. No grown-ups who will help. We've got this! We . . . got this.

CHAPTER FIFTEEN

A WORD OR TWO

We dive headfirst into a scramble session of planning. If it was just up to me we'd open up a Break right now and dive in, but Amari takes his sweet annoying time to think everything through.

"We don't know if she's right or wrong about Yo, but she thinks she's right and that's all that matters," he says. "If we don't help her find out for sure . . ."

"She'll keep trying," Dez nods resignedly. "Okay, whew. So about getting there . . ."

"The old covered bridge that crosses the creek," I supply. "We're on Peerless grounds—barely—but far enough away in case . . . something happens."

Dez blinks. "Something?"

"That's smart." Amari taps his lip. "Why did she open a Break inside the school, though? It's not like her at all."

"We'll just have to ask her when we find her," I reply. Leah's never thoughtless, even when she's upset. The Break *did* close by itself—neat trick, I gotta admit—but we're going to be as ridiculously careful as we can, before Wylie decides to snoop on us.

Between a visit to the courtyard for fresh fruit and some cold quesadillas left over from the dining hall, we're covered on snacks. There's nothing to eat in the radiant waste—nothing that we should eat, anyway—and we have no idea how long it will take to find Leah.

We creep to the Peerless entrance, then hustle for the bridge, food and Amari's drawing gear stuffed in our backpacks. Amari takes in the wooden wall of the covered bridge, picks his spot, and gets to drawing. Me and Dez serve as lookouts. No one has seen us so far. We left our tablets back in the room so they couldn't track us. I left Touré a note on my tablet's screen. So hopefully they won't be *too* mad when we're back with Leah in time for dessert.

Amari pauses, tongue squeezed between his lips. I steal a peek over his shoulder, holding back the urge to make suggestions. "That's, umm, a big door."

He cuts his eyes at me. "Yessir."

How should I phrase this? He's an artist, after all—they can get really touchy. "Umm, I'm sure you've—"

"It looks Ratchet sized!" Dez blurts out. "That's basically an invitation to tear up the school."

"Ratchet is *exactly* why it's big," Amari says. "I've seen pictures of these old rooms . . . called vaults. People locked up stuff they wanted to keep safe inside them. This door will be exactly like that—metal. Ratchet won't be able to bash through it."

"I like the sound of that."

"Metal *is* strong," Dez allowed.

Amari grins and turns back to the wall. Past time for his nickname. Helter Sketcher? Hmmm . . . nope. Scribble Lord? Definitely not saying that one out loud, either. Better cook on it some more.

"Nice." Dez nods approvingly as Amari steps back from the drawing with a bow. "We're ready for a rhyme, Keynan."

"A good one," Amari adds.

I glare at him, but time is wasting. Leah needs us. I got this. One deep breath. Once more my mind wheels over everything I need this rhyme to do. It's impossible to rhyme every little detail into my verses—Headmaster Kinder made me realize that. The intention needs to be locked tight in my brain, bright as the sun. I'll bet when I'm good enough, I can use magic with only a word or two.

Maybe that's how the Glories did it. But was that before or after they lost their minds . . . ?

Anyway. Focus.

> We're stepping out for Starbreaker through the vault door,
> Finding lost family so we can learn more
> But no one else can find the way back to our hearts' core.
> So no-permission-havin' creatures best ignore our secret school
> Don't cross over one step while we do what we do.

The air around the drawing shimmers as I rhyme. Amari's door shifts, the brown of the bridge's wood waning before a deep, intimidating silver-blue. Wow. It's definitely sturdy. I can imagine Slickback drooling over the sight.

"Nice work!" Dez hefts his backpack hesitantly. He grasps the steel handle and heaves. The massive door glides open on silent hinges, revealing a shimmering portal inside. "So who's going—"

A sudden groan cuts him off. The bridge trembles

beneath our feet. We back away in alarm as wood splinters and pops. The door jerks down, leaning crookedly to one side. "Hurry!" I shout. We've got to get through before—"

The door plunges through the bridge. A huge crash thunders up from the creek bed. We scramble out and pick our way down the embankment's chunky boulders, shouting in alarm. Somehow the vault opening is intact. A corner of one side is half submerged in the creek's flow. Cracked rocks and rubble from the ruined bridge lie broken all around the door.

"Great. Huge massive door—little bitty bridge!" I moan. "What were we thinking?"

"I said small," Dez declares. "Didn't I say small?"

Amari glowers at us. "We can still get through it," he snaps. "Help me! We're wasting time."

Me and Dez trade doubtful looks. "Maybe we should start over again," I say. "Make another one completely from scratch."

"If we do that, we could open a Rip."

I wince . . . he's right, how did I forget? The last time we opened two Breaks, they . . . tangled with each other, caught their magic in some weird tug-of-war. If it wasn't for Professor Touré and Mendoza, it would have torn Peerless apart.

The three of us lug the heavy door up and open. The Break still shimmers, inviting us in. I don't like how the other side is hidden in that silvery haze—especially now that we're about to just *drop* into it. But what choice do we have? Leah's waiting on us.

I take a deep breath—not exactly how I want to start this thing, but we can't go in there and not have each other's backs. I realize just how much I'm dreading going back to the radiant waste. Breaks and Rips. Loops in time! None of it makes sense. "Hey, we both could have done better on this one. That rhyme . . . not my greatest. My bad for getting snappy back there."

Amari blinks. "Me too . . . sorry. I just want this to work so we can get to her and get out." He grouses a bit. "I should have thought about the weight of the door. You were right about it being too big."

"We'll deal with it later," I say. "Y'all ready for this?"

They nod nervously as I step forward. Ain't nothing to it but to do it. I peer closer, my nose almost touching the wavery surface, but still can't make out the other side. I try to straighten, but my balance is upside down. The coruscating waves of light swallow me whole as I fall into the Break.

CHAPTER SIXTEEN

CONTRADICTION CANYONS

For a moment, everything around me squeezes down like a too-tight sweater knitted in a million colors. Before I can take in a breath to scream in panic, an impact jolts my feet.

I stagger but don't fall. Amari and Dez plop down beside me, appearing at the same time. Dez stops wheeling his arms with a sheepish grin. The ground beneath our feet is green and slippery. Massive yellow columns curve out of it on every side, so tall that I can't see the tops when I crane my neck. Strange spheres float above us, covered with bristling pearl-colored spines and blocking out the purple-orange haze of the radiant waste. Hmm. Are we back in the Pancake Plains? They are way different than I remember.

Dez swallows. "Anyone want to tell me what we're looking at?"

Amari shrugs helplessly. "I . . . got nothing. Keynan?"

"Whole new level of weirdness for me, too," I admit. "But at least my rhyme did the thing." I gesture up at our Break, and my hand disappears in thin air. My rhyme got that part right, it's invisible on this side. Go me!

"So how do we find Leah in all of this?" Dez asks.

I examine the sky, trying to look thoughtful. Inside? Slight meltdown. When I opened my first Break with Professor Touré, the rhyme took us close to some ruins in the radiant waste from the world before—something we needed at the time. Why didn't this one do the same with Leah? Not only is she nowhere in sight, I seriously doubt if anyone's ever stood where we're standing. Two of the spiky spheres float together. An arc of orange lightning sails between them. The bigger one explodes. Dozens of smaller globes burst from the collision.

"Let's stay away from—" Amari and I say at the same time.

"It smells so good here," Dez remarks. "Like when the courtyard flowers are all in bloom."

"Just be ready in case we need to put together a freestyle," I remind him. I pick a direction to search at random. It's not like there's a sign somewhere that says LEAH WENT THAT WAY. But we'll have to search for hints, maybe even use a bit of magic to help guide us. The radiant waste surrounds Peerless on every side. Touré never told us where it ends. I'm getting more convinced it's swallowed the whole world.

We weave through the curling columns for a while, but they're impossible to tell apart from one another. "I should make another Break," I say. "We're going in circles!"

"Let me try something first." Amari pulls a paintbrush from his bag before I can start up a new rhyme. "Pretty sure I can help us out."

He flips the handle of his paintbrush and scrawls on the stuff under our feet. Wherever he touches turns from green to yellow, and the dust that rises up makes us sneeze. I swear I hear something laughing with every new mark he creates. Dez tilts his head worriedly. Finally, I understand what I'm supposed to see: a shuttle. "A ride to get us around faster. This is genius!"

"I got the idea from you." He stands up with a wry grin. "Now can your rhymes do the honors? We just need a finishing touch."

Dez nods and I take off. I've got an idea that should fit with his perfectly.

Pull up with fly wheels to help us find Leah fast,
    need an expert driver who knows how to slip and
how to slash.
    Keep us good and safe until our search has
passed.

A searing glow crackles along Amari's drawing, and a full shuttle bursts into being before us. Any shuttle would be an improvement—the last one I rode in had pockmarks from corrupt Buster slobber. The only word that comes to mind about Amari's design is *zoom*. He couldn't be more pleased with himself. "Look at these lines. The paint is even better than I imagined. I don't normally do this, but it would be disrespectful not to brag."

Dez rolls his eyes. "Disrespectful to yourself?"

Amari goes on like he didn't even hear. "Built for speed, and wait until y'all see the inside. But Keynan, what was all of that about a driver?"

The door opens. Inside, a shadow of sparks coalesces into . . . Jocelyn. She splutters, staring at her hands, then back at us. "What! How am I . . ." Her gaze settles on me. "You again! Pulling me out of where I belong! This is wrong, Keynan—against the natural order of things!"

"Sorry, Jocelyn. We need you, though! You remember bringing me to Peerless, right?" I need to be sure it's really her.

"Of course I do!" she stares at her feet, crestfallen. "That mess has been the only thing on my mind since it happened. And I'm sorry I let you down, kid. I wanted to get the headmaster for you, I really did. But somehow . . ." Fear tightens the edges of Jocelyn's face, like she's remembering an awful dream. "I just *couldn't*. My . . . my brain would slip off what needed doing and onto something else every time I tried. By then she had you gathered without me."

Dez and Amari gawk as Jocelyn bounces anxiously on her toes. "You're good," I say firmly. "You did your best and we're not mad at you. But we need you again. Leah's in trouble and we gotta find her."

"Say less!" Jocelyn declares, rubbing her hands together. "Y'all buckle up. Not a thing made that I can't drive." She frowns down at the controls, murmuring to herself, focused. "Now look at my new whip. I'm about to flambé this."

We pile in, relieved. "You sure about this?" Dez asks. "Or is it not last-minute enough? Maybe a test run? Something?"

"No time. Trust the rhyme."

"And the drawing!" Amari adds with a sniff.

Once we're all strapped in, the shuttle glides forward silently. My heart starts beating again.

Amari daps me up excitedly. "I know y'all heard that, too!"

"Sure did!" I exclaim.

"She really remembers," Dez murmurs. "Kinder's reconjuring didn't reset her. Maybe she's proof we can get Peerless back the way it needs to be."

"Best news we've had all day." After the messed-up start at the bridge, things are turning around. I turn to the window to get my bearings. Jocelyn's weaving through those leaning stalks so fast there's not much for me to see.

"Don't worry, I'll find her." Her eyes touch mine through the rearview mirror. "I've got a knack for these kinds of things."

Which makes perfect sense—maybe my parents added a little extra to her magic? Some sort of homing compass? Amari and Dez sit behind me, heads close together. Parts of their conversation drifts my way.

"I told you he's the best to ever do it," Amari murmurs. "Jocelyn's taking us right to Leah. I don't know how, but he cooked it into the poem!"

Wait, they're talking about me? They can carry on with

the compliments! Even though this rhyme worked out well, I still have plenty to learn. Especially after our fight with Ratchet—I don't ever want my rhymes to mess with time again, not after Professor Touré's warning. But the more I practice freestyling, the better I get. Who knows what I'll be able to do once I'm *really* good?

The worst part about busted magic is the doubt. Are my rhymes all the way mine? There's no way to be sure, and I hate not knowing. Especially when folks are depending on me most.

"Keep your eyes open," Jocelyn calls out. "We way off the beaten path."

The shuttle clears the maze of yellow pillars, gathering speed. There's nothing but bristling spheres in the orange sky ahead. The lumpy green ground just . . . ends.

"Hey. Umm, Jocelyn?" Amari calls. She's humming to herself, driving straight toward the edge.

Dez makes a strangled sound and squeezes his eyes shut. "It's too much for her!"

"Jocelyn!" I yelp. "Don't you think we should—"

Our shuttle sails right off the edge before I can scream. My stomach lurches. But then glittering blue wings slide out of the shuttle on either side of us! They lock into place with a metallic clunk as we soar forward.

"Loving my new ride!" Jocelyn crows. "Relax, kids. I got this."

Dez flops back in his seat, panting. Amari peers out the window. "You did say fly wheels!"

"All part of the plan," I mumble. Jocelyn is sure of herself, but I wish we'd found a different way on the ground. The sky is so thick with spheres I can't tell up from down. Where are we? Those weird stalks still rule out Pancake Plains. And there's no fire tree anywhere. The air is clogged with smells, like every perfume and body butter and scented candle I've ever imagined all mixed together.

"That's what this stuff is!" I exclaim. "Pollen!" Globs of it.

Dez squints outside, where the ground should be. "Then those stalks must be gigantic flowers."

This is exactly what they'd look like if we had a big microscope. "Professor Touré told me about this place," Dez said. "They couldn't agree on a name! Contradiction Canyons, Relative Rainforest."

Amari's face screws up. "But those are nothing alike. They might as well be two different places."

"And they don't explain why we're smaller than fleas," I point out.

161

"Exactly," Dez says. "Perspective doesn't make sense here. Size and distance don't follow any rules. Headmaster Kinder argued that they shouldn't name it at all, because the name would just make it change."

"That's . . . helpful?" I manage. Size and distance can change up whenever they want? How are we supposed to find Leah with all of that going on? "Any other nuggets to share?"

Dez's face turns gray. "Touré said this is one of the most dangerous places in the radiant waste, and they barely made it out." He points. Ahead of us, three shadows bob and weave like smudges against the bright sky, somehow bumbling and graceful at the same time. They don't fly in a straight line, but somehow they leap closer with just a few lazy wingbeats.

"What are those?" Jocelyn demands. "My windshield wipers ain't enough for all that."

Dez moans. "I peeked at Touré's notes about the waste. I'm pretty sure those are toad bats. Not good."

"We're fine!" I insist.

"We are so not fine!" Jocelyn bellows. "Y'all hold on!"

The shuttle turns, hooking around the globs. Jocelyn climbs, angling toward long yellow-gold canyons that ripple and stretch. *Flower blossoms.* She swoops into one of the ridges for a place to hide, and we skid to a stop—the ground is soft as pillows. Jocelyn tugs urgently at her steering wheel and fiddles with the controls. "Keynan! It's stuck!"

Above us, the sky is darkening. The toad bats are multiplying, letting out huge thunder croaks that make us clap our hands over our ears. The sickly green creatures are horrid, with long legs dangling from bulbous bodies wide as a tractor tire, all held aloft by laughably tiny wings. Their bulging blue eyes gaze at us hungrily. Pollen globs plunge down like gigantic yellow hail. Every time one hits the ground, the fresh explosion of scents is overwhelming. Amari's eyes water nonstop, while Dez and I burst into sneezing fits.

It's up to me to get us out of here. *"A Break straight to Leah—"*

Another sneeze!

"Y'all, I can hardly—"

Sneeze!

"—rhyme! I need—"

Sneeze! Shoot!

"Move it or we'll get stuck!" Dez shouts. "Come on!"

We try to tug Jocelyn away from the shuttle, but she refuses. "I gotta get this flying again or we got bigger problems. Go! They ain't after me. Make one of those little doors to Peerless!"

"Are you sure?" I cry.

"I'll be fine. I can find my way back!"

We sprint off, dodging falling globs on every side. The ground is so soft our feet sink right through the yellow fluff with every other step. Amari's shoe gets stuck, and we stop to help yank him out. A sticky orange tongue snakes down from the sky and slaps into his back! He lurches into the air.

"Help me!" he screams. "I'm not that kind of snack!"

We seize his legs, pulling and shouting. The toad bat wobbles, still trying to drag us higher. More tongues zip through the air, trying to pluck us free. "Get off! Gross!" Two of them get their tongues crossed and fly off, angrily chirping and croaking at each other. Amari wriggles out of his backpack and we all crash into the yellow squish in a pile of arms and legs. We're all caked in yellow dust. "My paints! They took my gear! I'm always the one getting snatched!" he complains. "Carnivorous chandeliers, and now toad bats? Why am I a magnet for the weird stuff?"

The creatures circle overhead, croaking ravenously. We hop to our feet, ready to run. "Keynan!" Dez shouts. "You're not sneezing."

He's right! I inhale deeply, ready to spit fire as he starts beatboxing. The toad bats abruptly scatter, fluttering higher into the sky. "That's right! You better run!" Amari howls.

"I didn't do anything yet," I begin, but he barrels right over me, shaking his fist at the waste. Why so loud? They *could* come back. I keep scanning the sky while he hollers.

"Keymaster will rhyme you into Soup's next batch of black-eyed peas! You'll wish you'd never—"

Amari doesn't finish the sentence. He's standing stiff as a statue, fist still raised. So is Dez. "What happened to—" Oh no. I can't talk either. My muscles are frozen in place! My friends' eyes roll around wildly, begging for me to do something. It's like the museum all over again, except this time I'm caught up, too. I try to twist, to rhyme— anything! We need a Break to escape through, but my mouth won't move!

A deep growl vibrates through the air. Hot breath washes over the back of my neck. Ratchet is behind me—right in chomping range.

CHAPTER SEVENTEEN

SAME TEAM

Sneaking up on us! So unfair! We're completely paralyzed, like from a siren's song or spider venom. I can't beat Ratchet if I can't even fix my face to freestyle. Which is smart, I have to admit. Strategy. Something a Glory would use.

Tears stream down Amari's terrified face. Dez is mouthing words, although no sound escapes his mouth. I catch bits and pieces, *eat* and *too young* and *hate magic*.

Ratchet prowls around us lazily, close enough to nibble whoever is tastiest. Crystal scales cover every inch of the monster, from snout to those three sharp tails, shifting colors with every step like rainbows are snared inside them. I blink. Ratchet's four legs—no, six?—blur and rearrange themselves if I don't stare straight at them.

Now there's five. Amari gets one eyeful and squeezes his eyes shut. He slowly shakes his head back and forth.

Two long saber teeth poke out of the monster's massive upper jaw. A fever-red glow leaks from those catlike eyes. That's new—another remix. Is that what's keeping us paralyzed? Strange markings cover the blue fur on the creature's shoulders and back. If I was a little closer, I could . . .

A menacing growl stops that thought immediately—as if Ratchet knows what I'm planning. But one thing is clear: Ratchet is changing, just like Touré said—getting tougher every single time we fight back. Remixed. More powerful. Which gets me even more panicky. What else is Ratchet battling out here, to cause all of these changes?

I swallow. Ratchet won't . . . eat us, right? What do Glories eat, anyway? Is that what's behind all of this chasing me since the beginning? Am I a magical delicacy? A feast of Keynan McNuggets? The Glory's close enough to touch—I feel naked without my rhymes! Hopelessly defenseless. Nice leadership there, Keymaster. Failed to rescue one friend, and served up two more. I'm the worst friend ever—I should have waited, or tried harder to get past the homeroom professors so I could tell Professor Touré everything!

If there was ever a time to freestyle, this is it. But I'm so scared I don't know if I could rhyme something decent, even without Ratchet's weird paralyzing stink eye.

A paw scoops forward and gathers us all in like leftover scraps for the compost heap. The claws and scales don't shred our clothes to rags. The Glory's breath smells like garden herbs set on fire, eye watering and strong but not rotten. Probably some weird holdover from Amari's brick spider attack. The creature would be beautiful if it weren't about to eat us.

Ratchet sets off at a loping run, deeper into the waste. We're jostled along, clutched tight in the monster's new legs. Another remix. Just so it could carry us? The pinkish-purple sky blurs above us, and the giant pollen globs streak past until the ground is the same mushy color as above. Ratchet plods at the same steady gait but covers massive chunks of ground with each step.

Amari's mumble squeaks out behind me. "Great! We're about to be cat food!"

"You can talk! Hey! So can I." Barely. Whatever froze us is wearing off. "Dez, be ready for my rhyme. Dez?"

He doesn't answer. Oh no. I can't tell if he's awake or not. We might need to free ourselves without his help.

I take a deep breath, thinking of what to spit. Can we freeze Ratchet the same way the Glory froze us? Out-remix the monster? Or maybe my rhymes can crack right through that crystal armor again? I still don't understand how I made that happen the last time we faced off. I've thought about it plenty. The rhyme didn't even *attack* Ratchet. Nothing about it makes sense.

Suddenly Ratchet drops us in a heap. All the air wheezes right back out of my lungs. The Glory snorts at us and lopes off into the waste. We're not on the menu? I think? I recognize the weird bubbles floating in the air all across the horizon—none of them close, thankfully. There's nightmare things inside. Ratchet's pawprints send ripples of color surging through the spongy ground. We're somewhere in the Pancake Plains.

We're near the base of the most gnarled tree I've ever seen. Olive, maybe? Ancient, but normal. The ground around it is good old dirt instead of the yellow squish that creeps in just a few paces away. I twist around to check on my friends. The effort leaves me wheezing. What did Ratchet do to us?

There's more olive trees around us, a thick cluster that looks worn out, parched, and very old. But past them . . . "Amari, do you see that?"

He squints where I point. "Hey! Aren't those our saplings?"

"Ratchet *replanted* them?" Dez asks doubtfully.

I count the trees up. "Six of them. Umm, just like we

planned it." The saplings are definitely on the sickly side, but they're all alive. Corrupt magic isn't as strong here. Flecks of it dribble out of us, same as under the oak tree back at Peerless—but way slower. The only other tree I've seen in the radiant waste had leaves of fire, as if it had absorbed too much corrupt magic. I wish I understood *why*. There's something important here, and I'm missing it.

Dez stirs with a gasp. "We're alive?" He lets out a shrill laugh. "We're alive! I thought that was it for us!"

"It's past lunchtime. Maybe Ratchet's just saving us for dinner!" Amari moans. "Or there are Glory cubs around here, getting ready for a pouncing lesson!"

That gets us all peering around anxiously. But I get more hopeful the more I puzzle over this mess. "Y'all . . . I don't think Ratchet's going to hurt us. Why bring us here? This is probably the safest we've ever been in the waste."

Amari manages to sit up with a grunt. "I don't know, Keynan. If I was a Glory and wanted to lure Headmaster Kinder and Professor Touré out of the school—this is exactly what I would do."

"So we're bait?" Dez swallows.

Amari tries to flop a leg, but it's cooperating even worse than mine are. "We're definitely not competition!

We've gotta level up our magic somehow. If we get out of this, another remix will be waiting for us. And another one after that. The attacks won't stop."

"Scare Ratchet off for good," Dez agrees shakily.

"What if that's not enough?" Amari asks. "I . . . I could make something. Draw something that could break those scales—like Keynan did."

"Bro, I don't know," I manage. I can feel my fingers and toes again, though my head is still woozy. It's hard to think, let alone rhyme. But Amari's idea sets off a storm siren in my stomach. Using magic this way? It feels like we're inviting the corruption in all by ourselves.

Yolanda's old tablet video pops into my head. She was supposed to tutor us about the Wars of Illusion. *The elites won the war but lost it, too. Their weapons jacked up everything—broke magic. Shattered it.*

"I'm just saying . . . we might need more than beats and rhymes," Amari presses. "What if it takes magic to stop magic?"

I'm still not sure, but I'm scared to admit that he might be right.

A scrabbling sound comes from the other side of the grove. "Glory kittens," Dez groans. "Pretty sure I can walk. Try, y'all! Unless you want to wait around and find out how big they are?"

"He's right," I mutter. "And Ratchet could be back any second."

We totter to our feet with a whole lot of grunting and sweating. My legs protest like I just finished a hundred burpees, and sweat stains my shirt. But we're standing. Amari tries to draw in the dirt but scribbles it out with a frustrated snort. I slink through the trees, heart pounding.

"Keynan! *Toward* the weird sound? Really?"

"If they're small, we could trap them," I snap. "Maybe cut the fussing and get ready to beatbox!" Amari and Dez trade a weary look that makes my face burn. Okay, fine—my idea's ridiculous—but we need to get some advantage on Ratchet if we're going to protect Peerless.

I skirt around the biggest tree in the grove's trunk and gasp. "Leah!" She's grasping a low branch of the tree, trying to hoist herself up. Corrupt magic clings to her forearms and cheekbones like sparkling purple-and-blue scabs. Brilliant cracks shine through them, pulsing steadily as if the brightness is trying to burrow into her bones. A trickle of residue flakes from her pores. There's no way the grove will purge it all—even with our stolen saplings.

Dez swoops in and helps me scoop Leah up, one arm over each of our shoulders. "Leah?"

"Starbreaker, we got you," I murmur worriedly.

Amari waves a hand in front of her eyes. Leah's mumbling to herself, staring at the pinkish-purple void beyond the grove. "We need to get her to the oak tree," Amari breathes. "Right now!"

Why did Ratchet do this? I'm so afraid for Starbreaker my rhymes won't flow. It's like my eyes are stuck on the horizon, waiting for a distant sun to rise from below. But truth be told, that's impossible—because my friends need me. I'll do whatever it takes to keep them safe from harm. I wave my arm and the air obeys: blue, purple, and gold splays open with plenty of room for my Peerless crew.

"Y'all pick her up and carry her through," I say.

Now why are they both staring my way?

"Keynan, are you all right?" Amari asks worriedly, slipping in to hoist Leah up. She giggles.

"Of course I am. What are you waiting for?"

"You just made a Break and didn't even rhyme!" Dez exclaims. He's right. I remember the feeling of freestyle, the exhilaration of it coming together . . . but not the words.

What were the words?

The Break beckons; the soccer field awaits us on the other side of the glowing hole. A wave of dizziness almost sweeps me off my feet. What just happened? My magic didn't even bother with words—it came straight from my brain!

And . . . it felt amazing.

They both stare, fear and concern playing hopscotch on their faces. "Why are you just standing there?" Dez cries.

"Come on, Keynan!" Amari shouts over his shoulder, just before they disappear into the light.

"Right behind you!" Why do they sound so worried? I saved the day! Time for a victory dinner of—

Ratchet bounds to the ground between me and the Break. Crystalline wings sweep out from behind the monster's shoulders, tinkling like a forest of wind chimes and sharp enough to cut glass. The Glory spits out a clump of yellowing leaves and releases an enraged howl.

Ratchet twists around to face me, teeth bared in blazing anger. And something else . . . sadness? Why? None of it makes sense. My eyes flick to the plants Ratchet dropped. Vegetables. Pitifully small and wilted, but still food. Why feed us? Why bring us to a shelter from corrupt magic?

"What do you want?" I wail.

Ratchet snorts and turns back to the Break. Sizing it

up. Shoulders, ribs, haunches—the Glory's body is *elongating* like a snake. Another remix to squeeze through the Break.

I can close it, keep Peerless safe. That's what Touré would do. My magic could hurt Ratchet, too, scare the monster off permanently, like Amari believes we should do. I put those cracks in the monster's chest once—can more damage protect my crew?

But I don't do that, either. Right now my heart is telling me to try something different. I've gotta do *me*. I breathe deep. The rhyme swells my chest and rushes from my throat almost before I part my lips.

> *Is there any piece of you*
> *that's still breathing, still feelin'?*
> *I ain't dressed to be no villain,*
> *stressed we're on the same team*
> *Tryna find peace, wake up from the same dream*

Ratchet shudders, reeling away from the Break. Those new wings tense, ready to launch the monster free. One snaps from the shoulder, slaps into the ground, and shatters into a thousand glowing shards!

Silver-and-blue light bursts from the Glory's wound. The flash lances into the pink-purple soup above, sending clouds swirling. Leaves twirl down from the olive grove, caught in a rising wind. Ratchet staggers and collapses. The crystalline scales dim to muddy hues of green and blue. Shadows shift and twist within the massive rib cage.

I did it. My path to the Break is wide open.

But I don't escape. Pieces of the broken wing crunch under my shoes. I creep closer to the horrible wound. Worst rhyme ever! I was trying to reach out to Ratchet, not this! Maybe a different rhyme can heal, except—

Ratchet is *hollow*.

A person's bewildered face peers out at me through the glittering ribs. Her cheeks and forehead are crusted with corrupt magic's residue, thick enough for a second skin. Her locs glow with it. Her eyes are blue and brown one instant, pink and green the next. Despite that, she still looks exactly like my BFF, my homie, my ace beaucoup—just a little more grown up.

I don't believe my eyes. "Yolanda?"

CHAPTER EIGHTEEN

BECAUSE OF ME

Yolanda blinks. Her eyes focus and stop cycling through different color patterns, settling on dark brown. *"You again."* The monster's jaws speak in unison. The rumble nearly drowns out Yolanda's real voice. I can't help but back away. *"That little boy who keeps showing up around my sister."*

"Umm . . . yeah . . . Leah's my friend!" I squeak.

"What's your name?"

"Keynan, and my bad about the wing—"

"What's your *last* name?"

I hesitate. "Masters."

Ratchet's claws flex in and out of her paws. Yolanda doesn't seem to notice. Is she in control of Ratchet, or is it the other way around? We were all painfully wrong in believing Ratchet was a Glory. However Yo ended up like this brings more questions than answers, and she's still dangerous. I keep sliding toward the Break.

"I saw them once," she whisper-growls. "Your parents."

I stop short. "You did?" A thousand questions try to pour out of me at once, tripping over each other so nothing escapes my mouth.

"Yeah. So proud of their fancy school. Look where it's got us. I knew there was a reason I didn't like you."

Didn't like me—so it's fine to try biting my face off? I could've done with just a stink eye and still got the hint! Every problem at Peerless goes back to my parents. Everyone blames them for something. They can't all be wrong, can they?

Yolanda—well, the scary Ratchet shell around her— attempts to rise, muscles flexing beneath her glinting scales. She slumps over. Yolanda wheezes, glaring out of her crystal prison in confusion. "Is this a trick? What did you do to me?"

"Just getting your attention with a rhyme. And it worked!" I edge a little closer to the Break. If Amari and Dez come back for me, they could set off a whole new set of problems.

"Rhymes, in the waste? That's gutsy. Or stupid."

"Listen . . . Peerless is beat up pretty bad—" I leave out the part about how much of it is her fault. "But we're building it back up stronger than ever. Maybe we could help each other? Truce?"

Yolanda snorts. "You're not built for this. I have armor, and you're out here running around in—what? Your school uniform? Naked as a newborn baby. You have no idea." The monster's head shakes back and forth. The wound in Ratchet's back is steadily sealing. Filaments of crystal creep over each other with every breath. Will she recognize me when she's back inside?

"What happened to you?" I ask. "Leah's been worried sick since day one. She's the only one who believed you weren't one of Kinder's faux students, and she came out here to prove it."

A furious roar drowns me out. "Kinder! She conjured a construct of me?" Yolanda slams Ratchet's shell with both fists. Brilliant metal covers her hands—her body, too, where it's not swallowed in crystal. I take a few more steps toward the Break, but one of Ratchet's tails slashes in front of me. Great. The more the monster wakes up, the less Yolanda talks. I could freestyle a way out. But I don't want to hurt Yolanda again—or make her big mad. Madder than she already is. "I should have snatched her

179

armor, too!" she rages. I clap my hands over my ears. "When I'm strong enough, I'm going to—"

She cuts off, staring around the rib cage like she's never seen it before. "Didn't mean for it to go this far," she mutters softly. "Is Leah okay?"

"She will be. We took her back to Peerless." I lick my lips. "Why did you leave?"

"You know what Peerless is," she sneers. "How could you stay, instead of finding our parents? Some people think we can do this without a fight, and they couldn't be more wrong." My jaw works, but no answer comes out. "Anyway, it doesn't matter now. I . . . found them."

"Our parents?" I exclaim. Of all the things I expected her to say!

"No. *Them.*" Yo scrubs her knuckles across her eyes. The crystal skin has almost sealed her back inside the monster. "I messed up. They didn't know Peerless existed. They didn't know our parents hid *us*. But they saw me. One of them is inside the school. Inside Peerless, because of me." Her voice cracks. "They keep pushing me out! I can't tell which one of them it is, no matter how hard I try, even when I—"

Ratchet's crystalline shell ripples. Eyeballs of all shapes and colors squeeze out of the crystal, dozens of them, looking around wildly. They all pivot to me.

I can't with all the stares! So creepy! "We . . . we can help you!" If I don't faint.

"No, first-year. You'll only get in my way. I'm so close. I can beat them."

"Just come back home. We're doing magic totally different now. I can rhyme, and Leah's moves—"

"NO!" Yolanda's shout dissolves into a roar. Her eyes shift colors again, and lose their focus. Ratchet's crystal seals her completely back inside. The monster stands and glowers at me, scales regaining their brilliant turquoise fire. *"It's not safe. I'm not safe."* Yolanda's voice, melted into Ratchet's growl, curdles in my ears. *"Hard . . . to stay focused out here. Stay myself. Stronger. I've gotta get* stronger."

"Wait! Why is a Glory inside Peerless?" I press.

"I don't know. They're after something powerful—from before the Wars of Illusion would be my guess. Something only Peerless can get. Any ideas?"

I shrug helplessly. "Maybe? Most stuff is hidden away, so—"

Yo snorts. *"Then what good are you?"*

My mind churns over what it might be.

"Keynan!"

I spin around. Dez pokes cautiously through the Break. His eyes go big enough to fall out when me and

Ratchet—with Yolanda now sealed inside—both turn to him. One of her tails slashes for him. Dez yelps and disappears back into the Break.

"Hey! Be nice to my friends!"

"Your friends aren't your friends!" Yolanda snarls. "Not until you know for sure. A Glory can impersonate anyone. They've tried me out here, believe me. It's all a big game to them. You get my sister better. Then you both get out of Peerless! You're all in danger so long as *she's* inside. I'm not strong enough to take her on. Yet."

"But where are we supposed to go?"

Yolanda snarls, whipping her neck back and forth like she's arguing with herself—with Ratchet. She vanishes back into the grove of olive trees, branches snapping aside in her wake. Gone just like that, leaving more questions than answers.

CHAPTER NINETEEN

MONSTERS FOR FRIENDS

I trudge back to the Peerless courtyard in a trance, Dez chattering worriedly at my side. I barely remember closing the Break. After all this time . . . there is no Ratchet. Just Leah's sister, a hundred times scarier than her faux version. Telling me there's a Glory inside Peerless. How is that even possible?

We reach Leah, resting in a hammock near the oak tree with Amari at her side.

"How is she? Has she woken up at all? Has she said anything?"

"Still asleep." He claps my shoulder as I squat beside him. Leah's skin shimmers from head to toe as though she's covered in melted diamonds. Corrupt magic pours from her like some miserable, brilliant fog. My chest is suddenly tight, and my knees wobble. Amari glances at me sharply, then helps me sit cross-legged. I almost flopped over!

"Thanks," I say, embarrassed. Seeing Starbreaker—the toughest of us, the most fearless—taken out like this? I can't even deal with it. Magic keeps hurting my friends. I should be protecting them all, but I keep letting them down. "Even her sweat is sparkling. I've never seen it this bad."

"That's because you haven't looked in a mirror," he murmurs.

I glance down at my hands—they're shimmering, just like Leah's skin. I don't feel any different, though. Why is she asleep and I'm fine? Dizzy, but fine. I haven't been so worried over someone being sick since my mama, the day I left for Peerless. *My faux mama, that is,* I remind myself bitterly. We watch silently as corrupt magic leaches from her skin. "How is Jocelyn?" I ask. "Did she make it back?"

"Like nothing happened." Dez snorts. "She was chatting up Soup when I went to get cold water. I almost thought she wasn't our Jocelyn until she threw a yam at me when I asked how she got back. Told me no one likes snitches."

"I think there's some secret sauce in her magic," I

mumble. "Keynan, did Ratchet do something to you?" Dez asks worriedly. "You're not yourself."

"I'm fine," I insist.

"But just . . . maybe visit Nurse Manny? Until we get Touré down here?"

"No! Forget them. Y'all are *not* gonna believe this." Anger rises over me, enough that Dez blinks in surprise. Touré and Kinder . . . hiding Yolanda from us this whole time! I'm so sick of their secrets. My trust is reset to zero, and they'll never get it back. I take a deep breath and spill. Everything.

"Leah was right. Yolanda isn't a faux student. She's Ratchet."

Their mouths fall open as I fill in every single detail I can remember. I refuse to be like the headmaster and Touré—hiding things from the people I care about. *Then why don't you tell them how good the magic feels?* A voice giggles in the back of my head before I shove it away. *Or how freestyling is all you care about?*

The courtyard is quiet for a long time after I'm finished. Leah moans, tossing her head weakly. "I got you, Yo . . . You never gave up on me. I know you out here . . ."

Dez gets her to sip from a cup of water. "She looks way better than when we first set her down. If she'd been out there any longer, this might have been permanent."

Amari taps a finger on his chin. "Did Yo look this, uh . . . crusty?"

"Yeah. But she said something about armor, too. That we're like babies without it."

"Armor . . . wait. You remember that room we found in the hidden wing?" Amari says excitedly. "Touré's workshop? With all of those flat round things in the crates, and the weird skull? Wasn't there—"

"You're right!" I exclaim. "That's where Yo must have got hers. But the corrupt magic is wearing it out."

Dez snorts. "That's a nice way to say it turned her into a monster!"

"But it's still keeping her mind right," I counter. Amari's eyebrows raise doubtfully. "Well, mostly! She's not all the way cooked—she wouldn't have warned us about . . . you know. Y'all can't pretend like you didn't hear me say it."

Dez rubs his face with both hands. "That's a lot, bruh. We've thought Ratchet was a Glory this whole time. But no! That's *really* Leah's sister—just tearing up Peerless every other time she pops up?"

"I hear you—but now we know why."

"A Glory inside Peerless . . . I can't even." Amari squeeze his eyes shut.

"I know, but it changes everything. It could be any-body!"

"Saying we even believe her, Glories are supposed to be driven mad by corrupt magic." Amari spreads his hands. "Does that sound like anyone in Peerless to you?"

"Not really," I admit, a chill going down my spine.

"But that's just what Kinder and Touré told us," Dez says unhappily. "Should we really be depending on any-thing they say?"

I frown. There's no arguing his point—Yolanda said the exact same thing. *Your friends aren't your friends.* I push her warning stubbornly aside. No way am I going to start looking at my crew sideways. "That's fair. But what could a Glory want in Peerless?"

Amari shrugs. "If it's . . . really one of them, they know more about the school than any of us."

I sit straight up. "What if what they want isn't *in* Peerless?"

Amari's eyes go wide. "The turntable!"

"Exactly!"

We catch up Dez on the strange device we saw in the magical talking museum. We both felt drawn to it, and both Kinder and Touré perked up when we mentioned it. Which could mean nothing . . . or everything.

"It would make sense for a Glory to hide here, looking for something useful," I muse. "Then why not let us do all the hard work so they can snatch it from us the minute we find it?"

Dez shakes his head slowly. "We just need to . . . it's like Professor Okoro says about our lab work. Confirm or it's conjecture. What if Yo's trying to trick us?"

"She could be," I mutter. "Everyone else is. But she cares about Leah. And it explains why she's attacking Peerless. Before, I thought she wanted our magic. But if some piece of her is trying to protect her sister . . ."

"I guess," Amari says doubtfully. "If you're right, and she's telling the truth, how do we get Ratchet to stop tearing down Peerless without hurting Yolanda inside? She's basically a prisoner in that armor."

I shrug helplessly. He's supposed to be the answer finder, not me!

"We gotta do two things at once then," Dez says. "Because I'd *really* like to find out who the Glory is inside Peerless. Before they know that we know."

"I'd bet all my snacks for a year on Kinder being the Glory," I say. "Especially with how she's switched up our homeroom professors. They are downright spooky now. Gotta be Glory behavior."

"Same!" Dez declares.

"But Touré's been guiding us the most," Amari points out. "What if she's getting us ready for bigger plans? Can't ignore her, either."

He's right, too. I squeeze my eyes shut. This is a mess, everyone's doubts and suspicions slithering around. I can't imagine a better way to tear up Peerless. Ugghh!

Touré? Or Kinder? Either way, I have to admit Yolanda was right about one thing. I'm not built for this. I wish Leah was awake—she helps cuts through the nonsense, even if we don't always agree.

Dez and Amari exchange a nervous glance.

"What is it?" I ask.

"We . . . kinda told her what happened," Dez blurts out. "After we got Leah here."

My throat seizes up. "Who?"

"Who do you think?" Professor Touré's voice behind me nearly makes me jump right out of my shoes. "The same person who's always dragging you off the skillet!"

Professor Touré gets one look at Leah and tramples a cucumber vine in her rush to reach us. She kneels beside Leah's hammock and gently slides her knuckles along her cheekbone with a hiss. I blink. The shimmer on Leah's arms has already faded back to a healthy brown.

"Not even a scratch," Touré remarks. "Incredible. And lucky. She'll need to sleep here. All of you will." She turns to me, eyes narrowing as she searches my face. "How are you feeling?"

"Fine, just worried," I say stiffly. "I know we're in trouble . . . I just didn't want her to get lost out there."

"Wiley would have sat on us if we tried to get to you ourselves," Amari adds in a shaky voice. We're *nervous*. We're going to give ourselves away!

Touré grimaces. "They need . . . more calibrating. You all did a brave thing, going after her like that. But let me be real. Peerless is still bleeding magic. It won't survive another one of Ratchet's attacks. If repairs are going to work . . . we've got to be honest with each other. Why did Leah go out there?" Her eyes flit between us urgently. "The headmaster doesn't give y'all enough credit for being resourceful, but I know what you're capable of together. Did she find something? What could be worth the risk?"

I freeze. *She found out about the fake sister you tried to pull on us!* I want to howl. She's lied about Yolanda. Does that mean she's the Glory?

"Didn't she say something about that thing?" Dez cuts in. "A . . . turntable?"

"We tried to help, but Ratchet showed up again," Amari adds. "We didn't find it. Spent the rest of the time running for our lives."

"A turntable . . ." Professor Touré breathes. She's quiet for a long time. "How did you get away?"

"Keynan's rhymes," Dez answers quietly, staring at Leah. "He's getting better than ever."

Professor Touré's lip curls, but she quickly stills her face. "Keynan. Do you remember your freestyle?"

"I . . . um, mostly," I answer hesitantly. "It all happened so fast."

"But you *did* freestyle. You spoke the words for your conjuring?"

I choke out a laugh and bob my head. "What other way is there to rhyme?"

Touré nods, relief on her face. Dez and Amari watch me as she checks over Leah. Awkward. They know I'm lying. Dez saw what really happened for himself. How do I explain without freaking them out? I'm in control.

"Corrupt magic makes everything easier," Touré says suddenly. "If you allow it. Don't. If you feel anything . . . off, tell me at once."

"What do you mean?"

"If you can't remember your rhymes. Start writing them down. If magic manifests around you whether or not you speak it into existence. Most of all . . . if you're freestyling without intention—thoughtlessly, like your heartbeat. Tell me at once." She gazes down at Leah. "There are some things even the oak tree cannot purge."

"Okay," I say faintly. "Definitely."

"Good. Don't tell Kinder about any of this. She's pressed about enough as it is." She squeezes my shoulder and hurries off, more eager than I've ever seen. "I'm going to get some supplies from Nurse Manny. I'll be back. I want to hear everything the moment she wakes up."

Wow. We all watch her hustle off down the path. My head is spinning. Not only is Professor Touré lying to us, but she wants us to hide things from Headmaster Kinder. "Thanks for the save," I say to Dez. "Did you see her face? She forgot Leah completely once the turntable came up!"

"But she cares about Peerless. Really cares." Dez winces. "Doesn't she? This is so confusing!"

"She cares about us, if we're the ones finding that turntable," Amari muses. "She all but told us to lie to Kinder. That's nothing new, but with what we know now . . . is it Glory behavior?"

"I don't know what to think anymore." I rub my hands across my face. "But I saw Yolanda with my own eyes—I can believe that." *Can I, though?* I wonder. My eyes have lied to me before. "Neither one of them told us the truth about her. They let us believe Ratchet is a Glory, or some monster from the waste. That was foul."

"Easier to act like they're *both* Glories," Amari muses. "Maybe they are."

"I wouldn't go that far," I say. "But we can't trust them."

Dez lets out a miserable laugh. "So let me get this straight. Now the monster's on our side, but we gotta watch out for the grown-ups. Sometimes, y'all, I wish I'd never got out of bed for that midnight snack. That night you were trapping Slickback and Disco? Peerless sure would be a lot easier with just points and grades and homework."

"Yeah, but you would have figured it out eventually," I say.

"Better for that to happen with friends than on your own," Amari adds. "No wonder Yo's in such bad shape. She didn't have a crew."

"You're right." Dez sighs. "I'm just . . . kinda done with all of this. But I guess it's not done with me."

I feel the same way. First our neighborhoods, and now Peerless. It's just like Dez said. Monsters for friends. A grown-up Glory. Nowhere is safe anymore—unless we make it safe. I just gotta find out how to do it. Yesterday. My friends are depending on me, and I can't let them down.

CHAPTER TWENTY

ALLOWING ROOM

Brightness shimmers out of Leah for two whole days. I don't know how much magic a tree can hold, but the old oak soaks it all up. No one leaves her alone, not for one second. For classes, we decide the best way to get along is to play along. We do our homework in the courtyard. Peerless's magic still needs our lessons to hold the school together—according to the grown-ups, anyway—but at least two of us stay by Leah's side at all times. We sleep there, too; there's plenty of good spaces for hammocks around the oak tree. Wiley and the other cohort professors stalk us whenever we're not in the courtyard, but we don't give them a reason to pull us away. We've got to be there for Leah, be the very first ones to explain all of this when she wakes up. So she knows the truth.

Professor Touré checks on her twice a day, each time a little more worn down than when we saw her last, like those horrible circles under her eyes are only a few sleepless nights from becoming permanent. She's routed corrupt magic out of Peerless floor by floor, room by room, and locker by locker, slowly and steadily. The school isn't falling apart anymore. There are no black-outs, no signs of corrupt magic creeping into Peerless.

Why would a Glory do that? Maybe Yo was wrong.

One night I wake from a restless sleep. The courtyard is cool at night, but I'm thirsty. Leah's in a deep sleep when I flop over to check. Headmaster Kinder looms over her. She whispers softly, rocking her hammock. Her face is angry and grief-stricken at the same time. I freeze, panicked. What is she doing? Is that a rhyme? I'm not close enough to eavesdrop! She doesn't see me or look my way when she finally leaves. If she's the Glory who Yo warned us about . . . I'm nowhere near ready to take her on. Not alone.

When we're by ourselves, we constantly debate one thing.

"There's no point in arguing," Amari says after Touré finishes checking Leah the next evening. "Why would the professor work so hard to keep Peerless together if she's one of them?"

Dez and I groan. We're supposed to be reviewing Professor Okoro's lecture notes, but velocity equations are the last thing on my mind. We could at least get excused from classes while we're dealing with all of this, but no. We can get time at Nurse Manny's office for bubble guts, but not for magic that threatens our whole entire being. It makes zero sense!

"You could say the same thing about Headmaster Kinder," I counter. "She's grouchy, but mean ancient sorceress? Why even bother saving Peerless the first time Yo broke in?"

Amari shakes his head stubbornly. "We wouldn't know unless she wanted us to, right? We've got to surprise her while she's not expecting us."

"That's a plan I can get behind," Dez agrees.

"Surprise who?" Leah asks.

"Starbreaker!" I exclaim. We all crowd around her eagerly. "You're awake!"

"And hungry," she says with a shaky laugh. She touches her head, and confusion clouds her face. "I don't remember much. I felt like the waste just stretched on forever and ever."

"Food first! Then we talk." Dez and Amari hurry off to grab her some dinner.

"How bad is it?" she asks.

"Worse than my very worst. Detention until you graduate, probably. But it's not like they can send you home."

Her laugh ends in a groan. "I need a shower."

"Food first . . . and we need to catch you up on everything before they know you're awake."

She grimaces. "Can't wait." The crew soon returns with jackfruit sliders and roasted cauliflower, which she devours ravenously.

I still don't know where to start. "Leah—"

"I know I messed up, okay? Fake parents were hard enough, but my sister, too? I thought if I could just get back to that camp, maybe I could find some proof, or even her—"

"Leah."

"Can you shush? I'm trying to apologize!"

"You don't have to," I say quietly. "She found you. You were right."

Leah goes still. "Then . . . why isn't she here?"

"She's . . . she's Ratchet."

"What. *What?*" She shakes her head in disbelief.

"It's true. The Yo we've seen at school is a faux student. Your sister got . . . well, she lost herself in the waste, and . . ."

I stop as Leah's face crumples. "I knew it," she whispers

raggedly. "I knew it, *I knew it I knew it . . .*" We give her the time she needs, looking down while she furiously wipes her tears away. Dez moves as if to give her a hug, but I shake my head silently and mouth, *Wait*. He frowns, wiping his own eyes, but nods.

"Thanks," Leah breathes. "I'm okay. Let's hear the rest."

I start from the beginning, from making a plan after we found Leah's note, to the encounter with Yolanda. Dez and Amari jump in, too. I hate how much this hurts my friend, but I do my best not to miss anything. Every word, down to Yolanda's warning about Touré and Kinder. "She actually brought food back for us to eat," I finish. "She dropped you in a grove of trees. So even when she's full Ratchet, she still cares."

"That explains your rhyme, last time!" Dez exclaims. "You were speaking to Yo, we just didn't know it. That's why Ratchet cracked open."

"Yolanda wants out." I bite my lip. "She's not going to last out there too much longer."

"We'll get her back," Amari murmurs. "Won't we, Keynan? Peerless Pact."

"No doubt. Oh . . . Leah? I've been meaning to give you this. I left it at Peerless over break." I fish in my pocket and pluck out the small necklace I found in the dirt, back when we tried to plant Touré's saplings in the waste.

Leah's eyes brighten. "Oh wow. I thought I lost it."

"Sorry it took me this long." I shrug sheepishly. "Yo's gonna need to wait for our help, though. First things first. Right here in Peerless."

Amari and Dez go very still, watching me. "Kinder?" Leah asks finally.

"Kinder."

"She's the most likely," Dez admits reluctantly. "If Yolanda's right."

Leah rubs the necklace between her fingers. "So how's it going down?"

"We know our magic is still . . . basic." It stings to say it, but it's true. "But that doesn't mean it won't work. We're good at making traps."

"Slickback and Disco are way different than Kinder," Amari points out. "She was tough enough as a headmaster—and now we know why."

"Yeah, but we haven't all worked together," Dez presses. "Not really. That's got to count for something. A crew working together instead of one person alone? No limit to what we can do."

Leah purses her lips. "It's not like we'll be able to practice out in the open."

"Exactly." I stand abruptly. "We need to do this in a way she won't see coming. If we're wrong . . . well, we'll know who the Glory *isn't*."

"Touré's gonna be big mad about this if we're right," Leah says softly.

"Why?"

"Just . . . forget it." Leah sighs. "Well, we better come up with something incredible, or we're going to spend the rest of our time at Peerless cartwheeling around the halls whenever Kinder snaps her fingers."

"I've actually got some thoughts on that," Amari says, rubbing his hands together.

When we all finally climb into our hammocks for bed, I'm already cooking up a rhyme that will work with Amari's idea. I'm exhausted—we all are—but guilt won't let me fall asleep right away. I could confess how my verses just flow in my head now, but it's more than that. I remember the fear on Amari's face when they saw me make a Break with no rhymes. And I still won't stop. I can't. I don't care about the corrupt magic anymore. I love it. I love the freestyle. It's a little scary, sure, and plenty dangerous. But all will be forgiven after they see everything I can do.

CHAPTER TWENTY-ONE

THERE'S ONLY US

Leah gets back into a rhythm after another week. She's mostly okay—returning to classes, eating in the dining hall, catching up on missing homework. Homework! How is it still a thing? But Leah doesn't join in when we grumble about it. She says what Touré and Nurse Manny want to hear at her checkups. But there's something . . . off. She's here, but . . . not. Her laugh is forced.

Professor Mendoza even calls out the changes in class. "Leah, you're going through the motions," she declares. "Perfection! Class, look to her as an example."

"She's grieving over Yo," Amari says when I ask him. "We just gotta give her time." Which only makes me feel worse—I could have brought Yolanda back with us that very same day, if I'd gotten the rhymes right. If I'd really let my magic cut loose.

The only time Leah sheds that sadness is when we're all prepping for our Glory trap. She's so focused then, it's honestly a little scary. The whole plan revolves around tricking the headmaster into letting us use our magic—then surprising Kinder at the last possible moment. Everyone's part is important if it's going to work. We are talking about a Glory in disguise, after all. This is our first time using beats, rhymes, dance, and art, all in one big conjuring. It's going to be epic. Just hopefully not an epic disaster.

We agree to attend classes and pretend like everything is normal on the chosen day. I'm so nervous it's hard to focus on class, and I spend most of the time running lines through my head. When we all meet for lunch, we barely speak as we nibble at our bread bowls. I hardly eat; the last thing I want is Soup's Soup sloshing around in my stomach when we're trying to capture our headmaster.

We wait for the halls to clear of faux students after the last classes are finished, and march to Kinder's office. We're way out of bounds—students are supposed to stick to the dining halls or dormitory when class is over.

Dez licks his lips. "No turning back now." The headmaster's assistant, Miss Molly, is seated in the admin station just outside the headmaster's office, chewing gum. Short-cut purple curls frame her face, gaze fixed on her monitor. Her fingers clack away at a keyboard. I've never seen her anywhere else in Peerless, or even look up from her computer!

"Please wait in Headmaster Kinder's office," she announces.

We file nervously through the glass door. Kinder's painting is gone. She's not even bothering to hide her control room anymore.

Leah and I meet each other's eyes. "Ain't nothing to it but to do it," I murmur. Together we pad inside, Amari and Dez close behind. The glow of the monitors outlines Headmaster Kinder, typing intently on her tablet. I stop in surprise, stunned. She's dressed in full armor—the set of gleaming metallic clothes I remember from Touré's workshop in the hidden wing. The set is bluish silver and looks like it should weigh a hundred pounds. But she moves smoothly between the screens, peering up at them intently. Bronze writing in some language I don't know covers the armor's shoulders. Faint blue lines trace the seams, glowing faintly with hidden reserves of power. *That's what Ratchet is made out of,* I realize. *Peerless armor warped by corrupt magic.*

Amari swallows. "Umm, y'all? Slightly more dangerous than we thought. Should we—"

"That doesn't change a thing," Leah hisses. "We're still doing what we came here to do!"

"Act normal," I say. "Talk about normal school things like we planned."

"*Normal?* Do you not see today's outfit?"

Leah hisses. "No . . . what's she doing?"

I turn back to the screen—and the image Kinder is focused on makes my heart sink into my shoes. Yolanda, in full Ratchet mode, trotting across a patch of waste I don't recognize.

"Why did you have to make this so difficult?" Kinder mutters.

She taps a command into her tablet. The secret room's lights flicker and wink out—everything except Kinder's display. The intercom blares overhead, but she ignores it, fixed on Leah's sister. "*A storm is approaching the school grounds. This is not a drill.*" We watch as blue lightning sizzles up from the honeycomb ground and snags Yolanda's wings! She yowls in pain, twisting her way free.

"She's hurting my sister!" Leah hisses. We grab her before she can rush forward.

"Stick to the plan," Amari pleads.

Back on the screen, Yolanda wrenches free of the lightning and dashes away. Two glittering wings lie on the ground behind her.

"Stubborn child!" Headmaster Kinder flings her tablet aside in frustration. "You want power, but I swear you'll never get it. Not without me!"

All of my doubts about Headmaster Kinder evaporate in an instant. Hurting one of our friends—a Peerless student—over power? What more proof do we need that she's the Glory? "Y'all saw what happened after the blackout. She's using Peerless's magic against Yolanda!"

Leah's eyes flash. "Let's do this."

"Headmaster Kinder?" I call out, surprised at my steady voice. "We need to talk."

The silence stretches as she flicks off all of her monitors. The headmaster sets down her tablet and turns to face us, eyes more bloodshot than I've ever seen. "So. The crew's all here." Peerless's lights flicker back on, and her gaze swivels to Leah. "Stronger than ever," she says softly. "You gave us quite the scare. I'm glad you're safe."

"Are you?" Leah says testily. "Did you even know I was lost?"

Kinder jerks as if someone slapped her—someone

with a strong arm. "You're in the best place you could possibly be. Under my protection."

"Protection?" Leah splutters. "Who is really—"

"Such a great chat," I cut in. "Heartstrings and . . . bonding! Love this for us." Leah's supposed to keep Kinder off balance, not get her so mad we're all thrown into detention! I slide between them, breaking off their staring contest. Leah gives me an annoyed look, but she clamps her jaws shut. Kinder's eyes swivel to me. Eek. How did Leah handle this without flinching? I feel like I'm cooking under my shirt. "So . . . we had some ideas. About helping. Umm, with Peerless."

"Make it quick, Keynan. Peerless won't repair itself."

"That's actually why we came." I gesture her out past the reception area, into the hallway. There's caution tape along either side, where Touré is still plastering together new walls. "We know we're not ready for the radiant waste yet. But can we do more? If the cohort professors can step up, so should we."

"Between classes, of course," Dez adds. "Adding on to your great work."

"Oh?" Kinder pauses, peering at us as she considers. "You've got my attention." She winks at Dez. "Just don't lay it on too thick."

Amari clears his throat and nervously launches into his

idea of combining arts across Peerless, mixing together what we know, allowing real and faux students to play off each other, avoiding the same basic routines. This is the easy part of the trap, because it's all true—we could actually try it if the grown-ups weren't in the way. "Kind of . . . the opposite of what you're doing now," he finishes, licking his lips.

"Not that Peerless isn't great the way it is," Dez jumps in. "But we could be doing even more."

"So much more," I say. "Like one big crew. Same as when we stopped Slickback and Disco."

Kinder folds her arms. "This is all an intriguing . . . theory. But now isn't the time for . . . riffing. You all mean well, but your timing is awful. What's facing us out there is the only thing that matters. Later. Once we're whole again, I'll consider it."

"But we can show you!" I burst out. "Just a quick demonstration."

Kinder's smile vanishes. "You're going to miss dinner, children. I'd hate for you to lose cohort points." The headmaster turns back to her tablet, clearly telling us to scoot.

"Thanks for listening," I say. The four of us exchange glances. She didn't go for it. That's no surprise—the odds were never on our side. But she still thinks she knows why we've come, which means we can still surprise her.

This is it. Amari pulls out spray paint. Dez starts to beatbox.

Kinder goes rigid. "What . . . *what are you doing*? Stop!"

My rhymes leap out of me.

> *Sometimes there's no time, a demonstration is best*
> *We tell you we got skills, so now it's time for a test*
> *Of us—you—me—no rest, no sleep for what we going through*
> *Hard times, hard lines are what we need to pull us through*
> *So we've arrived to provide the glue, big bricks, strong plaster*
> *Cuz we're the Peerless Crew and I'm your Keymaster.*

As I rhyme, Amari paints over the walls me and Touré slapped together after Yolanda's first attack. And Leah . . . moves, her arms and legs melting into the rhythm of Dez's beat. I've never seen anything so sweet. Her feet ripple, her palms gesture, and polished floor soars over where cracks once festered.

Kinder is astonished. "That is . . . remarkable. I must admit."

"Trust, you ain't seen the half of it!" I answer.

Her eyebrows rise in shock. "Don't talk! Stop—"

"Why, you gonna dock points?" Something feels weird.

"Foul magic has seared into your joints, your bones! Keynan Masters, you're—"

But we're all in our zones. Leah's in full Starbreaker mode, dancing faster and faster. Amari pours paint over patchwork plaster. A new wall shudders forward, right toward the Glory—

"Y'all, stop!" Dez breaks the beat. A wave of dizziness drags me off my feet. The new wall topples around a snarling Kinder—it didn't even come close! The ground rumbles and—

"Oh no."

We race back into the secret office just as one of Kinder's huge displays cracks apart. Static spills across the ruined screen. The room buckles, brick and wood and plaster toppling on every side. Our trap slid right around her, as though the magic couldn't grasp hold of her—but still needed to fill itself with *something*. The entire station erupts in a wash of sparks.

Kinder shoves past us, aghast. "No, no, *no!*" she howls.

The last working screen fizzles. Yolanda is visible. Her loping gait halts and changes to a sprint, right before the screen winks out.

"Just like my map," Amari squeaks. "She saw us again."

Kinder goes very still. "She?"

"My sister." Leah plants herself before Kinder, fists clenched. I rise and stand beside her. "You lied to us about Yo! Twisted my head up with a construct of her!"

"Yes and yes!" Kinder snarls. "And I'd do it all over again! She's lost herself, Leah. Seeing Glories in every shadow, looking for someone to blame about her parents. They *aren't coming back*. They're gone!"

"You don't know that!" I cry.

"Sometimes I think I'm the only one in this place who does!" she snaps. "The only one who will accept the truth! I'd finally locked in a way to leash Yolanda, peel that corrupted armor from her before the damage is irreversible. And you chuckleheads just messed it all up! Go. Get out!" She glares at us . . . furious, but on the verge of tears.

Amari shakes his head slowly, and we touch eyes. "No way," he rasps.

He sees the same thing I do. *No way is she a Glory.* Wrong, maybe; salty, definitely. But an ancient sorcerer lost to madness? I don't believe it.

"It's not her," Dez moans. "We messed up."

An awful sick feeling radiates through my stomach. We completely guessed wrong on the hidden Glory. That means . . . Touré. Prodding us over the turntable. Hiding all of our mistakes from Kinder—from my very first Break on the soccer field to Slickback and Disco. Teaching us magic behind the headmaster's back. Taking us into the radiant waste—and leaving us there! It's all so obvious now I want to kick myself!

Leah rounds on us with a scowl. "After all of this? What else could she be?"

The headmaster searches our faces. "I don't understand."

"We . . ." The words are embarrassing to say out loud now. "We thought you were a Glory."

"I . . . do you need to go sit under the oak tree?" Kinder hisses. "How did such a ridiculous notion enter your head? No one's seen a Glory in years." She scoops up her tablet in trembling hands, a pleading note in her voice. "There's only us. Why do you think I'm never here? I promised your parents you'd all be safe. I've been trying to bring your sister home with all of the magic this place can muster! I'd bring down this whole school to get Yolanda back. I very nearly did! More than once!"

Peerless rumbles. *"Proceed indoors immediately. A storm is approaching the school grounds. This is not a drill."* Kinder lets out a defeated laugh. "And now we're all going to find out what she's capable of."

CHAPTER TWENTY-TWO

WORST REMIX EVER

Distant thunder trembles the ground. The walls, ceiling, and floor of Kinder's control room all vibrate with cold light, like someone poured a boiling rainbow over Peerless. Amari stares, mouth open, like he's never seen anything so beautiful. I drag him out of the room as it simply disintegrates.

Yolanda swoops down through the blinding halo of fire. Her wings are gone, but a sheen of metal glints on her paw pads, sizzling with every step. Bristling silvery spines cover her back. The beginning nubs of new wings sprout just behind her shoulders.

Another remix, some part of my brain realizes. *To stop Kinder's lightning.*

Radiant waste floods into the new hole she's torn

in Peerless. Warm wet air sweeps past us, syrupy as spoiling sweet potatoes. Kinder's ornate wooden desk suddenly collapses into a pile of brightly colored children's blocks. Glowing blue appendages like starfish legs wriggle out from beneath the floor tiles. All we can do is hunch and cower and crawl as corrupt magic twists reality around us.

Yolanda swipes for Kinder. The headmaster barely throws herself out of the way in time. Six lines of jagged light hang in the air like frozen lightning, throwing shadows over everything. The shadows themselves contort and twist into feline shapes, scurrying off deeper into the school. Wherever they vanish, deep cracks appear in the walls.

"She's too much for us!" I scream into the roar.

Dez is tugging valiantly on Leah's arm, trying to hold her back. "Let me go to her!" she screams. She pushes him aside and runs straight for Yolanda. "Stop this! I know you're in there!"

"Leah, *no!*" Kinder cries.

Yolanda releases a deafening roar. Amari and Dez are halfway ready to bolt, until Kinder plants herself between them and Yolanda. I'm supposed to rhyme, but I am *terrified.* Even the headmaster is afraid—it's plain on her face!

Leah flinches back, hands clasped over her ears, but she holds her ground. My breath catches as she digs in her pocket. Something glints in the air, a tiny chain dangling from her fist. Her gold necklace. "You're being the worst. Stop before you mess things up so bad we can't fix it!"

The monster hesitates, towering over her sister. *"Leah?"* An anguished voice ripples through those jagged monster teeth. *"No . . . I didn't want you to see me like this."*

"I don't care." Leah steps forward, sure and steady. She rests a trembling hand on the crystalline jowl. "Let us help you. Please."

"It's too late . . . She's got what she wants now. I messed everything up, but you gotta come with me. We gotta get out of here."

Kinder inches closer, stretching out a hand. "All I want is for you to come home, Yolanda. Come back to Peerless."

Yo bristles, rounding on the headmaster. Leah snatches her hand back as hundreds of bright spines burst through the crystal skin. *"You. This fake . . . place is even worse than out there. At least out there you can see it for what it is. But yoooouuuu . . ."* Yolanda roars and snaps her jaws at Kinder. Overhead, the ceiling collapses and Leah scrambles back to avoid it. Bits of wood and concrete and globs of water spin around Yolanda, shielding

214

her. Glowing spittle leaks from her jaws, burning through the floor. *"I'll bring down all of your lies."*

"You see it now, don't you?" Headmaster Kinder pleads. "She's too far gone. You kids *go*! Find Touré!"

Yolanda roars. The back wall of the administration room topples, windows shattering. Outside, more corrupt magic is eating away at Peerless. "Where are the soccer fields?" Dez cries. "The basketball court? It's all gone!"

"She's pulling corrupt magic into the school." Amari yanks at me and Dez. "Worst remix ever!"

Dez drags me back toward the main hall, but I shrug him off. "We gotta stop Yo!"

"I'm with you, but we need Touré! This will take all of us!"

Amari nods slowly. "He's right, Keynan!"

"But I—" We all stop as a steady rhyme sings through the chaos.

> *Lil sis, I know you listening but I need you to*
> *feel me.*
> *Somewhere through that glistening it's past time*
> *to heal, we*
> *let you down, lil sis, but this is far from the*
> *bottom.*

My failures walked all over me, shouldn't be you
who fought 'em.
   But you not alone anymore so let go of the pain
and sorrow.
   Call it even for today and train up for tomorrow—

The headmaster's rhyme washes over us like sunlight and stillness after a horrible storm. I've never heard anything like it. Yolanda stops, jaws writhing like she's arguing with herself. Kinder slaps her hands together—the crack reverberates down the hallway. The ground trembles again. "Keynan, get back!" Dez shouts.

"No! We've gotta help!"

"She's fighting it!" Leah shouts. "Yo, you can do this!"

The rumbling ground drowns out everything else. We press ourselves against the walls as faux students pour down every hallway. Third-years down to first-years. Dozens of them. Faces I've never seen before, and more that I recognize.

"We got you." Lacretia smiles at me as she flashes past. "I'll trade you homework notes later!"

Joey knocks Dez to the side as he charges into the battle. "This ain't for you, first-year. Go hide under your covers!"

Faux students leap and pounce on Yolanda, grasping

her neck and claws. They hold on to each other as well, snaring her in interlocked arms and legs. There's no punching or kicking . . . it's a giant group hug! Kinder rhymes the entire time, armor pulsing with power as tears stream down her cheeks.

She's desperate, I realize. *That has to be every student in Peerless!*

Yolanda twists and snaps her jaws—she's covered in so many faux students, they block the glow of her crystal. Even her roar is muffled when Lacretia bear-hugs her jaws shut. Kinder's rhyme rises in intensity, a hum that shivers through the air. The whispers of the faux students take up her flow, speaking to Leah as one. It's more than a rhyme now. The headmaster's squeezing out every last bit of love from Peerless. One beautiful singsong melody, meant for Yolanda.

We love you
We didn't do right by you, let us fix it
Come home
Come home
We're your family
Your sister needs you
Come home

Yolanda recoils. A tormented howl shudders through the air. The faux students roil and twist, a sphere of lovely words peeling Yolanda away from Ratchet's hold.

"She's calming down!" I exclaim. "It's working!"

Dez gazes at Kinder in awe. "She . . . how . . ."

"Magic starts with your art, your rhymes—but it doesn't end there." The headmaster's eyes never leave Ratchet, but I know her words are meant for me. "A single word uttered, or a phrase will do. A gesture. A thought. But you can't let it control you."

"You . . . you didn't hurt her," Leah mumbles.

"Thanks to you. You made me remember that even the Glories started out as people." Kinder relaxes. "If you keep your crew together, I promise you, this will all be child's play."

"Can we get Yolanda out of Ratchet?" I ask. "The armor, I mean."

"That will take more time." Kinder kisses her teeth. "Weeks, I'm afraid."

One of Yolanda's tails whips free. Two faux students go sailing into the radiant waste. She spins, lightning fast. More students lose their grip, slamming into the walls and wreckage. "So stubborn," Kinder growls. She takes a deep breath. The faux students redouble their efforts, dragging Yolanda back down.

"Headmaster!" I scream. "Watch out!"

Yolanda's shoulder contorts. A freed wing bursts out of her back, the membrane diaphanous and bright and twice as large as before. One last remix. The wing stretches high, casting the headmaster into a blue shadow.

Kinder squeezes her eyes shut. "Run, you chuckle-heads."

The wing crashes down, wrenching Kinder off her feet. Ratchet's tails zip out and send faux students sprawling in every direction. She's loose again! Her skin pulses brilliantly, a single orb of fire so bright it leaves spots on my vision. Faux students slough away from her like a snake's old scales.

Some spring right back to their feet, voices rising and falling as they fight for the fallen headmaster. Her rhymes still sing through them.

> *You were made fearfully and wonderfully*
> *For more than this heresy*
> *You are phenomenal, we all can see*
> *Never lose your inner mystery—*

I don't understand all the words. But Yolanda does. Her mournful howl ripples under Ratchet's roar. Shadows flicker on her ribs—palms. Yolanda's hands, slapping at Ratchet from within. Amari and I share a stunned look. "She wants out," he whispers.

Ratchet lurches back into the radiant waste. Glittering skin and wing and broken faux students litter the ground behind her. I stare in shock as Amari and Dez tug me and Leah back. "She . . . she took Kinder."

"Why?" Leah wails. "Why did she do that!"

"Come on!" Dez shouts. "We've got to get back to the oak tree!"

I stare at my arms in shock. Patches of them glitter brighter than Ratchet's teeth.

I stumble into something solid and look up. Professor Wiley. His hall pass—an electric green fly swatter—bristles in his hands. His sleeves are rolled up. He stares down at me, face unreadable. "Peerless no longer has a head-master. Get to the courtyard. That's the safest place! We'll make sure everything is just fine."

The other cohort professors join him, watching us. Fine? All of this? The school lights flicker; their eyes glow in the moment of darkness. They all carry hall passes of their own. The brighter they glow, the dimmer Peer-less grows. They're taking energy from the school for those . . . weapons.

We stagger on down the halls. Leah is sobbing, and

Amari and Dez both look as stunned as I feel. I can't believe Kinder is gone. What more could we have done? Professor Okoro emerges from the trophy room. He urges us down the hall with a huge hammer, crackling and dark as a starlit night. "We'll defend you as long as we can. Hurry!"

CHAPTER TWENTY-THREE

AN ITCH UNDER MY SKIN

Traces of smoke wrinkle my nose. Something's on fire, deeper in the school. A bank of lockers beside us bursts open. Cone-shaped jellyfish float out, choking the air with turquoise ink. We run past, shouting.

We finally get to the courtyard and stop in awe. Corrupt magic fills the air like a jewel-encrusted snowstorm. Flecks of tainted magic drift out of us to join the current swirling around the oak tree. Every plant and bush and flower is radiating light.

"Yolanda will tear down Peerless if we don't do something!" Dez splutters.

A door slaps open on our left. "In here!" Touré beckons us urgently from inside. "Now! Move your feet!"

Inside is bizarrely . . . normal. We're in the Horticulture

classroom. The latest set of sprouts is unbothered at our lab stations. Not an inch of radiant waste creeps around the corners of the room. Because of the plants? Or because of what Professor Touré is? "What happened?" she cries.

"Ratchet—" I start, then change what I was about to say. "Yolanda. Yolanda happened."

"Why lie to us?" Amari demands. "About her?"

He shoots me an urgent look, nodding toward Professor Touré slightly. *Distracting her,* I realize. *So I can surprise her with a rhyme.*

"What better way to turn you against Peerless?" A defeated sigh escapes Touré. "Yes, children, trust us even though we managed to lose Leah's sister to the waste for so long she turned into . . . whatever this is." She winces away from Leah's scowl. "I can't look at myself in the mirror most days, knowing that she's lost out there. Because of me. If your parents could see us now."

"But we could have helped—"

Touré snorts. "Oh, *please*, Keynan. If I had a nickel for every time you've said that. We knew if we told you the truth, you'd go racing off after her—exactly like you did! Then you'd all be lost."

Confusion holds my rhyme in check. She *cares* about us. A Glory? This is all off.

"But she's not lost!" Dez exclaims. "Keynan talked to her. She's not Ratchet . . . not all the way. She's *inside* Ratchet."

Touré uncovers her eyes from her hands. "That's not possible. The radiant waste—"

"She took your armor," I add reluctantly. "She's trapped inside it more than anything else. We could have freed her again with Kinder . . . if . . ."

Touré goes still. "Where are they now?"

"Gone," I whisper. "Yo dragged Kinder into the radiant waste."

Amari stares down at his palms. "The headmaster . . . distracted her long enough to save us."

Touré's hand closes around the door handle in a flash. "I have to go to her—"

"She's gone!"

"You don't know that!"

Touré squeezes her hands into fists, muttering angrily to herself. Leah continues pleading with her in low whispers. Touré's barely holding it together. She's torn between going after Kinder and keeping us safe. A Glory could care less about us. Is everything Yolanda told me a lie? Does it ever stop with this confounding place that my parents built?

"Yolanda fooled me," I blubber, sitting down hard on a desk. "Seeing Glories everywhere." I weakened Peerless to the point where she could just stroll in and topple it down! And now? I don't know what to do next. Who to trust. Everything I've tried just keeps falling apart. My friends are all scared, waiting for me to say something. How am I supposed to fix this? Peerless and my crew are counting on me.

"Professor," I say carefully, "we'll go to the courtyard like we planned. It's the safest place in the school. Take Wiley and Guerrero with you, and the others can stay and help us."

Touré blinks. She's actually listening to me.

"You know we can hold our own until you get back," Leah puts in.

"I wish I could," Touré says softly. "I don't even deserve you first-years. Bless y'all for even giving me the out. Go to the courtyard. I've got to salvage *something* from the control room if we've got a chance of getting either of them back. The magic for Peerless is too complex to manage without it. Be fast and be safe!" Her eyes catch mine. "Take care of them, Keynan. They're counting on you."

The hallway is churning with creepy-crawlies as Touré

225

slips off. I'm doubting now . . . pretty much everything. Leaving Touré by herself isn't a great idea—she's so shook up over Kinder she might do something reckless. But looking back at my crew, they need me just as bad. Leah's arms are squeezed tight around her shoulders like that's all that's keeping her from falling apart. Amari and Dez? They both might bolt if one more piece of weirdness surprises us.

"We're almost there!" I call out. The hallway no longer feels like a building, forget a school. We could be in some monstrous worm's gullet, with no way to tell up from down, doors opening in the ceiling and lockers puddling on the floor. A constant wind smells like overripe bananas and grows stronger the further we trudge, determined to push us back the way we came. But I'm stubborn too, dang it! The others can't know how shook I am. If I fall apart, we all fall apart.

We burst into the courtyard as if we jumped into a cool clear pond. The air is still. The sickly creeping heat of the radiant waste is gone from one step to the next. The walls stop curving like they're about to melt or wiggle away.

Corrupt magic chokes the air, a whirlpool of fractured light swirling around the old oak tree. The drift is so immense it feels like we're being pulled along on a river of magical energy. A glimmer of relief tingles through my arms. The courtyard is the safest place in all of Peerless, and I can *feel* the old oak working relentlessly against the radiant waste. We're gonna be okay.

"Can it hold it all?" Leah whispers.

"Are you kidding me? Our tree stood up to a swipe from Ratchet. We've got this!"

The crystalline crust is hooked on to all of my friends, tracing the edges of Amari's earlobes and eyebrows, stitched into the seams of Dez's clothes, burrowing under Leah's fingernails. We're a mess. We beeline straight for the oak tree.

"Something going our way," Dez murmurs in relief, holding up his arm. Busted magic is leaping out of all of us, faster than I've ever seen it. Whew. One small piece of hope, right on time! The oak tree is made of strong stuff—my parents built Peerless around it, after all.

"The tree is giving us a chance," Amari declares. "All right, Keynan. What's the plan?"

"Okay. Plan. Right. Let's round up the professors who are left. Jocelyn's on our team, right? Why not the rest? We can teach them rhymes. Take things back."

"Room by room," Leah says. "Just like when we came back from break."

"Sounds risky," Dez murmurs. "And exactly what we need right now."

Amari nods.

I face him reluctantly. "You were right about fighting. Even Kinder and Touré have armor. Can you come up with something like they gave the cohort professors?"

He purses his lips, then starts digging in his backpack. "Would be a whole lot easier if we could get to the art supply closet."

I frown, staring at the school beyond the courtyard. The walls creak and groan. Lights wink around the shadows like stars exploring the ground. "Let's make that the first place we take back."

"Got it!"

"Me and Dez can collaborate," Leah says, "while you get rhymes ready."

"Thanks, Starbreaker! Let's do this."

She smiles. "You took the words right out of my mouth. We're gonna have this school fixed up better than ever by the time Touré brings Kinder back."

Amari nods fiercely. "And your sister, too."

Encouraged, we all throw ourselves into our plan. My friends . . . sheesh. The absolute greatest. They trust me and deserve my best. I lose myself in the rhyme, half whispering and half scribbling notes on the tattered paper scrap Amari produced from his pocket. The magic should give the professors enough wiggle to act on their own when the radiant waste throws new weirdness at them, combined with specific rhymes they can spit without any extra directions.

It can work. It should work. *Please work.*

The whirlpool of light is still swirling above us—more corrupt magic than ever. A little more scribbling, and I'm ready. I need someone to test it on. Jocelyn is as good as anyone, I decide. Once that's set, we can take back the hallway leading to the first-year professors' classes. If each professor can at least keep their own class safe, the four of us can clear out the rest of Peerless. A tap on my shoulder pulls me out of the writing. Leah eyes me with concern. "Is it ready?"

"Not yet, but I'm close. I gotta get this right. Perfect."

Leah sighs.

"Why, what's up?"

"You've got to keep your head," she says. "There's so much corrupt magic around us, your rhyme isn't staying . . . you know. Home." She taps her temple, then gestures back to the oak tree. "See? They can . . . hear it."

Professor LaRue, the school's Horticulture teacher, wanders through the courtyard as if the radiant waste doesn't exist, staring at the bare strawberry bushes in a daze.

"That's fine," I croak worriedly. No. None of this is fine.

"Umm, Horticulture can be one of the first rooms we take back."

Leah brightens. "Hey, look who it is! This should make things easier."

Professor Mendoza picks her way toward us from the other side of the oak tree. She takes in the glowing foliage and trees with wide, uncertain eyes. "You've all worked so hard, with nothing to show for it." She circles the tree slowly.

"Hold on, Professor—we'll get you back in order again." Leah's right, my rhymes are skipping ahead without me. I haven't even started and I'm messing up already! Still, it feels like good luck to see Mendoza. Leah looks at me expectantly. "Might as well get started."

"Hi, Professor," I manage. *"Sit down for me, time to rewrite your story."*

Mendoza sits expectantly, tracing a hand along the tree's bark. "You poor dears."

Something in my chest gives way. Another faux professor trying to keep us safe, when they don't even know what's going on! I can't even stand the fake concern on Mendoza's face. I've got to change her—all of them—into something they're not, and hope I don't break them in the process. I bury my face in my hands. "I . . . I don't know if I can do this."

"Keynan, not now," Amari murmurs, clasping my shoulders. "Breathe. Don't fall apart on us. You're my brother, you'll get us through this. Tell us what to do."

"Just give him a minute," Leah murmurs. "Can't you see he needs a minute?"

"We can put the walls up again," Dez says, somewhere over my shoulder. "Maybe we try to do that first instead?"

Amari makes a doubtful sound. "Just me and you? Nah. The waste is already inside Peerless. The whole school will be like the hidden wing."

I just want to curl up in a ball while they argue quietly about what to do.

"We've got to try!" Leah insists, near tears. She sits beside Mendoza on the bench. "The professors can't bring my sister back to . . . to nothing!"

"And then what? Kinder's control station is busted— Peerless is done without it. Touré should have been back by now. It's probably too broken to save."

"Kinder and Touré," Professor Mendoza says absently, still staring up at the tree. "They never did quite right by this place."

Baby hairs on my forearms prickle. I straighten and frown. "What do you mean?"

"You should know better than most, Keynan."

Mendoza watches me, patting Leah's shoulder. The radiance in the air glints in her eyes. "The potential of you children, pushed into this basic understanding of magic. You should be *soaring*."

"What . . . what are you saying?"

"Exactly what I'm always saying," she says. "The words you need to hear."

Leah's snuffles cease. She recoils from Mendoza's touch. Amari squints at the faux professor, whispering silently to himself. But his lips are easy to read.

Oh no, oh no, oh no—

Horrid realization sloshes through my stomach. Screaming for me to do something. Anything. Laugh. Cry. Act. Speak. I have to respond. Even though I'm terrified of what will come next.

Words spill out of me on instinct.

> *There's an itch under my skin and I can't quite*
> *call it*
> *Mystery in the air and I'm about to solve it*
> *Knowledge—*

Professor Mendoza's lip curls in a snarl. She vaults to her feet. Dez lifts my rhyme up with a beat—the air around us flashes malevolently.

—evades us no longer, time's up—
Turn around, here comes the karma
Repeal what's fake, heat it up like a sauna
Skip the drama all day and show us the real!

Professor Mendoza's face twitches as our magic settles into her . . . irritation, then amused surprise . . . she laughs and—

Her face *splits* down the middle.

A seam of light stretches wide from her forehead down the front of her dress. Utter brilliance steps out, so luminous that I stagger back, throwing up my hands before I'm blinded. The others gasp and cover their eyes.

"What did you do to her?" Amari cries.

Movement within the light melts into something I can almost understand. Starbursts and reflected sapphires and electric shadows merge into arms and legs. It almost reminds me of Ratchet's crystal skin, but that's like comparing a melted, lopsided candle to the sun. She stretches, standing way taller than before. A deep, luxuriant sigh cuts the air, like crystals singing. The magnificence carefully steps out of Professor Mendoza as if removing an old comfy outfit. She even folds the faux professor's drooping skin and clothes like a discarded robe and sets it on the bench. The disguise's blank eyes stare at nothing.

Then . . . she looks at us.

Inside us.

Through us.

I can't decide what to do first. Howl in joy, cry for no reason, cartwheel in terror? I ignore the voice in the back of my head screaming how wrong this is. Wrong? *We* were wrong! To ever think that Yolanda or Kinder or Touré could compare to who stands before us now.

Because this . . . is a Glory.

CHAPTER TWENTY-FOUR

UNSPEAKABLE WEAPONS

Professor Touré dashes into the courtyard. "Children! Get away from her!"

Mendoza smiles, a crescent of cerulean brilliance. Her glittering arm rises. Her fingers pirouette—a quick, elegant gesture. The old oak shivers, then . . . explodes. We dive for cover as flaming leaves and dust and splinters rip across the courtyard.

The force of her magic slams into the study rooms and nearest walls, blasting them into rubble. The gardens, sapling fruit trees, and vines are reduced to shreds. The trees that aren't flattened lean dangerously. Yolanda's attacks nibbled holes in Peerless. Mendoza's have just cracked it open like an egg.

"Such a waste," the voice inside that brilliance sings. "I'm going to miss those fabulous berries."

Leah and I pull each other to our feet, knees wobbling. The air is hot and shimmering like we've been stuffed inside a boiling pot. Mendoza stands in the middle of the ruin, completely untouched, ignoring us. Quivering in the air beside her is our uprooted oak tree. Branches, trunk, and roots, thousands of splinters separated by countless radiant orange cracks.

"What's she doing?" Leah wails.

"I don't know!"

"We need to stop her!"

Sure, but . . . how? Even looking at Mendoza makes my brain stop working. Every rhyme I've ever imagined, even my best freestyle, simply can't compare to what I'm witnessing. But Leah's right . . . we've got to try. *"Show yourself out before I—"*

Mendoza blinks, like twin meteors fading, then flaring again. The rhyme turns to mush in my mouth—like the sound is stretched and pulled out, syllable by syllable! I try to finish, but all that escapes my lips is a dry hiss. She's stolen my voice! No rhyme. No words. Just a thought sent my way.

Touré staggers to her feet, but Mendoza slaps her aside with a flick of a finger, sending her sprawling. Leah cowers over me protectively, but disbelief clots her voice. "She . . . she didn't even need to speak."

"For so very long I've wanted to do that." Mendoza cackles. "If only you'd been Kinder instead." The glistening crystal where her face used to be shifts into an angry shade of bruised violet. She cocks her head as if listening to something farther away and gives a delighted laugh. "She's getting her own retribution, though. Far better than anything I could conjure."

Mendoza makes a fist. The shattered tree folds in upon itself, steam and heat radiating so strongly that we cower back. The cracks turn yellow, then white. Mendoza's fist quivers with effort. A stream of singsong words hisses through her teeth. Branches and roots crumple into the trunk. Bark sinks down into heartwood. I can't tear my eyes away.

The air around us crackles and snaps. A piece of sleek midnight wood drops into Mendoza's waiting hand. It's thicker than my finger, not so long as my forearm. A rapturous expression fills her face. She flicks her wrist experimentally a few times. "Not in a thousand years did I believe we would reclaim such . . . elegant weapons," she breathes. "I'm going to need whole new outfits."

Amari and Dez peek out from behind a collapsed wall. Mendoza beckons to us. "And I have you to thank, children. Well, Hector and Alicia, really, misguided though they were. Whoever thought the dross of humanity would usher in a more civilized age?"

I stagger forward. "You keep my parents' names out your mouth!"

Her brow wrinkles, a cloud passing before a perfect sky. "But they'll be remembered for all time, Keynan. Don't you see? This . . ." She rolls the stick in her palm again, almost lovingly. "Is a wand."

The word ripples through us like a half-remembered nightmare, echoing through the ruined courtyard. *Wand.* Professor Touré warned us about unspeakable weapons from the Wars of Illusion. And now a Glory just destroyed the heart of Peerless to create one.

Mendoza smiles again. "You understand, then. Good. You'll be praised, too—for pouring enough distilled magic into this place for my new tool. For your sister"— she nods to Leah, who bristles—"for leading me to this hovel to begin with. I'll think of you all as I forge our next world."

She rises into the air. Professor Touré staggers upright. Red stains her forehead. "I won't allow you to—"

"ALLOW?" Mendoza turns on her with a snarl. Her wrist flicks. A shroud of ice materializes out of thin air, binding

Professor Touré from head to toe. "I'll find a use for your . . . talents. But first, some manners." She glides into the sky. Touré dangles behind the Glory as if her ankles were caught up in invisible spiderwebs.

In moments they're both gone.

"She . . . did all of that, without one rhyme." Disbelief and betrayal shudder through my entire being. How did I miss this? More than any other professor, I had believed she was my friend—fake or not. But it's all so obvious now. A faux professor who cared less about her job, but knew plenty about busted magic? Then used her actual magic on *me*? "How could I ever match that?"

"It doesn't matter now!" Leah screams. "Peerless is falling apart! We've got to get out of here!"

"No," I mumble. "We can save it . . ."

"Open your eyes," Dez pleads. "There's nothing left to save!"

Amari holds on to him like Dez is the only reason he's standing. Corrupt magic drifts in the air around us like ash, directionless with no tree to draw it in. Some of it sinks casually into our skin. Leah's right. Without the oak tree, Peerless is finished. They're all waiting on me. All scared. But Leah's right, we need to go. And I'm the one with the rhymes. The only grown-ups who had our backs are gone. So it's up to me now. One foot in front of the other. We've always said we've got nothing but our art and each other, and now it is truer than ever before. I take a deep breath and lead us out of the ruined school, and into the radiant waste.

CHAPTER TWENTY-FIVE

HELTER-SKELTER

We clamber to the top of a leaning wall, snapped right in half, and slide down the other side. Rubble is everywhere. Smoky-gray leopard shadows dance and giggle and churn around us, whispering secrets of long-ago times in our ears.

"No!" Leah claps her hands over her ears. "Get out of my head!"

I jerk away whenever they creep close, and they laugh and somersault into the orange-purple sky. The air tastes like a storm, so strong and sweet I don't think I'll ever get the stench out of my nose.

Leah and I hold each other up, while Amari and Dez clasp hands as we trudge away from the ruined shell of our school. I check behind us to make sure they're okay.

What's left of Peerless is slowly being . . . consumed. Corrupt magic creeps over the grass and standing walls like squirming, multicolored moss. Dust and glittering motes of light swirl around us. This is worse than being caught in a storm. It's a normal day in the radiant waste. How the world really is without the illusion and safety and lies of Peerless to hold it back. This is where we live. Knots curl through my stomach. I want to curl up into a ball and squeeze my arms over my head. I'm not made of strong stuff. Maybe I never was.

A lone figure calls out in the distance to our left, waving urgently at us from atop a shattered toolshed. Leah squints in disbelief. "Isn't that a cohort professor?"

"You kids get back here!" Professor Osana's desperate shout barely clears the gusting wind. Her clothes are tattered, and grime covers her face. "Let us keep you safe!"

"Don't stop," Amari cries. "She doesn't know any better!"

"There's nothing left but waste! Where are we even going?" Dez argues.

"Please, we can still protect you!" Professor Osana's plea reaches us again. "Come back inside the grounds so—"

A long sinuous tail loops around Osana's ribs. She yelps as Yolanda stalks over to the toolshed and swallows her whole. Terrible violet burn marks scar the crystal along Yo's back and one of her new metallic wings. She's even bigger than before.

Leah goes rigid beside me. "Oh no. No, no, *no* . . ."

A low moan escapes Dez. "She's *eating* Peerless's magic."

I tug at Leah, and she reluctantly stops dragging her feet. Behind us, Yolanda picks through the rubble and springs on a faux student, gobbling them up with a rumble like cheerful thunder. She hasn't seen us yet. "Come on! I've got an idea of where we can go. The grove. Where Yolanda took us."

"But there's trees just in front of us," Dez points out. "Big, too. We can hide there!"

A series of sighs pulls me up short, examining the trees ahead. So close to the school? Can't be.

"With pizza for fruit?" Leah scoffs. "Don't believe your eyes. Don't touch anything!"

She's right, we're in trouble. Our first time outside of the Peerless bubble, Touré showed us this place. The foliage here used fruit and food like bait—tempting us closer to this breathing orchard. Now scorched birds sleep in the boughs overhead. If we creep past, will they attack us instead? Or will they catch fire and take flight—if we whistle their secret song just right?

"I don't see any birds." Amari frowns. "How do you know that?"

"Oh no," I whisper. Freestyle is twisting me into knots. I can feel it remaking my thoughts! I've tried to hide it for so long, believed I needed an extra boost, but corrupt magic has found a new place to roost. Now ain't the time to deceive. I didn't speak, but my friends still got a whole peek at my flow. "I'll be real with you. Magic told me so."

Amari nudges Dez, who quietly tries to beatbox. But we fit together like sweaty feet and wet socks. Smelly, instead of jelly and peanut butter. Besides, if I rhymed out of time right now? I would stutter. Fear is cluttering my brain, giving me the mush mouth. I figure one direction is just as good as any other. "Let's go south once we pass these trees."

My friends. They're still trusting me when I got no keys. Why? I've failed over and over again. I thought our crew's creations were unstoppably strong, but all I've been from day one is wrong, wrong, *wrong*. Keymaster? Please!

"Keynan, hold on!"

"Keep up, stay strong!" I shout back. "There's shelter ahead, with leaves like flame!"

"His brain's gone helter-skelter!" Dez screams. "And it's leaking into mine. Keynan—Amari's fallen behind! Stop!"

I spin around in alarm. Nothing but radiant waste, swirling green wind and purple rain. My brother's keeper? I didn't even keep him safe from harm! Then Amari stumbles forward, some wriggling creeper tugging on his arm. We're way past the orchard, plugging toward fresh places. Crystal encases our skin in patches, the same turquoise-violet as Ratchet's.

Dez races back to pull Amari close.

"Keynan, you are my *best* friend—but you are doing the most!" Leah snaps. "That tree was to the north. Don't you remember our map?"

She's right. "This place!" I rasp. "It's tricking me, taking us into badlands!"

Starbreaker clasps my face in both hands. For an instant there's no radiant waste, no corrupt magic except the flecks of gold glazed into the brown of her gaze. "Don't give up, I know you're enough," she cries. "Your name is Keymaster, and you're made of strong stuff!"

Dez's beatboxing pierces the rising wind.

*Poom click, poom
poom click . . .*

Tears stream down my face and over Leah's knuckles. I can do this.

Here with my crew and it's another day
Got my bestie Starbreaker helping light the way
Amari on my right—

I lose my flow. But the corrupt magic isn't running away with my brain again. I'm back in control—for now. A wink of light pierces the surging wind ahead of us. Too colorful, not the right shade for any Break I've ever seen.

Leah goes rigid. "Did y'all see that? Be ready to run!"

"More monsters," Dez wails. Another flash blinks, closer and brighter.

"I've been called a lot of things," declares a familiar voice, "but monster is a new low!"

I gape as Disco and Slickback emerge from the chaos! The talking gecko is bigger than I remember—mouth included. Slickback's brilliant yellow and blue skin is shiny as ever, and he looks us up and down with smug, black-slitted eyes. Disco flashes into being beside him, a dazzling flicker of yellow—the same flashing guide that beckoned us through the radiant waste.

"This weather!" Slickback declares. "I might catch a cold. Keymaster, your head's about as solid as an old sponge! Look at y'all!"

He's right. My skin's afire with so much purple and gold and glitter that I can't see the brown underneath.

Amari's shaken and barely standing, even though his skin isn't as encrusted as the rest of us.

"Please help us," I get out.

Disco flashes a sharp pattern of reds and golden greens.

"I know, right?" Slickback agrees. "We're supposed to be homies again, just like that? I do hate seeing scrubs punished just for being scrubs, though. Y'all owe us big for this one, but we'll square later. Follow that bird!"

Disco disappears. Slickback points a stubby gecko finger at another flash, barely visible on a distant rise of squishy ground. It sways beneath our feet as we climb, surging like an ocean wave. Another few steps and we'll be hiking upside down. "Don't fall for the illusion!" Slickback sings out, scampering around and through our legs. "I thought young folks had pep in their step!"

Another flash, more urgent this time. Disco still doesn't feel any closer.

"Almost there!"

My next step never touches the ground. I slip sideways into a waterfall of light. The rush threatens to drown me, blind me—

I stagger into calm and quiet. Familiar homes line a quiet street, ending in a cul-de-sac. Birdsong floats to my ears on a perfect fall afternoon with no clouds and a brilliant blue sky. Disco flits in the air above us, while Slickback leads us up a worn, cracked sidewalk.

"Where are we?" Leah asks in wonder. "Is this another school?"

"This is my neighborhood," I answer, stunned and relieved and suspicious. "Bizzy Block." But this can't be possible. It must be another illusion—I saw the radiant waste invade my home before I ran!

CHAPTER TWENTY-SIX

PARTS THEY LEFT BEHIND

Bizzy Block checks out with all of my best memories. My head spins as we limp our way down the cul-de-sac. My legs are trembling. It's well before dawn, there's no people out. Everything else? So normal it's creepy. The canvas tent in the middle of the street, Tua's shop. Old Zeph's rocking chair, next to his card table. The basketball hoop set up in the turnabout of the cul-de-sac, weeds poking through the asphalt here and there. The gap between our house and the Chandlers', where the old Jefferson house got pulled up by a storm. Eaten by radiant waste really; I know that now. The corn is harvested, clover covers the field. I'm still not used to the Delmar house being gone. A new winter crop covers that space, too. I don't trust any of it.

My chest tightens as my house comes into full view. I stop. I'm just not ready yet.

"But . . . I let the radiant waste in myself," I say out loud. "It was everywhere, just like at Peerless. How is any of this still here?"

"You young bloods sure got funny ideas about what's possible when magic is an actual thing," Slickback observes with a snort. "I mean, hello. Look at us!"

Disco flickers with indignant agreement.

I shake myself from my daze, a little embarrassed. These two just saved us, and I'm acting grateful as a rock. "We've done nothing but treat you both terribly since day one," I say to Slickback and Disco. "Thank you a million times for rescuing us. We can't ever really repay you, but I want to try."

"Me too," Leah chimes in.

"Same," Dez says. "It'd be kinda nice to have more friends to trust."

I nudge Amari. He rolls his eyes but bobs his head in agreement. "What he said."

What is his deal? "I'm sorry we trapped you, too," I add. "We didn't even give you a chance to make it work."

"Well now . . . is that what a little respect feels like? I must say, it's kinda nice. I shall ponder your proposal. I suppose fences can be mended, what with you being our creator and all." Slickback's stomach rumbles. "We'll make ourselves at home, for starters," he says. "Famished ain't the word."

I wince. "Can you please just not eat any of the metal that's . . . essential?"

"Honeymoon's over before it started," Slickback harrumphs. His beady eyes rest on all of my friends before settling back on me. "You and I need to have a deep chat about your circumstances, Keymaster. A private one."

Disco flashes indignantly.

"Goodness gracious, fine!" Slickback erupts at the bird. "Nothing essential. Whose team is you on anyway, bird? Catch y'all later. I'm sure you've got some soul-searching to do."

The whole thing makes my chest tight. Kinder and Touré kept us in a fake school—fake homes and a fake life. It's way different than what we did to Slickback and Disco, but the wrongness is the same. But these two found it in themselves to forgive us. Just like that.

"Just like that," Leah murmurs.

I blink at her. That was creepy. "I was thinking the same thing."

Dez clears his throat. "You gonna give us the rest of the tour?" I cross the street toward my home—my faux home. A plum rises in my throat. The magic-melted wall has been replaced, complete with a new window and siding. Buckets of paint sit beside it. Someone's been repairing it. All fake, yes. But why does that make me feel relieved and anxious all at once?

"Don't you think," Amari asks gently, "that y'all need to find the nearest tree?"

I could kick myself. We're all glittering like geodes turned inside out. I open the gate and circle the corner of my house, weaving through my mama's garden toward our orange tree in the back.

Behind us, the screen door bangs open. The moment I'm dreading unfolds like clockwork.

My faux mama strides for me, beaming, eyes only on me. Her braids are tied back, and her smile lights up her face. She's wearing long gloves. I forget to breathe, staring at them. They hide where her hands were eaten away by my rhyme, back when I started this whole mess.

"Keynan! I missed you so much!" Her hug feels like broken glass. But I can't help but squeeze back, even though it isn't real. My head and my heart can't agree on any of it.

"Hi . . . Mama."

"Tell me everything about Peerless!" Her eyes widen at my crystalline skin, then slide away from it. "Favorite classes, all of it. Is your roommate cool? And clean?"

"Yeah." These are her same words from the last time. The exact script. It's too much.

My faux mama rests her knuckles on her hips—I still can't help but check her gloves for signs of fingers. Maybe her hands are whole. "Did you meet anyone—"

"These are my friends from school," I cut in hastily. She jerks in surprise, as if they haven't been standing there the whole time. I make hasty introductions.

"Hello," she says uncertainly. "We weren't expecting . . . friends. Are . . . you all feeling all right?"

A sudden growl makes the hair on the back of my neck stand straight up. Buster edges around the corner of the house—hackles raised. The squash vines are gone— but he's still huge for a puppy. His back is almost to my mama's waist, and his eyes are glowing faintly blue.

"Buster!" I scold anxiously.

"Their magic only stretches so far," Amari murmurs under his breath. "They can only absorb so much unexpected stuff. They might attack us, bro."

My neighborhood wasn't designed to have friends over. It was only designed to take care of me. My faux mama is staring at my friends like she's having a hard time understanding what they are supposed to be doing.

"Umm, what's with the dog?" Leah asks.

"He's trying to guard Bizzy Block," I say aloud,

remembering how he attacked the radiant waste and swallowed it. "We'll be fine, Mama," I say quickly. "We just need to rest. I'm going to show them the garden, okay?"

"Oh. Okay." A lost, hurt expression blooms on my faux mama's face. "I'm just . . . so glad my baby boy is back home." She watches anxiously as everyone follows me to the orange tree.

"Oh! This is nice." Amari brightens as we draw closer. Buster stays with us, still growling deep in his throat as we pass the tomatoes. He cuts off abruptly as busted magic starts flooding out of my skin, sailing ahead of us toward the orange tree. His head tilts curiously, then he abruptly barks and leaps forward.

He's big enough to knock me flat on my back. "Gross! Not the face!"

My friends all bust out laughing. Buster won't be denied. He's *licking* away corrupt magic even as the tree helps purge us. Satisfied with himself, he snorts and darts off.

"Smart," Dez marvels. "Keeps the neighborhood safe."

"Let's hope he finds Slickback," Amari says with a speculative grin. He holds his hands up when we all frown at him. "Kidding, kidding!"

"No wonder everything's still here. Bizzy Block fought for itself." I let out a huge sigh. "So weird. This is all a lot more than I expected. Parents? Am I going to do chores now or something? My faux dad will put us all to work, believe me."

"You did better than I could," Leah says. "I'm glad Slick-back found your neighborhood first."

"Seriously," Dez adds. "Like . . . do we even listen to them anymore? They're just . . . copies. Constructs. You could unmake them with the right rhyme."

"I don't think I could if I wanted to," I reply quietly. "Part of our real parents is still in them. That might be all we ever really know about them. The best parts they left behind."

Busted magic streams out of us as we settle in the grass beneath the orange tree. Soon the air around us is on fire with corrupt magic.

A new ache stirs in my chest. I've gotta be honest with myself. After everything we've just survived . . . there's no way my parents are still out there. I scrape my knuckles over my damp eyes, but more tears replace them. I give up and let them fall.

Leah stares at her palms as corruption cracks and peels free. She's turned her back to us. She's probably thinking about Yolanda, but I can't bring myself to ask. Because it all leads to one obvious question: What can we do about it? Nothing!

CHAPTER TWENTY-SEVEN

PUT SOME SAUCE ON IT

My crew is in shambles. Alive, safe for the moment, but lost.

Dez is drowning in his own thoughts, fixated on scratching bits of grit from his shoes. Amari shrugs at me and snuggles on a patch of grass in the orange tree's shade. A nap? Now? I can barely sit still, after everything that's happened. It's like he found a power switch deep inside himself and turned it off. Leah's gazing up into the orange tree's branches as she twists idly at her locs. We're all worse than scattered. Afraid for a hundred different reasons. But at least we've got a second to breathe.

Ancient sorcerers and their awful weapons. Waste-lands that can turn your brain into a bowl of broken marbles. Corrupt magic that will flip your body inside out or transform you into a monster. What was I thinking to believe a crew and my rhymes could do anything about any of that?

My freestyling was the worst part. And the best part. My rhymes were everything. Perfect scores on a quiz without going to class. A first gulp of air after holding my breath for a hundred years. I was losing touch with my core the whole time, but also so close to truly grasping it. Leashing the magic. I can't help but wonder if that's what being a Glory feels like. Will poetry ever come so easily for me again? That's the scariest part of all. Because I want to try again.

We all stew in our own thoughts as the orange tree purges us. Dez finally pipes up. "So I never did get to try any of these snacks you were always bragging about."

"We've got you covered," a deep voice says behind us. My faux parents hold two platters and a pitcher of freshly squeezed juice. My faux baba appears unhurt— just as I remember him, smile lines crowding around his searching brown eyes, broad shoulders, plain work clothes already damp with sweat. He wears work gloves, too. My eyes slide away from them. "Your mama wasn't lying, you did get bigger." He frowns uncertainly, as if he meant to say something else.

The garden quiets as our parents fall silent, examining my friends intently. My faux mama's lips are pursed like she's about to whistle for Buster. What will they do if they decide my friends are trouble?

"Thanks for taking care of us," Leah says quickly. "The shuttle broke down and we all got caught in a storm."

Their faces relax. "A storm." My faux mama kisses her teeth. "You poor sweeties. A bolt of lightning hit Keynan's room, did you tell them, Keynan?"

I blink. "Yeah."

"Started that terrible fire. I'd never been so terrified," she continues. "Good thing Old Zeph had the wits to scoot you off to Peerless. Don't know how we managed all of that mess going on."

My faux baba squeezes her hand. "With each other."

Storms. Fires. They have to tell themselves lies to explain away my magic.

He smiles at me and raises a fist. I smile back. This part feels enough like home, almost enough to forget the illusion, until my knuckles bump the leather of his glove.

"I don't know if y'all heard yet," I say carefully. "Head-master Kinder might be closing Peerless."

"Closing Peerless?" My faux parents exchange a troubled glance.

"Power outages," Leah offers. "My neighborhood is dealing with the same thing."

"Been awhile since Bizzy Block had people from . . . outside," my faux mama says. "There's plenty of room here if it comes down to that. After we get the official letter from Peerless, of course."

"Right," I say hollowly. How could I forget? Letters from Peerless help bump the magic around in the neighborhoods. Headmaster Kinder's note in the envelope with the shiny golden seal changed their whole opinion on if I should attend. We can fake one, but who knows if they'd accept it or not?

Dez glances at me and jumps in. "I got mine. I'm sure it'll be here any day now."

"We'll keep an eye out for the drone." Uncertainty still tightens their eyes. They offer up stiff excuses about errands to run, chores to do, with promises to talk more later after neighbors bring over some welcome-back dishes.

"It's like they know somehow," Leah murmurs as we take the food back to the orange tree. Our skin resumes shimmering.

"That they're fake people?" Amari laughs softly, whisking a hand through the glittering air. He fondly pats our orange tree's trunk.

I shrug. "If they knew they weren't real . . . I feel like it would break them somehow."

Dez looks glumly at his sandwich. "I'm starting to wonder if I'm real."

We eat silently—except for Amari, who marvels over how fresh and delicious the fruit tastes. "It's the same food we had at Peerless," I grumble. "I doubt any of our faux neighbors are actually eating, so it has to go some-where."

"Drone deliveries," Dez adds thoughtfully.

"Oh." Amari's face falls a bit. "You're right. I should've thought of that." He's been more than a little shook since deserting Peerless. I'm just glad he didn't get lost in the radiant waste for good.

Corrupt magic still streams out of us when we're fin-ished eating, so steadily I worry if it will ever stop. The orange tree seems extra thirsty, somehow, and I breathe easier when the flow finally trickles to nothing.

I show my friends around my house to stretch our legs. Leah laughs softly when I pull up Mirror Maze Castle on the office laptop. Amari peers at it in fascination even though it's the same version we play on our tablets back at Peerless.

"What I wouldn't give to go back to complaining about *Build-A-Scholar*," Leah murmurs.

"Right? But we can't just stay here." The others edge into my bedroom to listen. "Professor Touré needs us. Yolanda, too."

Leah bites her lip. "I don't know if we can do any more for her."

I start to argue, but she shakes her head stubbornly.

"You tried once and she ran away. Kinder tried and she ripped a hole in Peerless. We used to get in trouble for dancing together, singing, as kids. And she . . . she didn't recognize me." Leah looks away. "Not when it mattered."

"Leah . . ." I can't believe my ears. She's fought so hard for Yolanda. Harder than any of us. I can't help but feel like we've all let them down. *I've* let them down. Dez and Amari shift uncomfortably as Leah glares at me, eyes begging me to drop it. So I keep my mouth shut, for now.

"What about our headmaster?" Dez breaks the silence. "If she's lost out there . . . her armor's strong, right? Shouldn't we help bring her back home?"

"She might end up like Yolanda," Amari whispers. "The professor version of Ratchet."

Which would be a thousand times more dangerous. I wince. "I didn't even think about that."

"Where would we even start?" Leah runs a hand along

261

the almost-rebuilt wall in my room. "It's so hard to know what's real anymore," she whispers. "Every time we go in the waste, something awful happens."

"We're real," I come back. "Our art, our music is real."

"Is it enough?" Dez demands. "You saw Mendoza. What a whole Glory can do. How do we get Touré back from just one? And if there's more . . ."

I've got no answers. Mendoza . . . she meant so much to me. Helped me with magic under Kinder's nose—but she was tricking us the whole time, and me most of all. How can I trust anything she ever said about rhymes, or magic? How can I trust myself?

Amari watches me expectantly. Leah's words from the radiant waste come back to me. "It's just like you told me . . . we're enough," I mumble. "Don't ever forget that." Leah squeezes my hand.

A tap at my bedroom door turns us all around. "Sorry, I couldn't help overhearing y'all mention music." My faux mama's eyes linger on Leah for an instant before she continues. "Keynan, do you remember that old nursery rhyme I used to sing you to sleep with at night?"

My whole face flushes. "Mama . . ."

"Can you sing it for me?"

"Right *now*?"

She just flashes me the Mama Look. Faux mama or

not, it still works on me. "Okay . . ." I start to recite it, but she interrupts. "Not like that. Put some sauce on it, like you might at Peerless. Maybe one of your friends can help."

Leah elbows me before I protest. "Keynan, let's do it. I'll help."

Doesn't she know where we're standing? The same place I first split Bizzy Block apart! My bedroom wall isn't even fixed. "I . . . the last time I used magic here . . ." I shoot her a desperate look. "I can't see them go through that again. I don't care if they're not real. I can't."

"I know. Trust me on this one," Leah urges. My faux baba enters the room and stands beside my faux mama, watching me intently. Leah takes a deep breath, then knocks out a beat on the new wall. Dez and Amari both tense warily, legs set to run. They don't trust my freestyle, not after the radiant waste. I don't blame them. My heart tightens with every bump of Leah's knuckles. My rhymes don't stop when I want them to anymore—and I don't want them to, once they start.

"Please don't make me do this."

My faux mama and Leah both turn to me. "Trust me like I trust you," Leah says.

Hard to argue with that. I rummage through my memories for the old lullaby. Okay. Deep breath.

Baba's dancing to the castle, so hush and close your eyes.

Mama's singing down the bastions, so don't you start to cry.

And if the Brights are calling, hush and close your eyes.

Mama and Baba love you, look to the sunrise.

I wince, afraid to breathe. But there's no Break, no shining orb to nibble my faux parents away again. They stiffen suddenly, trembling in place like stalks of corn the morning of harvest.

"What's happening?" Dez moans.

"I don't know!" If they end up being Glories, I'm going to pass right out! Their eyes flash blue. The shaking stops. Something about that tickles my memory. This is just like my first letter from Peerless . . . when that golden seal flashed and flipped their whole outlook.

"Keynan, we're so sorry." They speak at the same time, voices melding together, like they're both reading from the same source. "We're sorry for this awful lie."

So. Creepy. We all shy back. They grasp each other's hands, gloved fingers laced together.

"If you've gotten this far, you know"—they gesture

at each other—"we're not ourselves. You know about magic—but something has happened. Something we didn't plan for, and our friends at Peerless couldn't stop it. Now you're here. We'll answer your questions, if our conjuring allows it."

They abruptly stride out of my room. We all stare at each other.

"Is this really happening?" Dez whines. "I'm so confused."

"I don't like it," Amari mutters. "What if someone is controlling what they say?"

"That will actually be a normal thing," Leah says with a snort.

I nod ruefully. "True. We can at least ask questions and make our own choices, depending on what they say. Come on."

We file out to the dining room, where they're already seated and waiting expectantly. I swallow and sit between them. "Okay. Questions. How many other schools are in the radiant waste?"

"We're not sure," my faux mama answers. "Ten other academies joined our strike against the Glories. There may be more out there, hiding, keeping the waste at bay in their own ways."

"That way will never work," my faux baba adds. "Hiding. We can't take back the radiant waste without stopping the ones who caused it."

Leah and I share an excited glance. "Ten more schools," she breathes.

"Amari, show them your map!" I exclaim.

"I . . . I lost it," he admits sheepishly.

"But you can draw another one," I say impatiently. "I've got paper in my room."

His jaw works as Leah spins back to get it, but Dez's question to my faux parents stops her halfway. "How were you going to beat the Glories?" he asks.

They glance at each other and speak in one voice again. "We . . . worked for some time on a way to trap them. But if that failed and we had to square up, we needed weapons. Scepters, staves . . . and wands." They both shudder. "Wielding a wand is one of the nastiest things in all existence. For the person using it, and the world."

"Not as scary as having one used against you," Dez mutters.

"You made some?" Leah presses.

"Yes."

"Can *we* make them?"

The answer comes reluctantly. "Yes."

Leah nods thoughtfully. Dez stares out the window.

"Keynan. You have a tree right there. We all have trees in our neighborhoods."

"I don't know," I say slowly. "What she did to that oak tree . . ." I grasp for a word that fits. When something goes against everything you know is true, everything you've been taught? It was a . . . violation. "It felt worse than wrong."

Leah frowns at me. "When is the last time any of this felt right?"

"But our art is what heals the corrupted magic," I press. "Everything we've been told about the Wars of Illusion says that wands are part of the problem. Trees can still reverse the damage. If we start tearing them down to make wands, for a fight we don't even know we can win . . ."

"You really believe we can do both?" Dez asks doubtfully. "Keep using art *and* defeat the Glories?"

"We've got to protect ourselves," Leah insists. "This way might give us a chance."

"She's not wrong." My faux mama looks at me with a sad expression. "But just know these neighborhoods will break apart without their anchor trees. Everything left behind will be corrupted by the waste. Your crops, your homes . . . and us."

CHAPTER TWENTY-EIGHT

ANCHORED TO THIS LAND

My friends are actually excited over this terrible idea. My faux parents either can't or won't offer an opinion either way. They take turns listening to us and frowning at Slickback, who lounges on the kitchen counter like he owns the house, staring longingly at the faucet or the knives in the rack. He grumbles about Yua watching his every move—she probably caught him trying to snack on her tools. Disco is out in the street playing with Buster in some weird game of disappearing tag. Somehow they've become instant friends, which Slickback does not like. I almost wish he'd say something, if he's going to be in here while we debate, but I'm not sure he'd be on my side, either.

"Once our trees are gone, they're gone for good," I say.

"Better we're the ones who use them instead of another Glory," Leah replies. "And there's no guarantee my sister won't just tear them up."

I shake my head, frustrated. It's so obvious now, why Yolanda stole our saplings and tried to destroy the oak tree. Twisted up as she was inside Ratchet, she still remembered the power of trees. She was trying to keep Mendoza from getting her wand.

Dez licks his lips. "So . . . Yo could be coming for our neighborhoods next?"

"Yeah . . ." I admit reluctantly. "Unless there's another Glory out there that beats her to it."

"Don't we have enough problems?" Amari groans. "Let's worry about what's in front of us. Please?"

"Even if you leave . . . Mendoza out of it, I'd feel a lot better going into the waste with more than your beats and rhymes." Dez shoots an apologetic look to Leah before continuing. "We could go looking for other schools and end up like Yolanda."

"We could end up worse!" I counter. "We don't have her armor. If wands worked out for our parents, they'd be here right now."

"And probably telling y'all it's time for bed," my faux mama murmurs.

"So what are you saying, Keynan?" Leah asks.

"I'm saying . . ." My whole jaw stiffens and my words freeze up for an instant. I'm out in front, and I don't want to mess everything up again. "A Glory waited at Peerless for . . . all of those months? All for the oak tree to absorb enough magic. It was that important to them."

Leah crosses her arms. "You're making my point for me. Mendoza or another one of *them* could be spying on us right now. Ready to snatch another wand from us!"

Amari and Dez share an uneasy look that all but screams out their agreement.

Wow. It's really like that? "Fine. So say we fight them, and they fight back. Say we find other schools—use up their trees, too. Fight Glories until there's nothing left. Even if we win. There's. Nothing. Left." Slickback stops gnawing on an old baking pan, listening. My faux parents' gaze is expectant as I drag out my next words. Here goes everything.

"I say . . . we take back Peerless."

Silence stretches around the table.

"Bro. How?" Leah finally blurts out.

"The right way . . . with *our* magic. Same as we told Kinder, but forreal this time. Rhymes to refortify the walls. Art on the inside to protect against Breaks and the radiant waste. One room, one hall, one wing at a time."

Dez scratches his chin, thinking. "But the courtyard's gone. We don't have Kinder's control room."

"We've got something better: us. We'll build it all back, with beats and rhymes. Even stronger than before." I wink at Slickback. "Magic is an actual thing. We decide what's possible."

"You'll need more than saplings to fortify enough land," my faux mama points out. My faux baba stands off to the side, watching us all with a twinkle in his eye.

"I know." I take a deep breath. "We'll do it with our trees. Our orange tree here, and the crops and gardens around it."

"You're going to . . . transplant your whole neighborhood?" Leah croaks.

"Nope . . . *all* of our neighborhoods. Everything solid we're bringing to Peerless."

Slickback whistles. "Wild plan, young blood. I didn't think you had it in you."

There. I got it out. I watch as the idea trickles through my friends, from the rising excitement glinting in Amari's eye to the open doubt on Leah and Dez's faces. My faux baba flashes me a wink. He's not real, but I'm suddenly so grateful that this copy of him does these small things, gestures that feel right on point somehow. It makes me love my parents even more, and ache that much harder that they are gone.

Amari speaks first. "All right, fine. You're talking me into it. So long as I get to decorate the *whole* school."

"Keynan . . ." Dez hesitates. "What if Mendoza comes back?"

"Why would she?" I ask bitterly. "She got what she wanted from us."

"And if she does, we'll give her a good fight this time." Leah nods grimly. "Let's do this."

Three simple words send the kitchen churning with movement. We don't have long, everyone can agree. Not everything planted in the courtyard was destroyed by Mendoza, but I doubt it's doing much better than Yolanda's olive grove. If we don't hurry, we might as well start from scratch with the Bizzy Block Academy, which I don't think the neighborhood would be too happy about.

Amari sets to sketching a new courtyard. Disco adds color swatches with a touch of her beak, which sets him to muttering to himself about "respecting the grand vision" and "dull creatures." Artists. Such sensitive folk.

Leah peppers my faux parents with questions about other schools, Glories, and the radiant waste. My faux baba answers as best he can, while my faux mama inserts herself into Amari's planning, so the trees in the courtyard will be spaced for ideal growing. Before long he's grinding his teeth while secretly pretending to smile, and my faux mama is pretending not to notice. She and Disco get along just fine—knowing my mama, she'll snatch the whole project away if Amari isn't careful. I hide a laugh behind my hand as Dez and I head outside to smooth out how we'll actually make any of this happen.

"We're just going to have to try some things out," Dez says. We settle on a bank of old mailboxes that nobody uses. "Can you disappear it? Then make it show up farther down the block?"

"Disappear it. Sure. Sounds easy."

He beatboxes and I try out a rhyme. The mailbox wiggles in place and vanishes in a puff of silvery smoke. A holler spins us back to Old Zeph's. Part of the mailbox is half buried in his porch—melded right into the old wood.

"So . . . that's a no," I say queasily. "How about something more basic? Fly it through the air, maybe?"

"*Basic,* he says. *Fly it through the air,* he says." Dez squints at me. "You must want my lips to fall off. If the magic stops because I can't keep the beat, we'll have a whole mess."

"Could hurt the trees, too," I admit reluctantly. "We need to move through Breaks, fast. We need to be able to move fast . . . not carry a ton of stuff . . . and get all the trees there at the same time."

"Sure would be nice if we had a *wand* right now," Dez prods.

I stop tapping my lip. "Give me another beat. I want to try something."

He goes in on it, and I turn to Yua's workshop.

Keep me and mine safe and sure so we can move quick.

Stay tiny till I say the words: Bring back my bricks!

The workshop blinks in and out of existence and vanishes completely. Dez peers up and down Bizzy Block. The shop doesn't reappear. "This is definitely not working."

I stride into the street, squinting. A beige fleck that's out of place on the asphalt pulls my attention down. "Hey!" he exclaims. "That's as big as my thumbnail! We can work with this!"

A shriek rings out behind us. "Keynan! You are so dead!"

Yua stalks forward, nostrils flaring. Her long straight hair is tied back in a ponytail, and her work goggles are perched on her head. Before she's within range to shake me, I say, loud and clear, "Bring back my bricks!"

The air before us quivers and folds—we scramble back as the workshop leaps back to its normal size. Yua rushes inside with a cry. She emerges with a relieved expression.

"I . . . okay. It's fine," she pants. "We're fine. I don't know what I'd do without that workshop." Her face wilts for a second, and I feel awful. I just took away the one thing she does on Bizzy Block, and it left her in a panic. "Don't play with me like that!"

I check for myself—not one tool is out of place inside. "If it's good enough for her, we can do this." One step closer! Me and Dez bump fists and share a huge grin. We can really *do* this. We *are* doing it!

We work out the rhymes over the next few days, even crafting a way to hold our miniature trees in pockets of magic, kind of like the traps we made for Slickback and Disco. All of Bizzy Block helps out—trundling together wheelbarrows piled with tools, heirloom seeds, jarred preserves from our jam parties. It's not just the trees. All of Bizzy Block is coming back to Peerless with us.

"What will they all do there?" Dez wonders. "If this all actually works?"

"We'll figure it out." I hold in a laugh at the thought of Professor Zeph. The more I ponder rebuilding the school, the better the idea feels.

Amari saunters up to us with a big grin. "Y'all are gonna love this," he announces. "Check it out!"

Screeching tires pull our eyes down the street. A

gleaming blue shuttle zooms toward us. We leap back, but it peels to a perfect stop just inches from the curb. The doors hiss to reveal Jocelyn. "Heard y'all need a ride!" she croons.

"You made it out of Peerless!" I exclaim. She descends the steps, and I squeeze her in a hug. "How?"

She offers a laugh and a confused shrug. "You know I'm slippery when it comes to these streets. And somehow . . . I get a feeling when y'all need me, and I know how to find you."

"How's Peerless . . . ?" Leah hesitates. "Is there anything left?"

Jocelyn blows out her lips. "Can't lie. It's ugly. But so long as there's one brick on top of another, y'all got a place to start."

"And the trees to build around." Amari gives us a sly smile. "So . . . this shuttle has a few more upgrades, just in case we run into problems. My feet didn't appreciate all of that walking through the waste."

A sudden rush of hope squeezes tight in my chest. Jocelyn survived the chaos at Peerless? This plan can actually work! We can do more than plant the trees— maybe there are more faux students and professors to be saved.

Quiet falls on Bizzy Block. It's time.

Everyone I know gathers, pressing tight into our yard, whispering excitedly. Disco twists and flashes in the air overhead. Yua shifts eagerly on our steps, scratching Buster's ears. Every single person in our neighborhood watches me expectantly. My faux parents file out of the house and stand on the porch. "Everything of value from Bizzy Block is gathered up inside," my faux baba calls. "We're ready as we'll ever be."

"It might be weird for y'all inside the bubble," I say to our neighbors. "But we'll get you out as soon as we're back at Peerless!"

Dez beatboxes, giving me a thumbs-up. Leah joins in with a step to make sure our rhythm is rich and strong. The air crackles with energy as Amari starts up a clap, pulling in every last person from Bizzy Block, all on beat. I've never felt anything so wondrous, all of us locked in on getting this right—like we can fix the whole world with one good rhyme if we all believe in each other.

I release my freestyle, curling words through our crops, my faux family and neighbors, the trees, Yua's workshop, the gardens and soil. Magic swirls up and down Bizzy Block. Brilliant light engulfs the cul-de-sac from every side as rhymes pour out of me. I couldn't remember them if I tried. They just flow free and converge in the blue glow.

Then it's done. I stop, panting, dizzy and exhausted.

But I feel elated. It's the best rhyme I've ever done—ever performed. Even if I don't remember a word of it! All of our neighbors clap and hoot and holler, stomping their feet. "Maybe that's like the block party you're always dreaming about," Dez teases, nudging Amari in the ribs.

Amari blinks. "Yeah. Sure."

Leah frowns when the shimmering fades. "It didn't work. Why are they still here?"

All the faux kinfolk of Bizzy Block stand on a spreading patch of radiant waste where our yard used to be. My eyes dart in every direction. "No, no, no . . ." Yua's workshop is gone, like it should be—but our house and the Chandler place are still here. Ragged holes all up and down the cul-de-sac have replaced our crops, gardens, and the orange tree. My hands start to shake. "I . . . I screwed something up! I'll fix it, we just need to—"

"Keynan." My faux baba's voice cuts through the air. "The magic that made us is anchored to this land. We . . . can't go with you like this."

"You knew?" I demand, my eyes burning. "Why didn't you say something? I could've done something different!"

A great crack opens in the sidewalk and creeps up the side of the Chandlers' house.

"This is how it had to be," my faux mama says softly. "You already have what you need to return to Peerless. If you'd known, you'd still be wasting time here."

The streetlights flare on, then wink out. "Nothing else matters but keeping you all safe."

"We should go, Keynan," Leah whispers gently. My friends tug me toward the shuttle, where Jocelyn waits with a somber expression.

"Why are you so surprised?" Yua laughs and sits cross-legged. Little white-and-yellow flowers with grabby hands for leaves spring out of the honeycomb ground and creep up her jeans. "You're the whole neighborhood's little brother or nephew. When you rise, we rise."

"You finish up that schooling, now!" Old Zeph barks. "They finna be scared of you!"

"I will," I choke out. A biting wind rises, whipping the net on our basketball hoop.

"It's like I told you," my faux baba says. "Bizzy Block would run through fire for you. We take care of our own. Remember . . . make it yours." His finger taps his chest. "In here. Hear me?"

"Yes, Baba."

"So be it. See to it then!"

Disco flashes a sad pink, flitting in the air above Buster, who whines a goodbye. Slickback folds his stubby arms. "You hate to see it. We still need to talk, young blood."

"Come on, lizard," Amari says, squeezing my shoulder.

"Can't it wait?"

"Whatever." Slickback nudges my leg. "My needs can't be ignored forever. You and me. Later."

"But—"

"*Later.*"

Huh? Slickback and Disco don't follow as we climb the shuttle steps. What, do they not trust Jocelyn's driving? She closes the door behind us with a snort and we set out. As she rounds another massive crack forming in the street, I stare back through the window. All of the co-op waves us on. The Kwans' house sinks into the ground on our left. All of Bizzy Block is still waving as the radiant waste creeps over the neighborhood—this time for good. Everything that's left of it will be in my duffel bag.

Jocelyn's eyes flick toward us in the rearview mirror. "So who's in charge back there? Where to next?"

Everyone's looking at me—it's my plan, after all. So like my baba says . . . ain't nothing to it but to do it. I scrub away my tears and take a deep breath. "Okay, y'all. It's on us."

CHAPTER TWENTY-NINE

FEAST YOUR EYES

So we have the plan. We have the rhymes. Now we just need to do the same thing in everyone's neighborhood. Three more trees, and then we take our school back. We decide to go to Amari's next—Jocelyn claims it is closest. She's been amazing with finding her way to us, so there's no reason not to trust her now.

Amari's face is calm as the shuttle glides through the radiant waste, but his fingers are laced together so tight his fingernails are white at the tips. I can't remember the last time I've seen him this nervous, but I can't blame him one bit. Going back to Bizzy Block rocked my whole world—again. He can't be looking forward to that if his experience is anywhere like mine.

"Hey, you okay?" I ask, squeezing his shoulder.

"Yeah . . ." His smile cracks. "Okay. No. Not even a little bit. My parents . . . can you just get the tree for me? I don't know if I can handle it."

"Are you kidding me? It'll be fine," I say. "Your faux granny will probably make burritos for us."

He coughs out a laugh as the shuttle stops. "My granny. Burritos. Right."

He's so nervous I almost wish we'd picked somewhere else to go first—but it's too late.

"Next up!" Jocelyn calls. "Union Street Vista Apartments."

We get off the shuttle, following Amari out onto a tidy street lined with little shops stretching off in either direction. Across the street is a park with a playground complete with jungle gym and slides—and a huge cottonwood with a tree house nestled in the upper branches. Jocelyn has stopped in front of an oatmeal-colored building nearly as tall as Peerless, lined with three stories' worth of balconies, windows, and doors. The whole place is different from anything I know, but it's bright and cheerful and fits Amari perfectly.

Disco and Slickback beat us here. They dart through the archway leading into the apartment building—they refused to ride on the shuttle with us. I still don't know why; it's one more bother we don't need. Slickback has grown an attitude since Bizzy Block—maybe he's expecting more than my apology. Whatever's going on, I'll need to deal with him later. This is too important.

Amari glances back at us, gesturing hopefully at the cottonwood tree like we can just grab it and roll out. I shake my head.

He sighs heavily, and we follow him to an inner court-yard that reminds me faintly of Peerless. It even has a garden. "I can't imagine so many people stacked on top of each other," I murmur.

Leah snorts. "Where is everybody?"

There's a hum of activity just beyond my sight. People moving around, going about their routines—but nobody outside. They haven't seen us.

"Most folks keep to themselves," Amari offers. "You get used to it. Besides, it's early in the day."

Her eyebrow rises doubtfully. "So where's yours?"

"Sure . . . it's . . ."

Dez points before Amari finishes. "Gotta be that one."

A wall just off the second-floor landing is dripping with eye-watering color, a mini mural of a cityscape of floating pyramids. Vibrant fields fill the ground beneath them. "You got me." Amari lets out an anxious laugh. He's so nervous he's making me nervous.

On the stairs, we file past a stretch of wall with weird striped burn marks. It's warm to the touch. Two cans of unopened paint and brushes lie beside it. "That must be where you tried your magic." Amari looks down and nods. "At least you didn't take out the whole wall like I did."

The doorframe reads 24C in bronze letters. Amari knocks. No answer. He rubs the back of his head, then fiddles with the light beside the doorway. A key drops into his waiting palm. He flashes us a grin, unlocks the door, and disappears inside. "Granny? Are you—"

His voice cracks. Something changes in the air for a split second, so brief I think I imagine it. My ears pop. The hum of folks murmuring and moving ceases in an instant. I feel like someone wrapped a pillow around my head.

We all gape at each other. "Did you feel—?" I'm relieved I can still hear my own voice!

"What just happened?"

We hurry inside after Amari. Leah stops with a gasp. His faux granny is frozen in mid-stride, hand grasping a frying pan, balanced on one foot. Frozen, but awake. Aware. Her mouth is curled open, face straining. I swear she's trying to meet my eyes and fighting to speak.

Amari's face crumples. Sweat beads spring out on his forehead. "She . . . tried to hit me with that . . . when I was home before. She didn't recognize me, and I just ran out.

My . . . my art froze her. I didn't know she'd been like this the whole time. I didn't know!"

"Weird. Keynan's parents were fine." Dez swallows. "Is there anything we can do?"

"Doesn't feel right leaving her like this," Leah murmurs.

"We should try," I agree. "Maybe a rhyme will—"

"No!" Amari interrupts. "If we mess her up even more—I can't. Please."

The three of us exchange worried looks. "We won't be able to take her with us anyway," I say reluctantly. "Maybe it's better this way."

Leah screws up her face but doesn't argue. We stand there awkwardly while Amari disappears into his room, popping back out clutching a binder. He hesitates in front of his faux granny. "I . . . understand why you went off to fight them, even though it was impossibly foolish." He scrubs his eyes and grimaces. "I'm talking to her like she can hear me. Like she's not fake. Let's just get the tree and go."

He hurries out. By the time we catch up, he's already sitting inside the shuttle. "I'll talk to him," Leah says. "Just do this quick, okay?"

Dez and I cross the street.

"Let's hurry. I hate seeing him like that."

I gather my verse as we cross the street to the park.

The air flashes in front of us—Disco. "What's your problem, bird?"

"Your boy been holding out!" Slickback pops his head out of the cottonwood's tree house and scampers down the bark. "The best snacks. Y'all don't wanna miss this."

We follow him curiously to the nearest shop, right past a snoring, still cashier. The back is full of all kinds of random useful stuff. Soap, candles, shea butter. But Slickback flings another door wide. "Feast your eyes!"

We gawk at a huge storeroom full of delivery drones in long rows. "This . . . is huge!"

"Forreal!" Slickback smacks his lips over a drone set on one of the worktables. I spot a familiar burn mark next to one of the turbines. Smiley face in blue and pink on the front.

"Hey, don't you chew on that one. That's Eli! We've been through some things together."

"You," the magical talking gecko declares, "are one weird dude."

Dez circles the worktable doubtfully. "So Touré was working on Eli out here? For what, field testing?"

"Lucky for us. Who knows how they'd all end up at Peerless after—"

"That's. Not. Yours!" A figure in goggles rushes into the room, brandishing a huge wrench.

"Yua?" I squawk. "How'd you get here from Bizzy Block?"

"Who are you, and what is a Bizzy Block?" She pulls up her goggles, frowning. "Back off that drone. They need me."

All around her, the drones start activating, one by one, Eli included. The whine of their turbines fills the air.

"This isn't your Yua!" Dez shouts.

"I call dibs on the wrench if she knocks him out!" Slickback cackles. "You know what you 'bout to have, young blood? Rhymes with percussion."

"We don't have time for this," I growl. Yua's circling the table toward us, a feral light in her eyes. *Still and silent, best do what I say. Not a whisper of violence for the rest of the day.*"

Yua sits down, face blank. The drones are still rising up on every side! Several are blocking the way out.

"Umm, Eli? Still friends, right?"

Eli nudges me curiously. What does that *mean*?

"Do something, Keynan!" Dez is about to climb through a window.

I nudge Eli back. "Friends! Remember me?"

Eli abruptly spins around, between us and the other drones. They settle suddenly. Waiting.

"Not bad, Keymaster," Slickback observes. "See how

287

things go when you ain't trying to mind-control every-body?"

"It's about time something *finally* went our way," Dez exclaims. "Hey . . . there's a 3D printer over there! Let's hustle back before they worry."

Disco winks bluish pink, then back to gold.

"Seriously." Slickback nods gravely. "But don't trip. We'll be long gone before they figure it out."

Dez is already beatboxing, so I don't get to ask Slick-back what he means. The drone room, garden, and huge cottonwood tree—treehouse and all—easily bend to my rhymes. The pieces we need get wrapped safely in a magic bubble of air, and I stash them in our bag next to the orange tree.

Yua—this neighborhood's version of her—is still sitting in the middle of the new patch of radiant waste we've just unearthed. *"The work you've done is true,"* I murmur to her. *"Stay safe and find something new."*

She stands, still in a trance, and strides toward the apart-ments. Dez's eyes are on me, but he doesn't say anything as we get into the shuttle. No idea what he's thinking, but there's no time to ask or argue. I did what I thought was right. Who cares if a little magic made it go faster?

"Two to go." I sit beside Leah, glancing back at Amari. "Is he okay?"

"I don't know."

Dez slides next to Amari, but his eyes are fixed on the apartments. One of the walls suddenly sloughs off the side of the building, receding into shimmering dust. The collapse exposes more rooms full of faux neighbors, all frozen in mid-motion. Just like his faux granny, only going about their normal days. Leah and I stare, more than a little alarmed. How did his painting manage to do all of this?

Amari buries his face in his hands while Dez attempts to console him. Whatever magic Amari tried over fall break made the whole place . . . glitch. Frozen, just like my faux mama after the storm that hit Bizzy Block. Just one more reminder of how easy it is to mess things up. Ruin a home for good with the smallest mistake. My worry over what we'll find at Peerless sprouts tusks and quills as the shuttle glides away from Amari's crumbling home.

CHAPTER THIRTY

THE WELCOME SHE DESERVES

Light shimmers over the shuttle windows, blue and green and velvety silver. No telling where we are. Even worse is how long we've been away from Peerless. Every hour counts. Jocelyn drives confidently. I trust Amari's conjuring has the shuttle in shape. We eat the lunch my faux mama packed for us—veggie wraps, sliced cheeses, and fruit. Of course it's all delicious. Even Amari's mood is lifted a bit.

"These cookies are great," Dez mumbles between bites. "I guess I'm lucky we're even friends after I smashed up your care package. That feels like years ago."

"Old stuff, bro," I say. "I couldn't imagine the crew without you." And I mean it.

Leah grows quiet, but she's not nervous, just . . . ready. "Your parents seemed nice," she says. "I wish I could've met them forreal. We talked when you were out breaking things with Dez."

"Oh" is all I can manage, proud for not choking on my wrap. I'm glad the rest of the sentence didn't get past my teeth. It would probably just come out in a shriek. What could they possibly talk to Leah about?

"I asked why they think our real parents lost. Against the Glories. They said the plan was sound, but they were short-handed." She frowns. "They left without their best sorcerer."

"No way. *Kinder?*" She nods, and I purse my lips. "That actually makes sense. She doesn't seem to be in love with running Peerless."

"Exactly," Leah says.

"So why didn't she fight with them?"

"These constructs only hold so much information." She mimics my faux parents' spooky tag-team voice. We both grimace. "I . . . I wish Kinder was still here. Both of them. Even as mad as I am over Yolanda."

"Me too."

"Concord Towers!" The shuttle stops. "Y'all, please don't dawdle in there! I need my school back." Jocelyn pulls out a squeegee and some glowing window cleaner that boils green in the spray bottle. "This mess better wash off. Nothing worse than a dirty ride."

Even though she's fussing at us, I'm grateful she's here. Jocelyn's the only person left from the old Peerless—the reset didn't change her. She gives me hope we can really restore the rest of it.

We're inside an old parking garage, dusty concrete on all sides. Leah leads us to an elevator, and I gawk at how high up the numbers go. Sixteen floors! And I thought Amari's complex was huge. How? How do people live stuffed on top of each other like this? I can't decide if it would be better to live on the bottom, the top, or somewhere in the middle. Leah holds in a smile as she presses thirteen and the doors close. I jump a little bit when the elevator jerks into motion.

Dez whistles. "High-rise," he marvels.

"Never thought I'd see one of these," Amari adds thoughtfully.

"We're just lucky the elevator isn't out." Faux neighbors pass us when we reach Leah's hallway. A few even recognize her and wave. I'm just glad they're moving. Leah ignores them all, her jaw set like she's about to go to war against Mendoza all by herself.

Her door opens on the first knock. "Well. Look who's home."

"Hi, Mom," Leah mumbles. "It's me. Leah. I'm here with some friends."

A tight smile chases away the disappointment on the woman's face. Gray tickles her temples, her hair is cut short and curly, and she wears a plain shirt and jeans offset by long dangly earrings. Her resemblance to Leah and Yolanda is unmistakable—rich brown skin and wide, challenging eyes. Leah's faux dad is a stout man, bald with a salt-and-pepper beard, brown skin, and a mouth that pulls down at the corners as we shuffle inside. "Oh. Home early. Will you be helping out with chores?"

Amari and I exchange disbelieving, embarrassed glances. They're so *mean*. Couldn't they have at least made their faux selves nice? An exasperated growl gurgles in Leah's throat. "We don't have time for this. Keynan, can you . . . ?"

"I got you." I know exactly what she means. She slaps out a new beat on her hands and knees.

Her faux mom's eyes flash. "Young lady! *What do you think you're doing?*"

I jump in quickly and rhyme:

Honesty, we need that, so honestly let's peel back
The fakeness, replace it with the realness
No finesse instead of trust, transparency will be
a must
So go ahead, let's all discuss—what you know
about the real us!

Hmm. Could've been smoother. The magic settles into Leah's faux parents and their eyes flare blue for an instant—just like my parents' did with the lullaby. Did it work? They blink, then focus on Leah. She steps back uncertainly as they gasp and rush forward, crushing her in a hug. Overjoyed laughter rocks their shoulders. Leah's stiff at first, but then she squeezes them back.

I can't help but grin. This is the welcome she deserves!

"So much better," Dez murmurs.

Leah's faux mom squeezes her hands and kisses them. The two of them speak in unison, just like my parents did. "We knew you'd figure it out if things came to this," they say together. "You must have questions. We'll answer them, if our conjuring allows it. We'll do anything we can to help you, Yolanda."

Leah's smile shatters. Dez holds a hand to his mouth, mortified. I'm too stunned to say anything as her faux parents drone on.

"These constructs hold only so much information," her faux dad says. "But we wanted you to know, above all, how proud we are of you. You've made it so far."

Leah takes in a deep, shuddering breath. "What can you tell us about the Glories?" she asks in a too-steady voice.

The faux parents glance at each other. "We believed they were the same sorcerers who won the Wars of Illusion. We don't believe they can live forever, but who knows? They are still powerful and quite mad. We couldn't defeat them in a straight-up clash. Our strategy was simple: Create an illusion that worked like a maze. The deeper into it they fell, the weaker their powers would become.

"Obviously if you're here, we failed," she continues. "We should have never attacked their fortress. Not without Kinder. Heck Masters was so convinced he'd thought of everything, but if you're here, he miscalculated horribly."

Wait . . . what? My heart forgets to beat. It's awful enough that our parents all left us behind to go fight Glories—but their busted plan was my baba's idea? Just like Peerless was my mama's? They pulled all of my friends' parents into their grand plan—and lost it all. The people who told me I'm made of strong stuff weren't even strong themselves when it mattered most! And here I am, following right in their footsteps. Saving Peerless feels like a lifetime ago—I've done nothing but screw things up since then.

"But there's still hope," Leah's faux mom gushes fondly. "You're here, and that means we have a fighting chance, Yolanda."

"I wish you talked to me like that," Leah whispers. Her voice sounds exactly like how I feel, peeled right down to the core. "Just once."

Dez and Amari grab us and lead us toward the door. "Come on, y'all," Dez mutters. "There's nothing else for us here."

Back outside, I rhyme in a daze, pulling the line of palm trees from the middle of the extra-wide street in front of the building. There's an apiary—with real bees—and a greenhouse erected on an empty lot the next block over. After some grudging debate on if we can care for them properly, the bees go with the rest of our collection— they get their own separate bubble of magic, though. One step closer to getting Peerless back. The rest of the buildings on the street make me itch. Somehow I can tell they're all facades, hollow as Leah's faux parents.

We all wordlessly take our seats back on the shuttle. Leah hugs her knees to her chest, but I find her hand

and give it a squeeze. She doesn't meet my gaze, but she squeezes back. We've got our trees, almost exactly as we planned, and more good stuff besides, but somehow I feel like we're losing, just like my parents lost their fight with the Glories. Peerless is running out of time.

CHAPTER THIRTY-ONE

FORGET THE TREE

Jocelyn wheels us out, watching us all wordlessly in the rearview mirror, concern painting her eyes. Three trees down, one to go. I stare at the door, dreading the moment it opens again. Dez reads my face. "You're not coming?"

"You don't need me," I say. "Leah's parents didn't even see us."

"Didn't see her, either," Amari mutters under his breath. I give him a sour look. Thankfully, Leah didn't hear. I'm doing my best to shake off the crummy feeling after meeting Leah's faux parents, but it's impossible to get their words unstuck from my head, like a freestyle rhyme spiraling around in my brain that won't leave me alone.

Heck Masters was so convinced he'd thought of everything, but if you're here, he miscalculated horribly.

"Hey y'all," Leah says. "Someone please tell me I'm not the only who thinks they're glowing brighter."

We join her, crowding around the duffel bag. Every new globe of miniaturized neighborhood is pulsing brighter, like they are drawing strength from being near each other. That's got to be a good thing, right? Not something else I managed to mess up with my plan? We sure could use some good news right now.

"Definitely stronger," Amari agrees.

"So we have enough, right?" Dez asks hopefully. "We should get back to Peerless before there's nothing left."

I rest a hand on Dez's shoulder. "I get why you're scared, believe me." I force the words out, try to make myself sound encouraging when I can't even feel it for myself. "We gotta make this work. We need you."

"I'm with you. I just . . . hate going last. Especially for this. You'll come, won't you?"

I hold in a grimace. "We're right here with you."

The light glinting through the shuttle's windows gives way to Dez's neighborhood. A huge wrought-iron gate opens silently as the shuttle approaches. We glide up a drive paved with bricks that weaves past a rolling grass yard, ending at the largest house I've ever seen.

Jocelyn whistles appreciatively. "Okay, fancy!"

"It's an all-out mansion," I marvel. "Or a castle, even."

Amari's lips quirk. "How many rooms make something a castle?"

Dez's face looks hot enough to cook an egg on. "None of it's real anyway, right? I never felt quite right here. If magic weren't a thing, who knows? Maybe we'd live in a tree house."

A familiar flash greets us near the wide wooden door. "Disco." I frown. "Slickback's gotta be close, too. How come they won't ride with us?"

"Strange magical creatures, acting weird?" Amari smirks. "Too surprising." He's been a little grouchy about Disco after the bird's and my faux mama's feedback about his drawings. Two artists and their creative differences—and of course Slickback will take Disco's side.

I hope it doesn't cause us trouble. "Let's get what we came for. They'll be fine."

Dez's front door opens silently. We sweep through a foyer into a living room with a wall fountain gurgling contentedly in one corner and a couch the size of my bed. Floor-to-ceiling windows open to a rose garden in a backyard that could easily fit Bizzy Block, full of green grass. An old weeping willow tree with long droopy branches stands in the center of it. Delicious smells waft in from a kitchen big enough to hold a sleepover for all the first-years in Peerless.

"At least his parents thought of snacks," Leah mutters.

"Desmond, is that you?" A cheerful voice sails around the corner. "Can I pour you some lemonade? Welcome back from school, we—"

Dez's faux dad comes around the corner, followed by his faux mom. They're both dressed in fancy white shirts and pants, and she has a yellow flower pinned in her hair. She misses a step at the sight of us, pausing to take us in head to toe. "Dezzy. Who are your friends?"

"I'm sure there's a good explanation," his dad says with a grin. "We've got plenty to share."

Freely offered snacks? He'd be my new best friend, except something is off with Dez's faux mom. She breathes in small gasps, like she just sprinted around the house. Her eyes swivel between the three of us. "Come down from the Prismatic Asylum, finally?" she rasps, glaring at Amari.

"Umm, sorry, what?" he squeaks.

"You won't take what we've built. We won't allow it!"

"Dez, what's her deal?" Leah asks.

"I don't know!"

His faux parents stalk forward, planting themselves on either side of us. Words hiss through his faux dad's snarl. *"Starlight in one flash, bring a big splash to my fist-fight!"*

The hair on my forearms shoots up at the rhyme. A surge of light flickers in the high ceiling. Leah pulls me down. An arc of lightning zips through the air—right where my head had been. The blast sinks into a wall, licking its way through the foyer ceiling like a centipede. Part of it snakes back around toward us. We fling ourselves down as the couch bursts into blue-and-orange flames. More lightning glances against the kitchen island, exploding in a shower of marble dust.

"Get away from them, Dezzy!" his faux mom shouts. "They're Brights!"

"No, they're my friends!" Dez cries. His voice grows shrill. *"Dad, what are you doing?"*

I risk a peek around the couch. His dad is outside, arms raised, shouting at the top of his lungs. Another lightning bolt splits the sky. A huge, awful cracking sound fills our ears.

Amari scrambles over to us. "Keynan, *the tree*! He's trying to burn it up!"

An idea springs to mind. "Draw us a square, hurry!"

"Can I get a little more direction?"

"Just do it!"

He pulls out a marker and, on the tiles, quickly draws the sloppiest square I've ever seen him draw. I start rhyming over it before he's finished.

> *No need to see us, look—your son's home*
> *Time to spill everything, let your knowledge roam*
> *Be free so we can rewrite this whole tome*

Amari's square shimmers and rises from the floor. We yank it up like a windowpane and crowd behind it just before Dez's faux dad stalks back into the living room. He blinks in confusion—eyes flashing blue. "Dez? You're home early? What's going on?"

It wasn't the cleanest, but my rhyme worked. He looks right past us.

Dez peeks out from behind the kitchen island. "Dad, you must be confused! The tree!" They rush outside. We trail behind carefully. Smoke tickles my nose, teasing for a sneeze.

"Oh no," Leah groans under her breath.

The weeping willow feels even older than our oak tree that Mendoza destroyed. One of the branches is completely singed and hangs on by a thread of bark. Half the tree's leaves are spread across the ground from the lightning strike.

"So. You see us." His faux dad surveys the damaged tree. His voice grows cold. "For the constructs we really are."

"Yeah," Dez says shakily. "I know. About magic, the Wars of Illusion. Everything."

"Everything." His dad shakes his head. "If that were true, we wouldn't be having this conversation. You'd absorb our knowledge and be done with us."

"Okay, umm . . . whatever. I need to take some things back to Peerless."

His faux mom snorts. "That means Heck Masters failed us all. Touré and Kinder, too? I doubt they sent you here on their own." She shakes her head ruefully when Dez doesn't answer. "Take some advice, son. If you see a Glory? You run." She gestures back in the house. "You run and hide. Forget the tree. Forget Peerless. Take all the food you can carry and find another school."

"How?" he asks.

I'm so shaken I don't even hear his faux dad's answer. *None* of my parents' friends had their backs. Why? How were they supposed to take on the Glories if they didn't believe in each other? Am I a dummy for thinking we'll do any better?

We sneak outside and hide in the rose garden. The willow tree has stopped smoking, but Amari looks at it doubtfully. "This one might not be worth saving," he says.

Dez hurries back out. He's spooked—and I just now realize one of his shirtsleeves was singed by that lightning conjuring. "Dez, your arm! Are you okay?"

"What? Oh. It's fine. Listen, I've talked them down, but . . . Keynan. They aren't Glories and they almost took us out. If there was ever a time to rethink wands, this is it. No offense, but I'm not going to sit here beatboxing while you come up with a rhyme the next time we get attacked!"

"He's not wrong," Leah says quietly. "There might be enough trees left for all of us to have one."

Amari clears his throat. "I'm sure your rhymes can cover the basics."

How did we get here? I feel like someone set a giant kettlebell on my chest. I'm just reliving all of my parents' mistakes. My friends' faith is leaking away with every new stop we make, every choice that's ahead of us. They're hearing all this doubt about Heck and Alicia Masters, too, and probably wondering what I'm made of.

"I get it, y'all. This was scary—but we still got through it. We'll still need a place to stay—who knows if another school is any better off than us? If they've even got food, walls, and people?" I look at each of them in turn. We're a crew, and we can do anything together if we believe in each other. "I'm tired of all this running. Let's get Peerless back . . . *make it stunning—so strong that before long we'll be the ones doing the chasing instead of the hiding, running things like—*"

I clap my hands over my mouth when I realize what I'm doing. The words came out on their own. Not my friends! It was an accident! I didn't mean to freestyle on my friends like that! I'm stressed, desperate, I only wanted to convince them.

But before I can fix my mouth to apologize, there are nods all around.

Leah blinks like she just woke up from a long nap. "Running things," she echoes. "I like the sound of that."

"Okay," Dez says, shaking his head like he's surprised he was even disagreeing with me before. "I just wish we were doing everything we could, you know?"

"Hmm . . . wasn't expecting that," Amari says, peering at me like a bird. "But what can I say? I'm all in."

"Don't forget the turntable," I offer. "We weren't even looking for it—imagine what else we could find. We just gotta deal with this messy part first."

"Why is the right thing always so hard?" Leah mutters.

"All right, Keynan. We'll stick with your way. Let's go back to Peerless."

"But wands later," Dez says firmly, and I'm a little bummed that Amari's nodding eagerly. "We're going to need them."

"Later," I agree reluctantly. I'm still hoping I can convince them, eventually. The radiant waste wouldn't stand a chance if we surrounded Peerless with a forest of real trees, instead of a handful stuffed in the courtyard.

Amari looks at me like he's never seen me before. "That would really be something."

Oh. Oops. Thinking out loud again.

I couldn't be more relieved—or feel more *guilty*—over how this turned out. They're all on Team Keynan—because I rhymed them that way. *I used magic on my friends.* Sure, I got what I wanted. We saved some time arguing. But this is worse than back when Mendoza rhymed me out of a fight with Dez in the lunchroom. I *have* to be right about this now—it needs to work after doing something so foul!

Is this where the Glories lost their way, too? When they lost control of magic and went with whatever felt good—the easy way, like Touré would say? I can imagine how ashamed she would be of me in this moment. This isn't any better than Kinder making the faux students cartwheel around the halls. I'm relieved I don't have to convince anyone now, but it's still not right. I'm doubting myself more than ever before—and sick about it, because my freestyling has never been better.

I'm afraid my plan is going to blow up in my face. But my name isn't Heck or Alicia—I'm Keynan Masters. The Keymaster. And I'm going to keep doing what I know is right. Trying to, at least. I gotta stand for something, even with the mistakes I make along the way. I only hope it doesn't cost me everything.

CHAPTER THIRTY-TWO

TOO LATE NOW

The glimmering light outside of the shuttle grows turbulent. We're close. The shuttle slows. A gust of wind rocks the shuttle. A spray of grit and bright flecks of corrupt magic thrum over the windows. That unforgettable tang fills the air, even though the doors, and everything else, are sealed tight. It takes me right back to my first bike ride through a storm, holding on to Eli with everything I had—trying to get to Peerless. I feel even more powerless now than I was then.

Jocelyn clears her throat. "Last stop."

Strange patterns flash through the heavy mist surrounding us. We're all pressed against the glass, looking for a sign of anything familiar, walls, fields, even a professor strolling by. But it's all eerily still. Dez swallows. "Keynan, I don't think there's anything left."

"Our memories are left," I say firmly. "We'll build it from scratch if we have to."

"You haven't really given us any other choice," Amari says with a sigh.

Jocelyn swings the door open wide. We step out. There's no sign of Yolanda anywhere. The mist is thick and pink. My throat tingles. Corrupt magic is remaking me from the inside out with every breath. I nearly trip on something hard underfoot: a step. We're right at the front entryway. The outer wall is still standing! The letters are dark. Striped vines snake over the wall like glowing purple snakes. Cracks spiderweb across the brick. The huge double doors hang from their hinges, inviting us deeper.

Slickback and Disco await us at the stairs. The lizard lets out a low mournful whistle. "Never thought I'd squeeze out a tear for the place I was born," he says wistfully. "You blink and things get worn down, just like that."

"No thanks to you," Amari snorts, glaring at the duo.

Disco takes on an affronted shade of orange.

"Say that again," Slickback observes. "You can't choose family, after all."

I stride over to him before things get worse. "You all actually want to help with the school? Really help?"

"Not really," Slickback replies. "But you can ask anyway. I do adore telling people no."

"I actually—"

"*No!*"

"—had something else in mind for a . . . uh, being of your immense talent."

"Oh? Flattery? This has promise. You may speak."

"There's a . . . place in the radiant waste. A building, a museum really. There's something there called a turntable. If you were to locate it for us . . . you'd be the hero of Peerless. We'd need a monument of you in the courtyard."

"So long as you don't eat it," Leah murmurs.

Slickback rubs his chin. "A chance to avoid this danger? Yes. Gain all the acclaim, while my colleague here does all the work? Yes and yes. You, my friend, have got yourself a deal." He wrests a hinge from the door. The whole thing topples to the ground in a spray of corrupt magic. "Road snack. Disco! Let's go hunting. We're skipping the battle with that mindless feline. Hopefully there will be something left of y'all that ain't bedazzled by the time we get back."

Disco flashes a bluish red with golden edges, which

I can only interpret as good luck. "Thanks," I whisper. "You too."

I turn to face my friends. "We're here now, y'all. No more putting it off. Let's do what we came to do."

My heart sinks as we pass through the broken doors and into the school. Radiant waste swallows everything like a colorful, creeping mold. The grand stair leading up to our dorms is still intact. Beyond it, a whole wing has collapsed in on the main hall. Little glowing eyes peer out at us from within the rubble.

"Heads up!" Amari shouts. A pair of faux students scrambles through the wreckage, panting. I recognize a third-year, Joey. A huge bug clings to his head. Glowing wings drape over his face like some sort of emerald veil. The other third-year is covered with orange and blue spots, like little mouths ringed with square teeth. The two of them stagger closer to us, moaning.

Dez snaps into a beat before I can even think to squeal. I pull myself together and rhyme.

> Buzz off fall back and fly away!
> Get up out my face because we're here to stay!

The mothlike creature flutters up through the collapsed ceiling's hole in a whisk of dust, dragging a squealing Joey with it. The other faux student flees on foot.

Leah shudders. "They . . . it's eating them?"

"It'll be us next if we don't move!" Amari hisses.

Faux students ghost out of the broken halls as we press forward. More creatures hide at the edge of my sight—slithering and clambering and lurking in the ruins on every side.

Leah sweeps into a rhythmic dance, twirling and spinning. The halls lurch around us as if Peerless is trying to keep up with her moves. Faux students go tumbling in every direction.

"Nice, but there's way more of them than us!" Amari stops and scrawls on a patch of cracked concrete. "We need more than this."

Before I can even throw a rhyme at his drawings, he grabs them and pulls them right out of the concrete. A staff for each of us. Tall as me. Their surfaces crackle with magic. There's so much corruption floating in the air it's starting to make me sick . . . even though I'm feeling extra quick with my rhymes, extra slick with my—

Not this again.

"Hurry," I mutter. I reluctantly accept one of the . . . weapons. There's no question that's what it is. Dez takes one eagerly, while me and Leah hold ours like they might bite us. What will these do to Yolanda? We're going to face her eventually. Maybe these are what we need to finally stop her.

"Are you sure about this?" Leah asks.

"Dez's parents gave me the idea," Amari admits. "These will help us, promise!"

Right or wrong, it's too late now. Our staffs crackle and sputter with blue fire as we press through the main hall. I keep expecting mine to burn down to my fingers.

Faux students creep out, sniffing the air like we're fresh snacks. Dez jabs at one that gets too close—she goes flying down a side hall, green energy pulsating over her body. "Yes! That's what I'm talking about!"

Amari grins. "Not so bad, right?"

I groan. "But you stirred them up!" The broken walls boil with fresh movement. Shadow creatures dance out of the cracks and pluck at our shoelaces. A toad bat's tongue loops around a corner, snatching for Leah's arm. "Go! Move it!"

We run and fight and jab our way to the courtyard.

Corrupt magic drifts through the air like feathery clumps of soapsuds. My arms tingle in patches, glowing with the stuff. Crystalline slivers dust my friends' skin, too, taking root in their pores. We hastily survey the courtyard. Most of the bushes and flowers are ruined, blasted down to their stems. Some smaller trees that weren't snapped at the trunk might make it, if corrupt magic doesn't swallow them first. A gaping hole in the ground is all that remains of the old oak. Even the roots are part of Professor Mendoza's wand.

"Where do we even start?" Dez croaks. "It's completely wrecked."

"No, it's not!" I cry, feeling a lump rise in my throat.

"There's the greenhouses still," Leah says hopefully, but her heart's not in it.

I'm suddenly as unsure as I've ever been. "The dirt is still dirt!" I unsling the duffel bag and unzip it. Our collection is glowing so brilliantly it almost hurts to look at it. Leah pulls one of the bubbles out. Dez and Amari peer at the planting instructions my faux mama wrote for us. This has got to work—or we're lost.

CHAPTER THIRTY-THREE

SPEAK LIFE INTO THE LAND

Amari sets the cottonwood tree's globe in the center of the ragged hole where the oak tree stood. He scrambles back. I push out everything else, focused on this tree and my rhyme.

> *Speak life into the land because it's all borrowed*
> *From who came before us and who will be here*
> *tomorrow*
> *So we do our part, partners, push back these*
> *Glories*
> *Leave behind the sorrow and tell our own stories*
> *Name this ground hallowed until time don't tick*
> *And now for my first trick—bring back my bricks!*

The cottonwood tree twinkles and flashes to full size in a blink. Free-floating magic in the air quivers. I hold my breath. The flecks of corruption immediately twirl toward the tree's trunk. The boughs tremble, but the tree holds—even Amari's old tree house is still intact.

"It's working!" Dez shouts. "Let's plant the others!"

I manage a small smile. This is a good start. But even if we replant all of the trees . . . none of it matters if we don't stop Ratchet.

"Where's the rest?" Leah cries. We look around in alarm for the duffel. "It was right here!"

I skirt around to the other side of the cottonwood. Did something go wrong with the rhyme? Amari gives a surprised shout, and points. "Y'all, heads up!"

At the ruined courtyard's edge, Professor Wiley and Professor Valiant watch us with cold eyes. They are tattered and filthy—I can't believe they've lasted this long. Valiant holds the duffel. My heart sinks. Our miniaturized trees still glisten within.

"Students! We're confiscating these . . . materials." Wiley's voice is a dry hiss, singed around the edges. "For your own protection. You don't have permission for extra credit."

Is he serious? "Listen to us!" I shout. "We need that bag. It can set everything right!"

"Students should listen and obey," Valiant replies coolly. "Points docked from Wiley Squad."

Professor Wiley flashes her a glare.

I can't believe this—they are so wrapped up in Kinder's conjuring, they'll stick with it even with Peerless falling apart around them. Amari makes a disgusted sound, gesturing at the faux professors with his staff. "What are you waiting for?" he whispers.

The professors eye our weapons and retreat past the study rooms, fleeing down another convoluted hallway.

"Stop them!" Leah shouts.

"Stay and guard the courtyard," I say to Dez.

"What about Ratchet? If she comes—" He grips his staff anxiously.

"Don't let her destroy the cottonwood tree!"

"But—"

The three of us race after the professors. My heart is vibrating. We could lose everything if we don't stop them. Amari raises his staff, giving me a questioning glance. I nod grimly—what choice do we have?

Green electricity peels out of the weapon. Arcs of lightning wrap around Wiley's and Valiant's legs. They drop to the ground, moldering radiant waste sending up an orange mottled cloud around them. Hungry scrabbling sounds echo down the hall. We all flinch, eyes darting every way for Ratchet. The faux professors edge away from the honeycombed walls, clawing feverishly at the lightning binding their legs.

I dart in and snag the duffel away from Valiant. "The trees are okay," I say in relief, then turn to Amari. "Hey, too close! Those are still our professors—and you could have messed these up!"

"My bad," Amari mumbles. "I thought they were going to destroy them."

"Those . . . saplings belong in the greenhouse," Valiant insists, glaring up at me. "Give them to us, and we'll make sure detention is fair."

I hesitate. They recognize the value of the trees, but they don't understand what they are. Not completely. Professor Wiley stops struggling with his bonds when Leah pokes him with her staff. "Don't even try it," she warns.

"Weapons," Valiant muses. "Kinder would be proud."

Leah and I share a disheartened look. Grabbing the staves, using them. It was so *easy*. We got the trees back. We stopped the professors before they could hurt us. But now what? Let them go, and they'll come right back at us. Then what?

Leah searches my face. She nods. That's all the signal I need. I dive into a rhyme without a second thought, knowing she's got my back.

Reversing Kinder's conjuring
Do the dirty laundering
We got no time for wandering
When home is right here, old school
New tools, hope is what we gonna bring!

The professors glower at us. Nothing happens. *"Laundering?"* Leah growls. "Who says that? Could you just do something simple for once?"

"We could still just lock them up," Amari adds. "Pretty sure this school has a dungeon somewhere."

"Just give it a minute," I snap. The professors shiver as the rhyme settles into them. I can't tell if it's working or not. Their electric bonds cast shadows over the warped hallway. "We . . . gotta let them go."

Leah and Amari share an alarmed look. "Why?" she demands.

I search for the words. "The rhyme . . . it isn't Kinder's way. I gave them a choice. But it's not a real choice if they're tied up."

Amari mutters something under his breath but flicks his staff forward. The bonds crackle apart and vanish.

"How do we know we can trust them?" Leah asks.

I shrug and take a deep breath. "The funny thing

about family is that they don't stop being family when they mess up."

Wiley stands slowly. "Especially when they mess up," he says quietly.

"We could really use your help," I say. "Kinder's not here, and we'll need to do what we can without her. Can you grab anyone you can find? Bring them back to the courtyard?"

Wiley blinks. Valiant gives me a surprised glance. "Count on us, Keymaster."

A determined light in their eyes, they stride deeper into Peerless. The corrupt magic shrinks back from them on every side.

"How did you know they'd do that?" Amari demands.

"I didn't." I shrug. "But if we go forcing our way on anyone who stands in our way, we're no different than the Glories. Now come on . . . we've gotta get back to help Dez. We've got more trees to plant!" Battered faux students stagger toward us through darkened halls and over collapsed walls. Some of them are still glowing where a blast from a staff knocked them down. I'm exhausted from running and fighting. I feel weary down to my bones—like the staff's magic is using me instead of the other way around.

Just ahead, Dez anxiously waves us back to the ruined courtyard. "You got the trees back! Yes!"

"My sister?" Leah pants.

"No sign so far." Dez's eyes widen. "Look out!"

Faux students lunge for us—and freeze in bursts of light. Corrupt magic rips out of them like the willow tree seized it. But instead of pulling the faux students apart at the seams, the corrupt bits and creepy-crawlies from the radiant waste scamper away or get pulled into the tree if they get too close. Dazed students stare around at each other in wonder.

"Criss cross applesauce!" I shout, because I can't think of anything else to say. They sit obediently and wait.

The others stare at me in surprise. "Why not just . . . you know, wipe them out?" Amari gestures with his staff.

"That's not what we're here for," I retort. He really needs to calm down! "The students can't be part of Peerless if we blast them to scraps! Let's get started on these trees!"

I go to our next hole: the orange tree.

Leah whistles loudly. "Hey y'all! Extra-credit project over here, come help us!" One by one the faux students come over and help us dig better holes, with shovels and buckets and hands. I nod at her gratefully—now I just need to restore the tree to full size.

"Bring back my bricks," I whisper. The orange tree

322

springs back to size in the hole. We position it carefully and cover up the root ball with soil. Not great—but not awful either. The green oranges are still small. If we do our job right, they might actually ripen enough for us to eat in a few months.

"One more down," Amari proclaims, patting the trunk affectionately. One by one, we get the rest of the trees in the ground. By the time we finish, every single one is gleaming as it pulls corrupt magic from every side.

"That's it, right?" Leah says excitedly. "They'll push out the radiant waste! It's starting already!"

She's right, the corrupt magic is leaching out of the air! I allow myself to breathe a little bit. The ground under our feet is nice normal soil, and broken bits of the school. The courtyard itself feels more solid somehow. More safe.

"Ummm, if it's working, why are they still coming at us?" Dez asks in alarm.

Shoot. He's right, too! It's like the radiant waste knows what we're doing. It refuses to give back the land. Even more faux students lurch toward us, busted magic seeping from their bodies. I don't know if the trees will be enough.

"Wrestling practice!" Leah shouts. "Submission holds—go!" The faux students respond to her again, pouncing on the corrupted students, the trees absorbing magic like bottomless drains.

"That'll buy us a little while," Leah says. "But I'm not sure if we can fight them all off."

She's right—the trees need *time* to purge the school. "This won't be enough to save Peerless. We need Kinder's office back to fix what's broken!"

That means going through the main wing, where the radiant waste is worst.

CHAPTER THIRTY-FOUR

ROASTED

"I hope your rhymes are ready," Leah says. "Let's do this!"

We press forward through the main hall. The walls and floor bend and loop and twist like overcooked spaghetti noodles. We slip and slide until I rhyme the walls straight. Soup springs out of the trophy room, his eyes glowing blue. "Smart guys! Let's get some food in ya!"

He tosses spoons at us that hum and spark. Whatever he's spooned onto them is bubbling and giggling. Big. Nope. "Run!" I yell.

We cut through a broken wall that gives us a path to skirt around to the gym. Leah and Amari slam the doors shut. Spoons clang out, bouncing off the other side. "Everyone okay?" I pant. Inside, everything is almost normal, if we ignore that the gym's roof is cracked open to the sky. Roiling, radiant waste clouds crackle and swirl above us—they seem close enough to touch.

"I feel funny." Dez's face is a little gray. "I . . . I think some of it got in my mouth."

"Look out!" Leah cries. Dodgeballs rain down on us like hail. Amari draws a huge umbrella that protects our heads—but one still smacks his arm. "Ow!" he yelps.

I fling open the doors. "It's a straight shot to Kinder's office! Let's go!"

We head out the gym's side exit and run back for the main hall. Fresh faux students hiss out of cracks in the wall, their bodies hidden in shadow. A side wall explodes into the hallway and Professor Okoro lumbers out, blocking our way! His eyes are a mottled shade of green.

"Time to turn in your science experiment!" he growls.

Dez chokes over his beat. "Foh no! My mouf . . . ain't . . . working rife now!"

My rhymes trip over themselves, and Professor Okoro seizes my arm. I squeal in pain. We're in a tug-of-war and he's winning! Leah and Dez leap forward to help pry me loose. Amari's trying to draw, but the radiant waste swallowed his marker. He's clutching his arm—shining flakes of magic stick to his skin where a dodgeball hit.

We're in trouble. I can feel corrupt magic bubbling

into my brain, clotting my thoughts like a stain. I could freestyle my way forward easy as a baby in a stroller, if I just listen to the magic that's already within.

Is this how we win? Like Yolanda, do I just . . . give in?

An insistent honking echoes through the hall. The faux students spin around in confusion. A wall disintegrates in a flash of multicolored light.

Disco zips through the explosion, followed by Jocelyn in the shuttle! She screeches around us, knocking aside any faux students too slow to leap out of the way. Professor Okoro leaps on her hood with a growl. "I got this!" she shouts as the students turn to her. "Go! You can make it!"

We press forward, quickly reaching the admin office. Corrupt magic glints in our pores like diamond dust, glittering even when the halls turn dark. We're running out of time.

Miss Molly sits still, as though Peerless isn't falling apart around us. Her face has no eyes and no mouth. I flinch back, but she just points us to Kinder's secret room. I dash past her, ready with a rhyme. We made it—we still actually have a chance! The trees are in place, we just need to do a little more with the school itself to get things right.

Curled over the ruins of Kinder's display is Yolanda, wings spread wide. Her crystal scales shine so bright they hurt my eyes. She stretches languidly, like she's been waiting for us. She stands and shows her teeth.

"Oh no."

Yolanda roars. Her long rainbow teeth are all I can see. She swipes at me before I can react. I fly back into the assistant's desk. The wood bursts apart in a shower of glitter and magic. I can barely breathe. The others back into the broken hallway as Yolanda prowls out of Kinder's office, snarling at us.

I hoped things wouldn't go down like this. There's no escaping it. We have to fight her.

"Yo, I know you can hear me!" Leah shouts. She strikes up a beat with her hands and feet. "Keynan, help us!"

"It's too late for that," Amari groans. He can barely lift his arm, but he thrusts his staff into my hands. "You know how we've got to end this!"

The staff might as well weigh a thousand pounds as Yolanda stalks toward me.

"Oh no you don't!" Disco appears beside me, Slickback riding behind her wings. "Get out of here, young bloods!"

They zip around Yolanda with Slickback spitting a singsong rhyme:

You ain't ever seen magic burn as hot as us,
Better freeze where you stand before I start to cuss!

The hall turns slick with ice around Yolanda's feet. Dez jumps forward with his staff, magic crackling dangerously. Blinding cotton-candy-green flashes shoot from Disco's wings, forcing Yolanda's eyes shut. Radiant waste creeps toward her, strange vines with leaves like crab pincers snagging her rear legs. Only . . . that doesn't make sense.

"Keynan!" Amari shouts. "She's caught! Use the staff or there's no getting Peerless back! The rhymes aren't strong enough!"

My staff's yellow spark turns sharp, all teeth and danger like a hungry shark. It's time for me to decide which path to take. Use weapons, break with Touré . . . or keep my rhymes? Is the magic knotted around my thoughts leading me to something tragic?

"Please," Leah whispers.

Yolanda breathes in deep. Tinkling bells swell the air, a beautiful sound until her rainbow scales freeze. She exhales. A plume of blue *fire* from her jaws sweeps across the room! Every surface it touches is consumed with a crust of purple-and-green frost. Disco wobbles in broken circles, the light of her wings lost. Dez screams as Yolanda swipes him across the knees.

"Please," Leah says again. "What are we going to do?"

"She's your sister, and that makes her part of our crew."

I drop the staff.

Yolanda rounds and stares me down. Each one of her steps shakes the ground. We both inhale at the same time—she's about to spit fire, so I better spit mine.

We made a Peerless Pact to keep you whole
You acting up real bad and it's taken a toll
On us, so now the crew is low on trust
But this family must do what family gotta do!

Yolanda recoils like the rhyme slapped her in the ribs. I see the girl shudder inside the crystalline crib. Fury flashes in the monster's gaze, and she lets loose a purple blaze.

There's no place to hide. I'm roasted.

Until Leah coasts between us. Time slows as her legs ripple, a cool autumn breeze. Her feet flow like the floor is glass instead of lava. I cower, but flames pass beside me, redirected by her hands, mesmerized by her dance, light as flower petals and pencil shavings. Amari gasps, caught in the same trance. Despite his misbehaving, he's finally seeing what Leah and me both know: Yolanda is not beyond saving.

A high-pitched squeal suddenly shrieks through my bones. What the what?

Boom.

"Y'all? Ish shish fing even on?"

Boom boom click.

Boom boomboom click.

Dez is nowhere to be seen—but he's found the Peerless intercom! The beat he drums thunders around us. Slickback appears beside me and presses a strange cylinder into my hand; it has a sphere of puffy blue foam on one end.

"What is this?"

"A mic, of course! Speak into it. Get your friend!"

I press in on my freestyle. My voice *booms* through the space, ten times louder!

> *We're family now and that means you too*
> *Always room for one more in the Peerless crew*
> *Your sister holding us down so we can fight the*
> *Glories,*
> *But you gotta come out and be part of the*
> *story.*

My voice thunders through the halls, shaking up the walls! Best of all? I know it's all me—not a touch of corruption in the words I bring! Yolanda staggers back, lashing her three tails. Crystal fragments shudder free of her scales and wings, but Leah sails out of the way, and then . . . Starbreaker, my BFF, my homie, my ace beaucoup . . . *sings.*

> *This isn't who you are or what you do*
> *We'll get our parents but I need you too*
> *So believe in us like we believe in you*
> *It's a whole new start to the Peerless Crew*

I've never heard anything so wondrous. The radiant waste stills on every side. Glimmering magic swirls around the sisters as Leah's last note fades. She walks forward and gently takes Yolanda's jowls in her palms, face inches from those monstrous teeth.

"Little sis?" Yolanda's voice rumbles from her jaws. Amari and I slide back as her tails whip back and forth.

"Hi, Yo. I'm here for you."

Disco is solid teal. I've never seen a bird faint, but this might be the day. Slickback gawks. "You been holding out!"

The scales crack and flake apart in glimmering chunks, until wings, legs, and the monstrous head all fall away, crumbling to the floor. Leah doesn't flinch as the monster dissolves around her. Yolanda blinks, staring at us all with brown eyes. Her gaze settles on her younger sister. She suddenly ruffles Leah's locs and giggles. "If you need a touch-up this bad, I can't imagine what I look like."

The two sisters envelope each other in a crushing hug. "We got you," Leah murmurs, rocking her sister back and forth. "I knew we could."

I share a triumphant glance with Amari—he looks bewildered and amazed all wrapped up in one as we gather in close.

"I . . . I lost my way," Yolanda whispers, tears pooling in her eyes. "I'm sorry I left you by yourself. I just wanted to find Mom and Dad."

"I know."

"Thank you." Yolanda's eyes find me through the glittering magic that swirls through the crumbling hallway. "Thank you all for freeing me. I'm scared that . . . I've done something terrible."

"We'll figure it out," Leah says firmly. "Together."

"Umm, hello? Whash happening?" Dez's voice peels over the intercom. "Did ish work? Ish anyone shtill in there?"

"We're here!" I shout. "We did it . . . we won!" I can hardly believe it. We saved Peerless. *Again*. Used the trees to take back our home from the radiant waste—and not for something even more awful. We did it the right way. "Come down here and meet—"

"Thash great and all, but can you get back here, please? We've got bigger—"

We glance at each other in alarm. "Dez?" I call. He doesn't answer. The intercom is dead.

CHAPTER THIRTY-FIVE

COME FIND ME

Amari and I share a bewildered look before we race off for Kinder's control room. The sisters limp after us determinedly. "Yolanda can barely stand up," I shout over my shoulder. "Just stay here!"

"No way," Leah calls doggedly. "Go. We're right behind you!"

I could shake them both, but we sprint ahead. Yolanda lopes along awkwardly like she doesn't remember how to use two feet. She stumbles and falls, but we can't wait. Getting Peerless working again will take time. But with all of us together, we'll bring the school back even stronger than before—even with whatever new problem Dez just uncovered.

"Something else creeped out of the waste," I murmured worriedly. "Or Mendoza's back."

"I doubt that," Amari says. "We'll be fine. It's probably fine."

"We've worked too hard for something else to break down now."

Dez stands frozen as we rush in. He reaches out and squeezes Amari's hand. "I'm so sorry," he whispers. "I didn't know what to do!"

We gape around the room—it's completely restored, just like how I remember it! Perfect consoles, brand-new screens.

"How, bro?" I exclaim. "This is amazing!"

"Not me," Dez moans. He turns as a figure moves from behind the nearest workstation, and my entire heart sinks through the floor.

Headmaster Kinder is back.

She mutters over Peerless's controls as if we're not even there. Her neck and hair are encrusted with corrupt magic, glistening like frost. Her armor is still intact, but the edges glint dangerously, as if lightning is coiled inside the turquoise metal. We watch her in disbelief. Amari's still holding his staff, a grim expression on his face. The headmaster speaks. "Such a sacrifice, Keynan, to do what you've done." Pain rumbles beneath her voice, malevolent and cold. Fresh fear sinks into me with every word. "I didn't think you had it in you."

"You're sick," I croak.

"We can help you," Amari says nervously.

"Oh, children. No." Kinder stills and finally faces us. "I don't think you can."

I can't help but flinch. One of her eyes is milky white, flickering like there's a raging storm trapped within it. Slivers of corrupt magic swirl around her like broken moons orbiting a turbulent planet.

"Headmaster, we've almost got the school back," I say carefully. "We replanted the courtyard with all the trees from our neighborhoods. See?" Radiant waste doesn't cling to the floors around us so strongly now. "It's already working. We just need to scour the rest of it out!"

"It will never be enough."

"How can you even say that?"

"The Glories, Keynan. I thought of nothing else. Look at the destruction Yolanda's caused, and with only a fraction of her potential. If we're ever to stand against the Glories, defeat them, we must wield the same power." Her smile deepens at the staff in Amari's hand. "But you already know that, don't you?"

I shake my head. "We brought Yolanda back, and we didn't need weapons to do it." I hold out the device

Slickback delivered so she can inspect it. "If you stand where I stood, you could probably understand."

Kinder goes very still. "The mic feels like a million dollars in your hand . . . ?"

I shrug hesitantly. Our words . . . definitely new to me, but somehow tried and true. Like they were a gift handed down from one of the best of the best crews. "You've got to trust us."

Kinder's smile returns as she gazes past us. The homeroom faux professors file in silently. Amari tenses, but I put a hand on his shoulder. Wiley gives me a terse nod as the faux professors line up behind me.

"What?" Kinder shrieks. "What is this?"

Wiley's stare is unblinking, but his voice is not unkind. "Peerless won't survive without a whole new set of rules."

"A clean slate is needed. For the good of us all," Valiant adds.

A gentle whir rumbles through the space as Eli appears, whisking in with a dozen more drones. Even Amari's jaw drops at that.

"You've . . . turned this entire place against me." Kinder's voice cracks. "I only ever wanted—you have to understand. I—"

"We know, Headmaster." I stride forward. "Just come

with us to the courtyard. We gotta heal you."

She laughs mirthlessly. "I'm that corrupted, am I? Very well." She steps forward, then stops with a hiss of fury. "You!"

I spin around. Leah and Yolanda have edged into the room. Kinder takes Yo in from head to toe, her face painted in a fury as her gaze drinks in what's left of the battered armor that Yo took from Touré's workshop. "That belongs to *her*," Kinder snarls. "You don't deserve to wear it! If she had it when she needed it, she might have been *saved*, she might—"

"She can take it off!" I blurt out. "It's cool, right? Yo! We're all friends!"

Yo stares at Kinder as if nothing else exists. She stops leaning on Leah and stands with gritted teeth. "You can try to take it off me, Headmaster."

"Corrupt magic is coursing through you still, Yolanda—I can see it now." Kinder taps her temple. The storm within her eye swirls faster. "I can use it. *And I will have it . . . !*"

Kinder swipes one of the control screens. The walls flash white. A whine fills the room, so high-pitched my teeth ache. Yolanda pitches to her knees with a scream. Corrupt magic bursts from her pores, ears, nose—absorbed into Kinder's outstretched fist.

"No!" Leah screams. "Stop this!"

Dez lunges for the screen, but Kinder tosses him aside with a flare of magic. *"Step aside, little dove, while I fix this, remix this, nothing in the way of bringing back my lost love."*

Dez hits the ground and lies still. Amari holds his staff in two hands, advancing forward. Behind me, Leah leaves her sister's side and charges for Kinder. The headmaster smiles. Her lips part to deliver some new awful rhyme. In horror, I realize she could knock all of us aside without thinking twice. Fighting her won't stop this, just the same as when we tried to stop Yolanda.

I've gotta do things my own way.

I throw myself between Kinder and Yolanda—right into the magic streaming from Yolanda. Blue-and-gold heat swallows my vision. My teeth clench together before I can set myself to scream. The pain is so much I can't rhyme it away, can't think. My body crumples, and cool floor kisses my back.

"Keep her away!" Somewhere I hear Leah's voice. My head lulls to the side. Dez and Yolanda and Guerrero are dragging Kinder down. Yo's hand is clamped over her mouth, but Kinder wrenches free. Peerless students and faculty surround her, as tight as when she set them against Ratchet.

"No! I never meant this for you, Keynan! Let me go, I can help him!"

"You've done enough!" Dez growls. "You're not your-self!"

"He's hurt bad!"

Leah and Amari come to my side, concerned faces shimmering with corrupt magic. He gasps.

"Leah . . ." Yolanda spasms and collapses, falling away from the headmaster. Crystal creeps over her arms and legs. Scales. I can only watch, like a bad dream I can't wake up from no matter how hard I try. "I . . . I can control it," she pants. "The armor reacts to threats. But I can't do it in here! Not next to *her*."

"Yo, no!" Leah cries. "Don't leave me again!"

"I'll be okay, little sis." She glares down at Kinder. "No thanks to you!"

Kinder crumples, misery and awe in her eyes. "You . . . built a school around yourself. I only meant to bring you back, and I made it worse. I'm . . . so sorry."

"Yeah. You are. But I forgive you. And I'm not going to undo all the work Leah's done here. No matter how much it hurts. Help keep her safe." A convulsion nearly doubles her over. When Yolanda straightens again, her eyes are glowing and mismatched. "Mom and Dad were busters sometimes, Leah. But they would be proud. I know I am."

They embrace. Yolanda's eyes fall on me. "When

Peerless is ready, come find me at the fire tree. I'll be waiting for you!" She presses something thin and square in my palm. Closes my fingers around it. Then she takes a deep breath and marches through a cleft in the wall. In moments, she's disappeared into the radiant waste.

Leah extends a hand after her sister; she even takes a step in the same direction. I wouldn't blame her if she followed. Instead, she helps me sit up.

"Peerless Pact," she whispers, squeezing my hand. I squeeze back as everything goes dark.

CHAPTER THIRTY-SIX

THE WILDEST PART

I wake up to the sight of familiar leaves overhead. The orange tree. The branches look strong and healthy, and there's no corrupt magic in the air. Beyond the tree, there's clear, open blue sky. Yeah, I know I can't trust my eyes, but I never thought I'd be so happy to see the illusion. It's not real, but at least I'm in on the secret. I'm a part of the lie.

Anyway. I'm feeling good. Really good.

I check my hands and arms, touch my face. I'm actually grateful for bruises and normal brown skin. No magic buildup . . . that I can see. I didn't let my friends down. My rhymes came through—with no notebook, even! And when it came down to it, I didn't let corrupt magic take control of my freestyling. I'm proud of that, most of all.

You might even say . . . I mastered it.

"About time you woke up, brick brain."

I sit up and almost tumble out of the hammock. Leah smiles over at me.

"I heard there would be snacks. For saving the school and all. Pretty sure I earned some."

She rolls her eyes. "We'll get Soup right on that. At least have some water."

I notice a tray beside me for the first time, with a glass of cool, clear water. I drink it gratefully. The tray abruptly zips off. I barely hold in a shriek and almost spill the water.

"What is that?"

"You've never seen a garden snail?"

"It's big as a kitten!" I shudder. "Tell me it didn't *pour* the water!"

"Would it matter?" An annoying voice howls, "Ohhhh, boy! Your face! I am in tears!"

Slickback and Disco appear in the foliage, cracking up. So annoying.

Leah shrugs, hiding a smile. "The prank was the bird's idea. Apparently there's plenty of magic creatures still hiding in Peerless. These two are . . ."

"Ambassadors! Mediators of the highest caliber—"

". . . helping us deal with that." Leah glowers at the pair, who promptly scurry off. "You feeling okay?"

"Good. Great." I'm a little achy, but I sit up and gaze around. Our trees are strong and healthy . . . the rest of Peerless is in shambles around it, but the kind of mess that we can clean up with hands and shovels along with our beats and rhymes. "And you . . . Slickback was right, you've been holding out! Your voice, Leah!"

She's suddenly very intent on picking at a fingernail. "Well . . . I wasn't in Creative Writing for nothing. It's silly, really. My parents always said Yolanda was better at everything. Especially singing."

"I've never heard anything so . . . beautiful." She flushes furiously, and I stammer. "Is that the right word? Amazing? Marv—"

"Would you. Please. Stop."

"Sorry. Okay. But I'm just saying." More of what happened rushes back to me. "Kinder! Is she—"

"She's fine." Leah shakes her head, like she's not sure if she's speaking the truth. "She won't stop apologizing for Yolanda. We're already working on how to bring Yo back for good. Touré's armor is protecting her—even as messed up as it is—but Kinder is worried that her attack on Yo damaged it. Cracked it somehow. She can't be out there long."

"It's hard to believe that Ratchet is just twisted-up armor. Yo was so scary that way."

"I know! But Kinder thinks we can all do the same thing. Make more, like what your parents had, but with Yolanda's style—still conjuring, but remixed."

I let out a low whistle. "Wow."

"She's . . . changed, Keynan. I . . ." Leah shakes her head. "You'll just have to see it for yourself. Anyway. That's not even the wildest part you've missed."

Gravel crunches nearby as Amari and Dez enter the courtyard. "Look who's awake!" Amari exclaims. "Keynan, you're not going to believe this."

"Believe what . . . ?" I ask carefully.

They're not alone. Trailing after them with a plate of snacks . . . is Ian! "You . . . you're not . . . ?" I stammer.

"A construct?" Ian lets out a shaky laugh. "I'm really here. They caught me up on everything. Actual magic? Sorcerer battles? Some roommate I turned out to be—I was done after our Extra Exclusive Hall Hop went sideways. My memory is honestly really foggy about a lot of it." He frowns and holds the tray out. "But I'm good for snacks, at least."

"But the radiant waste should have gobbled you up!" I splutter. "How did you make it through all of this?"

"Hiding under the bed, duh! And . . ." He nods across the courtyard. A bonsai tree is freshly planted beside the koi fish pond. "My parents begged me to take it to school

346

when we came back early from break. I guess they knew I needed it. Kept the . . . bad magic from swallowing up my room."

I shake my head in wonder.

"Looks like our crew is getting bigger," Amari says.

"Right? I vote your next mural is a group portrait."

He offers a crooked grin. "I'll see what I can do."

We dap it up: *slap, knuckle, crackle pop—*

"Forreal? That's not how it goes!" I exclaim.

Leah rolls her eyes. "All that practice wasted. Tragic."

Amari lets out a shaky laugh and shrugs it off. "Whatever—it's tiny stuff compared to everything we've gone through. And everything we're about to do. Pretty soon we'll have things exactly back the way they were."

"The way they were?" I hobble to my feet with a smile.

"No homework," Ian says immediately.

Leah gives him the side-eye. "Well, maybe no points. And so long as we're learning, can't we just skip getting grades and doing tests? The whole thing could be a lab."

Amari and Dez nod approvingly.

"So we should make some upgrades? Get it? Up*grades*? Do you see what I—"

They all groan and boo until I let it go. My baba would be proud.

CHAPTER THIRTY-SEVEN

DELIGHTED YOU SURVIVED

With a few tough weeks of sweat, rhymes, and magic, we transform Peerless from the inside out. Room by room. We do more than clean up the mess that Mendoza and Yolanda left behind. We reimagine the whole school. Touré and Kinder had chopped all of the arts into little pieces, so it was easier to chase corrupt magic out of the school. Keep the illusion.

But that's all over with now. Art and magic should be intertwined. They don't always do exactly what we want. We make mistakes. We argue over Amari's murals, suddenly infusing life into the stark, plain walls—he insists on adding abstract shapes and colors instead of the epic fight scenes and landscapes he used to daydream about before the recital. Not my fave, but I stay in my lane. He's already prickly over the help from Disco and more than enough mouth and opinion from Slickback. He grumbles a lot over not getting to execute his vision—whatever that means—but he relents whenever he's outvoted by the bird and the lizard.

Dez's beats drift over the intercom while Leah sings order into the courtyard. Headmaster Kinder and I exchange verses—she calls it the start of something called a cypher—as we walk the halls, chasing out pockets of radiant waste. Slickback wiggles his tail into this, too, and after a whole lot of convincing, Kinder allows it. With practice, we adjust. Innovate. Improvise.

Freestyle.

The headmaster is quiet now, but somehow even scarier than before. We spent a week's worth of days and nights together in our new courtyard. I didn't think the corrupt magic would ever stop pouring out of us—and I linger extra, just to make sure it's all the way gone. It's not that I don't trust our new trees. I don't trust myself.

But when we're both finished, her eye remains different—that same turbulent storm. It takes me two whole days to work up the courage to ask her about it. Kinder's silent a long time before she answers. "Sometimes magic is like hurt. It can get pushed down so deep, there's no getting it out again."

Well, I'm pretty sure I hate that answer, and it's the last thing I want to accept. But I can still love her for who she is, however different she is now. I know we'll probably never really agree on most things, but it's the least I can do after everything she's done for us. "Maybe . . ." I admit grudgingly. "For now, at least you've got a whole new way to accent your clothes? It's all Amari and Leah talk about."

Her jaw works silently for a moment. "You . . ." She laughs softly. "You are your father's son. Don't ever change, Keynan."

If we're going to heal the radiant waste or *really* help Yolanda—let alone face the Glories or find our parents— we need to build a space where art and magic are all in the mix together. Even including our new made-of-magic friends. Slickback is determined to find the turntable for us now—he won't say how he got the microphone, but he's sure salty about it—and Kinder encourages him to go, too. Part because we need all the help we can get, and part so that he won't gobble up every door handle and bit of metal left in the school. He finally agrees to leave after the headmaster bribes him with an especially fancy pair of her dangly earrings.

When Kinder brings back the faux students, classes are different, too. For every subject, we're encouraged to try new things. We sing to the plants in Horticulture, show how beats and math fit together in Physics. We get plenty of messes to clean up, when magic pops out unexpectedly, but it's worth it.

Our new and improved courtyard's trees protect even more land than the old oak, even beyond the covered bridge that leads to the school. The breathing orchard is part of Peerless now. The corrupt magic is drained, and if the monsters living there haven't fled, they're not luring us with impossible snacks. We've transplanted gardens to the soccer field at Peerless. With a few tweaks to our faux students, everyone helps take care of it under Soup's watchful eye. We restore the professors, too. I never thought I'd be so pleased to watch Professor Wiley fold up his tie and slip it into his pocket.

Ian and Dez retrofit our drones with new mechanical arms and diggers—I can't tell if they are more excited about the code or the welding. My old homie Eli stays in the mix. The drone isn't quite as aware as Slickback and Disco, but the others lead where Eli follows.

We all decide not to treat Eli any less—not just because of everything we've survived together, or the fact that I wouldn't have made it to Peerless without Eli dragging me here. It's just the right thing to do. When we're ready, the drones will help us plant new saplings in the radiant waste. Eli will be the first drone to try, so I know we're in good hands. Err, turbines.

Jocelyn took Amari and Leah out to our old neighborhoods to see if there was anything left. The people were all gone, just like I was afraid of. I'm glad I didn't go. I couldn't bear to see whatever was left of an empty Bizzy Block. But they brought me a surprise: me and my parents' old books. Every neighborhood had something real, left behind for us.

I'm finally making time to organize the stack in my dorm room, but one book stops me cold. One with no writing on the plain white cover, but I know the title inscribed on the first page.

Collected Poems from the Lost Century.

Professor Mendoza's book is real, too. She gave it to me as a reward, for doing her silly little bribes.

How much of the words from this sank into my head, into my bones? Was Mendoza pushing me and manipulating me through it somehow, too? Should I finish reading it, or burn it? Neither feels right. I wish I had someone to ask about it, but who is going to feel good about a gift from a Glory?

I hide it under my pillow at a knock on the door. Leah pokes her head in. "Hey! You good?"

"Yeah . . . I really am. You?"

"Yes and no." She fiddles with her gold necklace. "Everything we've done with Peerless . . . I wish she could see it. We saved her, but she ran right back into the waste."

"I hear you. But she's awake now," I say. She nods dubiously. "Besides, what'd you expect? She's twice as stubborn as her sister."

"Such a brick brain—no doubt you're feeling better." Leah's eyes twinkle. "Come on. It's time for Sunday session."

Did I not mention this? It's my favorite thing. On Sundays we eat together in the gardens of the courtyard and work on our beats and rhymes and songs together. Tonight Soup's made us a special tray of his legendary spice tarts while we wait for dinner. We joke and laugh about our work, try new things, and just be silly together. Not worried about magic, just enjoying what we create.

Amari nudges me, motioning toward the main hall.

We all still as Kinder emerges. She glides over the stepping stones and joins us, sitting cross-legged in our half circle. The silver vortex in her storm eye is wistful. "Y'all have brought such soul and joy back into this space—I never thought I'd witness it. I only wish she'd been here."

Leah nods to herself. "Keynan's parents told me you

were their best sorcerer. You and Touré must have loved each other a lot."

"So much."

My jaw falls open, until Dez nudges me to get myself together. Leah rolls her eyes at us, as Kinder blinks her tears away. "It was foolish, really. She would explore the radiant waste on her own—trying to find pockets where magic didn't hurt us. Going shopping, she called it. She got sick right before I was supposed to lead the strike against the Glories, and I couldn't think about anything else . . . I couldn't go." She lets out a bitter laugh. "And look where that's brought us. People might have shaded your parents, Keynan, but if they failed us, it's because I failed them."

I don't know what to say. I'm ready to kick myself for not realizing why Headmaster Kinder is even looking after Peerless. It's been hiding in front of us the whole time, right down to Kinder's last rhyme: *Step aside, little dove, while I fix this, remix this, nothing in the way of bringing back my lost love.* "We'll find Touré," I promise.

"Spice tarts always cheer me up," Dez offers. "Have one before Ian eats them all."

"It was just that one time," Ian complains. "And I'm never gonna live it down?"

"Nope."

Kinder accepts and turns the tart over in her hands, not even taking a nibble. She casts a hesitant look at Ian, like she wants to say something, but she doesn't. We all grow still at the awkwardness. Ian gazes forlornly at the dessert in Kinder's hands.

"Keynan, this is yours." She extends a flat device with a simple screen, small enough to fit in my hand. "It belonged to your father."

"What is it?" I faintly remember Yolanda giving this to me before she left.

"A . . . way to store music. Thousands of songs."

Dez whistles softly.

"But it's not just another keepsake from your neighborhoods." She fixes me in place with her gaze. "She found this . . . out there. It's damaged, barely holds a charge. But the last playlist . . . it was made well after your parents left Peerless. Not long ago, in fact."

"What are you saying?" Leah asks hoarsely. "That my sister found—"

"Our parents are still alive," I say. I knew it. I *knew* it.

"You said it's damaged," Amari points out. "Those dates could be wrong."

"They could be right, too," Dez whispers.

This changes everything. The new Peerless is far from finished. But we've got so much more to do.

"I just wanted to . . . thank you," Kinder says. "You've reminded me what this place is meant to be." She stands, face hardening. "Come with me, please. There's something I need you to see."

The five of us exchange mystified looks and follow her into Peerless. The halls are silent; no faux students or professors are around on a Sunday. Our footsteps echo back to us. My heart skips a beat once I realize where she's leading us: our Creative Writing class.

Professor Mendoza's old room.

We shuffle inside. I can't think of anywhere else I'd rather not be. Kinder flicks on the light. Gasps escape us at the words burned into the room's whiteboard.

So delighted you survived my farewell kiss,
But if you come for the queen, then you best
not miss.

The bold, flowing script still glows with magic as though it was freshly seared into the wall. *Mendoza.* Something tightens in my chest. I imagine her napping in class, sipping her tea, accepting my bribe of blueberries for some extra credit. She must have been laughing at me, at all of us, the whole time—while she waited for us to get the oak tree exactly how she wanted it.

"If paint doesn't work," I growl, "if rhymes don't work, we'll take the whole wall down and start fresh."

Leah's hands are squeezed so tight they are shaking. "I know that's right."

We bump fists in agreement. Ian swallows nervously, eyeing us all. Dez glares at his shoes while Amari taps his lip thoughtfully.

"No," Kinder says.

"So she just threatens us and gets away with it?" Leah erupts. "We'll be ready next time."

"That's precisely why. So we *stay* ready." Flinty determination lights Kinder's eyes. "Next semester, I will personally teach a new course at Peerless . . . Introduction to Magic. Her words stay, so none of you forget what we're up against."

"And then what?" Ian asks.

I speak up before Kinder. "Then we go get our parents back."

★ ★ ★ ★ ★

ACKNOWLEDGMENTS

For all of the people, my village, who made it possible for me to tell this story of my heart . . . what a journey. I'm grateful for every step.

This project never leaves the ground without my agent, Mary C. Moore. Shout-out to the original Inkyard crew for all of the love you poured into this project! Thank you to Liz Agyemang and Erica Sussman for snatching up the baton to see this story through. Gratitude to Godwin Akpan for another stunning cover.

All my love to the NSS crew, especially B. Sharise Moore, Eden Royce, and Veronica Henry. Y'all are my port in the storm, and I am so blessed and humbled to share this timeline with you. Thank you for being there for a brother when I needed reassurance the most.

For Wil Ralston and the *Just Keep Writing* podcast family, you reminded me of who I am and what I was sent here to do. I'm forever in your debt, and I ain't done yet.

Azure, Dakari, Tamika . . . I adore you and I hope I make you proud. Best fam in the world!